BETTER IN THE ZAK

MFF ROMANCE

JESS SAVAGE

SPECIAL & EXCLUSIVE DEALS

Love. Steamy romance. Triangles with happy endings.

Join JESS SAVAGE'S NEWSLETTER to stay up-to-date with new releases, special offers, and one-day-only sales.

https://landing.mailerlite.com/webforms/landing/s2g8h3

PROLOGUE

A YEAR AGO IN A FLOWER-STREWN, BACKYARD ceremony, I married Chance Zak.

Yeah, THAT Chance Zak.

Maybe you know him as the hunky star of SHIP-WRECK HIGH. Maybe you know me from that show too. I played his love interest in Season 3, which inspired a small sub-genre of fan fiction and one hilariously bad porn, DICKWRECKED HER PIE.

Maybe you've discovered him more recently thanks to his move to global sex symbol status as the smoking hot addition to those superhero movie franchise. Or maybe you caught the Clio winning, panty-melting, cologne commercial he did.

Or perhaps you know him our reality show, GOOD IN THE ZAK —the romance our characters had teased on the small screen, twisted in with our real lives, who we are behind the act.

Of course, from the engagement on the beach to the intimate wedding at Chance's Hollywood Hills mansion?

It was all a hash-tagged, orchestrated lie.

But Chance did love me.

I never doubted that. Even though we both knew I could never love him back.

Because everything in my life has been based on two promises I intend to keep:

I would make it big in Hollywood or die trying.

and

I would never let another person control me ever again.

PART ONE

ONE

—FIVE YEARS AGO—

"POSTURE." My mother jabbed a finger between my shoulder blades.

A casual casting room observer might've mistaken it for a pat on the back, even emotional support. I stood taller.

"Tits out. Let them see that first. Don't look up until he speaks to you."

I tipped my head down to hide the line of my jaw. Once, I had been the spitting image of my former child star mother. But last year, my lower jaw had started to grow too large, until my bottom teeth jutted past my top ones.

I knew I didn't look right, not even for a normal non-beautiful non-Hollywood type. She kept sending me on calls. Only now as a character actor, a teen villain.

I snuck glances around the packed, stuffy room, checking the competition. We were all trying for the pilot episode of SHIPWRECK HIGH.

The script sample was goofy clean fun: a class of freshmen take a school cruise to the Galapagos after winning some world-renowned science contest. But of course, disaster strikes and the class ends up shipwrecked on a deserted island, where they use their mad high school science skills to survive, all while learning important life lessons and falling in and out of love with each other.

"Now which one of you lovely ladies are here to audition?" A bored 20-something fellow patronized my mother and me as we signed in.

My mother laughed uproariously. "I'll be reading for a part!" She fixed her hair. "Kidding, of course. I'm much too..." Her face soured and she gestured at me. "Daphne, my daughter."

"Age?"

"Seventeen," I said.

"And contact number," he concluded.

I reeled off my digits and gave him my headshot. Just beyond his table, a set of doors. The doors to my new life. I hoped anyway.

An hour later, he motioned to me. "OK, Daphne, let's get you in front of the camera."

Lines clutched in my hand, I went in, head tilted down. If I kept my chin at the right angle, my eyes were the first thing you noticed; big and hazel. Or my skin, which had always been good. Or my strawberry blonde hair. There were so many pretty parts of me.

Maxillofacial surgery— breaking my jaw so I wouldn't have an underbite anymore, was $40,000. We didn't have that kind of money.

"Every TV show needs a villain, that makes your underbite a feature, not a bug." My mother had doggedly repeated the past few months when I'd tried to bring up surgery.

The millions she'd made as a child star haunted our dingy apartment like a ghost. When she got high, my mother would rage at the manager who'd siphoned it all off, leaving her nothing but a lifestyle she couldn't afford. Less often, she'd get teary-eyed over her parents, who lived quite middle class on the investments they'd made from their cut, and now told her to 'first straighten up and fly right' when she asked them for her money back.

When she was happy, she'd make plans for a comeback, even though everyone in town knew she was uninsurable for big projects.

We never spoke about what had happened to the money I'd made in toddler commercials. It was simply known that it was gone now. To food, to acting lessons, to years of dry spells between gigs. To buying entrance to high-end Hollywood events on the chance of reigniting a connection with an *old-friend-turned-producer*, or a showrunner on the prowl for the right washed-up actor to cast in a gritty budget flick.

It's a hard thing to love someone and still promise yourself you will never be like them. You'll die before you let yourself be like them.

Now, as I stood in front of the camera, waiting to say my lines, the casting crew behind the table conferred with each other. My cheeks prickled.

One said, "Can you look up for us? Straight into the camera."

No shame! I told myself. *Show business it too hard as it is. Be shameless.* So I lifted my witchy, jutting chin, and stared each of the four down.

One wasn't an adult. A teenager. Dark gold hair over one eye, curl like an ocean wave.

I knew instantly he'd already been signed for the show.

He was here to read with potential castmates to test their chemistry. The adults whispered. Subtle head shakes.

They were going to reject me without even letting me read.

I focused on that cute boy. He was probably my age, 16 or 17, perfect skin, that star quality some people have... or don't. I couldn't take my eyes off him, he seemed like the best thing in the room, just a little more perfect than everything and everyone around him.

I hated him. All he had to do was sit like a dope in that chair and success would be his. I would get sent away with nothing. Our eyes locked.

From memory, I called out the first line of the script. "No, Leo, you've gotten some bad advice."

A momentary stillness from those shuffled papers and the showrunners getting ready to bounce me without an audition. The boy said nothing.

For a heartbeat, I died. He didn't know the lines. He was going to leave me hanging, like an asshole. I tried to send a psychic vibe through the space between us:

Please. Please just let me show them I can act my ass off. That I can make people love me. I've got that in me.

"I don't think so," he said slowly, and I breathed again. The line from the script. "Look, you gotta get out of here, Martin's supposed to meet me to collect driftwood for the campfire."

I flushed with relief, my newfound adoration for this guy coming off me in waves.

Better yet, the absolute silence from the showrunner's table. They were paying attention to us. I had them, that charisma I'd inherited from my mother glowing in me, captivating them.

"Okay, I'll go. But not before I get a goodbye kiss." When I said it, something crackled between me and the boy paying Leo. The subtle swallow, the way his eyes seemed to darkcn.

"Kissfire? I mean campfire!" The boy said it with such beautiful dorky showmanship, his head bobbing, cheeks flushing.

The table laughed, even though they must've heard him read that line dozens of times already. Laughter bubbled up in me too.

"Great read," the showrunner called, studying papers on the table. I'd been cast in stuff before, this was going great. He tipped his head at the handsome teen. "Nice job, Chance. And nice job too, uh... Daphne?" He consulted my headshot. "Could you give us your profile?"

That sinking sensation. I turned, the boy reading Leo's lines disappearing from view, but not before I caught the stunned expression on his face. This must not be his first acting gig either; he knew something was wrong.

"OK, thanks for coming in, we'll let you know," thc showrunner said, flat and dismissive. "Have them send in the next."

"Thank you." I turned, pageant-style, making eye contact with each like I'd been trained since I'd gone in for toy commercials at 3-years-old. None of them looked up. That was it, then. I'd been rejected.

Mom pacing at the door. She only had to see my face. "Oh, no-no-no. I heard you. They laughed. Was that Don Straden in there?" She nudged open the door. "Don?"

"Mom, don't." I tried to claw her back. The 20-something manning the doors chased after her. But my mother was already in the room.

"Don, can I have a moment?" She said in her most commandingly friendly tone. "It's me, Heather Conover. We worked together on—"

He was already coming around the table, rushing toward her in an embarrassed but smiling way.

"Yes, of course, Heather, how nice to see you. Is this your daughter?" He gestured at me, and in doing so, got my mother to turn back to the doors. He then walked with her toward them.

"I'm sorry, Mom," I said on the car ride home. Not because I was sorry — it had been my face that had jinxed the audition, not anything I'd done— but because my mother needed the soothing.

"Don't be," she said, knuckles white on the wheel as we drove LA's gritty streets, looking for an onramp. "You're gonna get that surgery. You've got what it takes. But with that face, you're not even going to pass as Hollywood ugly."

* * *

THEY SENT me home from the hospital with a bottle full of liquid codeine and instructions to buy a bulk supply of Ensure. Or at least that's what I remember aside from the blinding pain of broken bone.

"You are truly hideous." Mom glanced at me between driving the stop-n-go traffic.

Thanks, I tried to say. Because the bands kept my jaws bound in place, it came out, "Shannnks."

"Guess this is as good a time as any to tell you," she said. "You know we couldn't afford that surgery."

My stomach sank, queasy and bleary with drugs and injury and the stop and go lurch of LA traffic. When she'd made the appointment, my mother had told me she would take care of everything. I'd let myself believe her. Some nest egg she'd been holding back.

She tittered nervously. "It's a hell of a bet. Only a truly good guy would foot the bill for a thing like this."

"Mmmmmhhm" I said: *Mom?* But part of me knew already. And that part wanted to vomit. I wondered how that would work with my jaw wired shut.

She cursed at the bumper in front of us. Someone honked and she gunned the engine, switching lanes, cutting them off to the shriek of breaks.

"Lloyd paid."

Lloyd. Her boyfriend of five years. Lloyd, who would throw his keys or his beer bottle against the wall, scaring Mom so bad she'd tell me to pack up so we could stay somewhere else for the night. Even though Mom owned the condo.

I groaned.

"You better cram that attitude real quick," she snapped. "I did what had to be done. You weren't ever going to make it with that face. Now, look at you. You've got a real chance now, baby."

She flicked the visor in front of me down so I could check the mirror there. I didn't. I knew my face was a blood-caked, purple, bruised potato.

"Be nice to him," she said. A loan from Lloyd wasn't as low as Mom might've gone to secure funds... "Because until you pay him back, he's your new manager."

My heart stopped. I shook my head, breathing hard. My whole life, my mother had been my manager. That was the one thing she'd taught me from her failures in this town: you never, ever let anyone else control the money. Or else like her former manager and her parents before him, they owned your career. I punched the dashboard until my knuckles bled and she slapped my thigh and screamed for me to stop, but it didn't change the facts.

My mother had sold me to her boyfriend. For $40,000.

TWO

—THREE YEARS AGO—

I stood in an audition room for SHIPWRECK HIGH, my insides on fire with excitement. I clutched my new head-shots so I wouldn't nervously pick at my best causal outfit; low rider jeans and a t-shirt that clung perfectly to the undersides of my breasts, emphasizing my waist.

What a difference a little time could make. I'd thought of this room countless times as I'd lain in bed, binging episode after episode of SHIPWRECK HIGH as I recovered from surgery, memorizing their lines, fantasizing that one day, it would be me on screen.

And I'd had plenty of time to watch them. It had taken me a full year to heal properly from the surgery, for the swelling to go down, revealing newly implanted cheekbones and freshly aligned jaw.

A full year of unemployment. Of wondering if I'd made a horrible mistake, of whether or not I'd ever get a job.

Because let's face it: the kind of education I'd gotten

between so-called homeschooling and a boatload of absences due to acting lessons, casting calls and late nights on Sunset? I might be able to get a GED if I really put an effort in. But unless I managed a dollop of fame acting-wise to prove my worth, no college would take me. Without any other skills or education, I was looking at waitressing for life, maybe spend my weekends working as eye candy at a car show.

Objectively, the doctor had made me *Hollywood beautiful*, the symmetry of my features perfected with a bone saw and silicone.

Since honesty is important in any relationship, I'll tell you I had no connection to this new face, any more than putting on a mask for Halloween. Thanks to that liquid diet I'd been on with my jaw wired shut, I also had a newly rail-thin body.

The real me still lurked underneath the mask. And in case I might forget my true lantern-jawed ugly duckling nature, Lloyd made sure to remind me.

And like me, so had SHIPWRECK HIGH come into its own. The show was a hit now, which meant Chance Zak was waaaaayyy too big a star to be caught trading lines with the cattle calls. Still, I thought of him, that zing of chemistry between us, and it soothed my nerves.

"Ok, you're up," the bored and harried woman said from behind the casting table. But her eyes were on me, considering.

I said the lines I'd practiced in the mirror hundreds of times in the past week. A casting assistant said Leo's.

The call came that afternoon, but I'd known by the light in her eyes as I'd spoken, as I'd tossed my head, showing off every mesmerizing curve and angle. I'd landed a reoccurring role on Season 3 of SHIPWRECK HIGH.

"Congratulations!" Lloyd smirked when he overheard me telling Mom I'd gotten the part. "Sounds like you owe your manager a night on the town." And then, "We'll be tracking down potential leads, networking," he'd told my mother. Even when you had a job in this town, you were always looking for the next one.

Lloyd took me out to the bars on Sunset.

Didn't matter I wasn't 21. With my face, we could cut to the front of most lines.

They tried to send Lloyd back to the velvet ropes, so he kept a firm grip on my upper arm, or a hand firmly wedged in the back pocket of my jeans, so we couldn't be separated.

See, Hollywood is about who you knew, about hearing of an upcoming audition or show, getting in front of someone important. For Lloyd, it was also about scoring drugs, or maybe a quick scam to make a few bucks, some jobs for me that slid into the grey area between acting and maybe something a little more sleazy.

"I'm her manager," Lloyd would snarl until the bouncer rolled his eyes and either sent us both away or allowed us both to pass.

"Flash your tits," he'd sometimes whisper in my ear; his equivalent to greasing a palm with a fifty.

"Fuck all the way off," I'd hiss back. His grip on me would go so tight I had to grit my teeth so I didn't flinch.

I'll tell you true. Sometimes I did flash my tits. Because nothing was going to stop me from getting where I wanted to go. Lloyd was a good teacher that way; I learned quickly that grown men would part with all kinds of valuables just for the rush that comes with seeing a bit of skin.

But the worst was at the end of the night, when we'd stumble home and Mom would be waiting, drunk on the couch, eyes bleary and red, ready to pick a fight. I was taking her place and it showed in how she stopped putting herself together, stopped eating, stopped moving. I was the new young face, on the arm of her boyfriend, prowling Sunset with him as she had done. I felt like a vampire.

But I did it all, even if it meant stealing her place in the world, even if it seemed like putting the drugs in her body myself. Because with each step, I got closer to those two things I desperately needed: To being famous and to paying off my debt. Once those happened I'd be free of Lloyd, her, and anyone else, forever.

Even when I discovered Lloyd, genius manager that he *wasn't*, had managed to negotiate exactly union standard for my pay: three thousand dollars an episode, my character in every three out of five shows. Still, each dollar put me closer and closer to paying him off and getting the fuck out of there. Even when Lloyd started deducting 'rent' from my money on behalf of my mother. And then charging 'expenses' as my manager, until I could see my life turning into my mother's. But even then, I knew if I'd made it on to SHIPWRECK HIGH, all I had to do was keep working and eventually, I would pay him and escape. I kept a ledger; every dime I made, every expense Lloyd claimed. At night, I did the math over and over— how many shows until I belonged only to myself.

So maybe you can see how my world was dark and bright all at the same time. They say in space, stars can explode and cause a black hole. I totally got that, how something could be full of light and energy and also so dark and empty inside it only seemed logical everything would collapse in on itself.

That's what I was when I met Chance for real.

* * *

My first day on the set was pure freaking magic. I mean, everything.

Security at the gate? Magic.

Diesel and bougainvillea perfumed the air as I hurried across the parking lot and swung open the heavy door to get to the studio? Yeah: magic.

This ridiculous theme song rang in my ears as I stepped foot into the building. It went like this: *The Staaaaaaaarrrrrrrt of Daphne's New Shiny Perfeccccct Liffffeeeee.*

Breathless and blinking at the change between the Los Angeles sun outside and the commercial fluorescents inside the building, I followed the well-placed signs to the set, heart racing so fast my cheeks had to be pink. Everyone I passed got my very best movie star dazzler.

And then, holy magic of all sparkly freaking magic. I found myself on the set where my dreams would start: SHIPWRECK HIGH. And with it, I found Chance Zak.

He was bullshitting around with two crewmembers, sharing a casual laugh and pointing at the bright overhead lighting. Tight white T-shirt, jeans that hung perfectly from his hips, suggesting those perfectly sculpted abs every SHIPWRECK fan knew well. Let's be real, it was why the show was a hit. They always had the actors stripping down at the beach for some key plot point.

I stood in the dimness off-camera, perfectly still on the outside.

My insides were another story: heart pounding so loud all I could hear was the blood rushing through my body, timed perfectly to the echoes of my theme song.

It had to be my nerves, my excitement about my first day. But when I saw Chance Zak waiting there, golden-haired, muscles chiseled and flexing with his every casual move? I wanted him more than I'd ever wanted anyone before.

Not in my sweet and tender heart either. I felt it right between my legs.

I looked away, shocked at my reaction. I tried to reason it was nothing more than misplaced excitement for the job. My body stubbornly insisted it was him I wanted, and in the worst possible way. Tingles cascaded across my skin, puckering my nipples, lifting the tiny hairs just south of my navel. My movements, restless, tilting my ass a little.

I flushed, nervous anyone who saw me would know. But my eyes were drawn to him again, my tongue against the inside of my bottom lip, fighting this mad, impulse to get closer to him, to touch him.

Rub against his leg like some hungry cat, whydon'tcha? Lloyd sneered in my head.

I hated that he narrated my most punitive, self-loathing thoughts. But his words did their work. Whatever madness stirred in me went out like it'd been doused with a bucket of water. What on earth had gotten into me?

On set, one of the crew members said something and they all laughed again, joking around. I could tell they were a little attracted to him too. The guy who'd spoken gave himself away with a small shift closer to Chance, a lingering glance when Chance spoke to the other guy.

With a more level head, I could see the possibilities glimmering all around him, like an aura. Of course I'd been attracted; top-tier celebrities lived in their own realm of sex appeal.

Chance had been a stunner when we'd first met, but in the time since, he'd perfected his art. Even as I lectured myself, insisting I was merely observing him now to learn his trade, shifting my weight from one leg to the other sent off sparkles between my thighs.

He noticed me then. The instant his easy smile faded, distracted, made me feel powerful. And then helpless. Both.

Then he said something to the crew, patted one on the arm, and walked toward me.

Holy shit. Holyshitholshitshollllyyyyyyyshhhhhhheee

With his success on SHIPWRECK HIGH, he had the fan base to launch into movies. Maybe become a leading man. Even if he never made the transition, he could still be doing autograph signings in Las Vegas for the next thirty years, supported by an endless stream of aging hipsters who'd had their first die-hard crush on his character. In our world, he might not yet be a superstar, but he would always be made.

"So you landed Vanessa," he said when he got near enough there was no mistaking he meant me.

Up close, the star quality of him radiated like the sun. His shoulders impossibly broad, muscles cut like someone had chiseled him. The masculine scent of him, warm and pleasant as he studied me.

Since I'd become beautiful, I'd made lots of men nervous, their sweaty palms and flickering glances like I was too much to take in all at once. Not Chance. Easy, level, sea-green eyes landed on me and stayed there.

"You know, this is actually the second time I've tried out for a role with you," I said.

I don't know why. Maybe I wanted to fill the silence.

Or maybe I wanted him to know the face that had brought him across the room with that sexy smile was not really mine, and so he might as well fuck right off flirting with something that wasn't anymore the real me than the lights above our heads.

He grinned, wagging a finger. "I *thought* I recognized you!"

His lie felt like an insult. Pretending he knew me. It seemed obvious I should remember him; at my audition, he'd been the big star. But there was no reason for him to remember me. I'd just been one failed audition among countless others.

But this was Hollywood, where everyone put on a big smarmy front like they were your best friend. I laughed, rolling my eyes. Obligatory flirtation. He was about to be my coworker, might as well play along.

That finger he'd been wagging touched his bottom lip as if he were solving the world's sexiest puzzle. "First year. You read for Bethany Bimmel. They'd just signed me. Man, I thought you knocked your audition out of the park."

Holy shit, he did remember me.

I didn't know how to feel, except naked, and speechless. He'd seen right through the mask to the real me.

I gestured at my face, feeling a blush come on. Plastic surgery was nothing to be ashamed of in this town, but it did feel as though he'd caught me playing dress-up. "Guess I look a little different now."

I could sense him then, noticing the differences, the way his gaze crept over my features, giving me those shivers at being observed so carefully. "Oh yeah."

I didn't know whether to laugh or be offended.

"For your information, this," I circled my face with a perfectly manicured index finger, "cost me 40K and a year of looking like Mrs. Potato Head."

As soon as the words were out, I wondered how the hell I'd gotten into bragging about my surgery to this guy.

Because he was too beautiful. Because with his looks, he

didn't even notice how hard the rest of us had to work to get here. I scowled at him.

"That's not what I noticed the first time," he said, leaning in conspiratorially.

"Oh no?" I leaned in too, folding my arms across my ribcage to push my cleavage up. He wasn't the only one who could play the sex appeal game.

I had zero regrets about using my body to get ahead. This was show business. You learned to wow them with pizazz or baffle them with bullshit, but you don't let yourself be forgotten, overlooked, or overshadowed. Especially not by some pretty boy born on third base.

Especially if he was the prettiest boy you'd ever seen.

To his credit, Chance's eyes only dipped for a moment. Then they were right back on me, that self-assured half smile flashing a glimpse of dazzling white, straight teeth.

"You're like me," he said.

"Oh really?" The blush was real, him reading me like that.

"Yeah. That's what I remembered. You didn't audition scared. You were pure ambition walking through those doors, no apologies for everything you were, no shy, unsure bullshit. They were fools not to snap you up for something."

All my charm drained out of me. I imagined how he must've seen me; so ugly he'd known, like the rest of the casting crew, I'd get kicked immediately. But able to admire my spirit for trying in the face of certain failure.

I hated him. He'd seen the real me.

But... I liked it too— the way it felt under his microscope. In this world of cotton candy and bullshit, somehow he'd seen the real me.

"I, uh." He pulled back, confusion and a hint of a blush

on his face. "Sorry." He finally just copped to it. "Sometimes I say things I should only think."

Relief washed over me, that at least he felt normal human emotions: awkwardness, embarrassment, sticking his perfect foot right in his beautiful mouth.

So not a god then, just a really hot mortal. That meant I had a fighting shot with the guy. Although whether I wanted him under my thumb, or just under me, I wasn't quite sure.

"You ready to go over lines?" I smirked.

He grinned, and once again became Chance Zak, TV hunk with burnt gold hair, perfect skin, and dazzling eyes the color of the sea, too impossible to be anything but a fantasy. "Yeah."

THREE

—TWO YEARS AGO —

"You're good," Chance said.

We were at the wrap party for Season 3, which was strategically being held at The Lilly, a café more famous as the place where starlets went when they wanted to be 'caught' by the paparazzi than anything on the menu.

All those candid celebrity shots of couples eating normal meals in intimate patio settings? Yeah, that's The Lilly. The cast of SHIPWRECK had strategically rented the place for our cast party to drum up cheap publicity shots for any photographers who wanted to make a buck selling our candids.

Chance and I were supposed to hang together as much as possible, because our love story had gotten traction with the fans.

The only problem was, Lloyd was still negotiating my contract renewal so I could come back for next season.

"Yeah, well, I don't know if the show wants me back that

bad." I shrugged, covering for Lloyd even though I hated to do it. Worse would be Chance asking questions about why my manager was such an inept loser.

Chance nudged me as we huddled together at a table. "Well, definitely play hardball, Daph. Get paid your worth."

I leaned against the table, glancing toward the sidewalk, hoping we were getting a little paparazzi attention. Also because I couldn't look him in the eye. How did he do that? He always managed to be so encouraging, even though not signing a contract yet probably made me look like trouble.

I'd spent a season of taping with Chance, and I was completely attracted to him. But more than that, I needed him in my life.

I decided then, I'd sign the contract on my own. I didn't need Lloyd's permission, and as my manager, he'd get his cut no matter what I did.

It scared me to sign the contract alone— the loads of papers, the technical, small print, the fear maybe SHIP-WRECK would take advantage of me somehow. But...

"I will." I grinned at him. "I will play hardball."

From the corner of my eye, a photographer seemed to spot us. He lifted his camera.

"'That's my girl." Chance gave a sly nod and reached out to nudge my leg under the table.

The instant he did, that familiar jolt of chemistry sizzled my insides, and my breath caught. I nudged him back, keeping the contact pressure of my leg against his. The muscled flex of his calf against mine, scratchy hairs brushing my smooth skin.

In moments like this, I wondered why we'd never hooked up.

Except I knew: I couldn't risk this job going south, pissing off my famous costar, or worse, having a disastrous time in the sack with him, and losing our on-screen chemistry. Besides, this throbbing need for him? It sold our romance on screen. Always being on the brink of tumbling into bed with him was our secret recipe. I reigned in my raging pussy, mentally muzzled it, and crossed my legs, Chance and I separating.

"You're really a nice guy." I leaned over and stole a sip of Chance's Big Mean Greenie, which as far as I could tell, was entirely made of blended spinach and cucumbers.

"The fan base is screaming about our story. The studio would be crazy not to sign you." Chance stole his drink back, grinning, and took a sip.

His eyes moved somewhere beyond me, a frown wrinkling his forehead. "Hey, isn't that? Is that guy your business manager?"

On no.

Slowly, I twisted, distantly aware the paparazzi was taking more shots now than when Chance and I had been flirting. There. All the way in the back of the room, at the bar, Lloyd was standing too close to SHIPWRECK HIGH's showrunner. I couldn't hear the words, but the body language was clear. Lloyd was angry, and the showrunner was looking for an escape from the conversation.

"I gotta." I was up and speed walking across the restaurant without even finishing my sentence. There were tons of cast and crew, their family, and Plus Ones schmoozing, which slowed me up as I tried to dart through them, to Lloyd. He stood up too forcefully, the slight stutter-step backward to maintain his balance.

Fuuuuuuuuuuu. He was drunk.

Three feet away, I heard the showrunner say, "Look, call the office Monday, I'm sure someone can—"

My heart sank. Calling the office? Someone else? Two bright red flags the showrunner was trying to get away from the drunken, belligerent asshole who was supposed to be negotiating my contract.

"Hi! Hi Don," I simpered, touching the showrunner's arm. He looked down at my hand like I'd soiled him somehow with my touch, but when our eyes met, he seemed to soften. "Everything OK?"

"This asshole." Lloyd stage whispered at my back. I took a quick step back very purposefully on his toe with the spike of my high heel. He hissed and tried to pull away. I leaned my entire body weight into that one-half-inch square. He yanked his foot and freed himself, making me stumble a bit. But thankfully, he didn't say anything more.

"Hello dear," the showrunner said, a mix of frustration and pity on his face.

"I'm so glad you're here," I said. "Lloyd hasn't given me a copy of my contract yet, but I was just telling Chance how thrilled I am to be part of the SHIPWRECK HIGH family. If you have a copy available, why don't you send it directly to my email? I could sign it and drop it off today."

The showrunner's eyes ping-ponged from me to behind me, where Lloyd still stood, reeking of desperation. He wasn't the only one. I could feel the showrunner on the fence. I threw a smile on him I hoped conveyed I would do anything, absolutely anything to sign that contract.

But that was a mistake, my desperation, and his face closed against me.

"Look, you're a lovely girl." He patted my arm consolingly. "But this isn't really a decision I can make myself, and like there's some... complications with your contract. Why don't you call the office Monday." His face soured, and without looking anywhere near Lloyd, Don hurried into the crowd toward the back exit.

Call the office Monday? My stomach sank so hard I had to swallow to repress that feeling I might puke. I had no doubt they were pulling my contract. By Monday all the emergency meetings would be made and I would be out. He was probably having his assistant make the calls right as he trudged through LA traffic in his moneymobile.

I spun to Lloyd, painfully aware we'd made a scene, that the first ripple of gossip spread all around us, people's eyes wide, their conversations paused.

"What did you do?" I demanded as quietly as I could.

"Nothing. I didn't do," Lloyd started. As I turned away, he grabbed my arm. I froze, not wanting to draw attention, to make more of a scene. With his free hand, he gestured rudely at Don's back. "Look. I just... He could've written in a cameo for your mom. It wouldn't've cost him anything. It would've boosted her spirits, you know."

So many emotions.

Weird, unwelcome tenderness for Lloyd, who was apparently actually looking out for my mother. Aggravation he was going to tank both our careers with his demands. Pity. Doubt; the story sounded noble compared to Lloyd's usual motives. Loathing I was tied to him.

"Get out of here." I hurried through the party without looking back, knowing Lloyd would never leave on my say-so. But after ruffling the showrunner's feathers as he had, some bouncer would toss him in a hot minute anyway. And anyway, I had bigger fish to fry. If there was an opportunity to save this, it wasn't with him.

I weaved through the crowded room, searching for anyone who might help me. A producer who might be persuaded. One of the writers. Chance.

"Daphne Conover?" A young woman about my age stepped in my path, flashing a huge, lip-glossed smile. "I am soooo sorry to bother you," she giggled, shoulders hitching with nervous energy, her eyes bright. "But I was wondering if I could maybe get your autograph?"

"Wow, that's so sweet of you. Sure."

I needed a moment to get my plans in order anyway. I could swirl a signature as I figured out how to fix this as easily as I could walk and think.

Besides, being wanted, even if only for an autograph, soothed my nerves the tiniest bit. Especially being wanted in this room full of influential people. And, apparently, the Plus Ones with stars in their eyes.

"Who are you here with?" I asked as she handed me a neatly folded SHIPWRECK HIGH t-shirt she must've brought with her. Or maybe it was in the swag bags waiting for us at the door when we left.

"I'm Don's niece," she chirped, tucking flat-ironed hair behind her ear, nervously glancing down at her cleavage before grinning at me again.

"You're a terrible liar," I told her as I searched my purse. "You have a pen or something?"

"How did you... OK, practically like family. My dad and Don go way back."

"Oh yeah?" I raised an eyebrow. She was actually kind of cute. "What's your name?"

"Audrey." She sighed heavily, the scent of bubblegum sugar. I wrote:

To Audrey.

How do you really know Don? :D

XO, Daphne Conover

"Here you go." I handed it to her. As she read, I started moving through the crowd again.

"FINE." At my back, Audrey sighed heavily again, as if overexerted by the truth. "My dad's his dermatologist."

I laughed despite myself.

She pulled a folded piece of paper from her pocket. "Call me sometime. We could have some fun."

She pressed it into the palm of my hand. I took the paper and slipped it into my front pocket. I mean, I definitely had other things to occupy my thoughts, but who doesn't swoon a little at being wanted?

As I moved away, the warmth of being recognized cooled into dread. I was about to lose my role on SHIP-WRECK. I wanted to believe they needed me, that the chemistry and storyline between me and Chance was so important, they couldn't possibly cut me out.

Except I'd seen countless stars bigger than me fall into obscurity thinking they could leave a hit TV show and make it on their own, or hold out for more money only to find themselves unemployed.

Chance. I decided as I was walking. *The person I need right now was Chance.*

I caught a glimpse of him from a distance. He'd moved from our spot, and now stood in a small group of people, but his head craned. He was looking for me. I just knew it. Like touching him under the table, knowing no matter how casual we seemed, both of us were focused entirely on those few inches of flesh pressed together.

Our eyes met across the room and he smiled.

I hurried to him. "I'm sorry," I murmured to the others standing with him, and to Chance, I said directly, "I need you."

"Excuse me." Immediately, he stepped away from the others, even as the woman by his side reached out as if to draw him back, he smiled his goodbyes and came to me as if I were the only person in the room.

It was good PR. Both of us were more famous for our TV entanglement, the fantasy that our on-screen romance was true. Even to people who should know better, Chance was Leo and I was Vanessa, and when we left this Holly-wood café, presumably we took a flight to the Galapagos and lived in a beach shack and used utensils improbably fashioned from coconut shells.

And I reminded myself that, lest I forget it was probably an act, because damn, it was easy to be charmed by a guy like Chance.

"What's up?" He said when we were away from the others.

I told him.

He squeezed my hand. "OK, let me make a few calls."

* * *

WE ENDED up in the parking lot for privacy, sitting in the front seat of his car, trying to undo Lloyd's fuckup. But as Chance discovered, Lloyd hadn't just asked for a cameo. He'd asked for a producing credit on the show. He'd missed a deadline. He was everything an arrogant, self-important actor would be to get written off a show. And he wasn't even technically on the show!

By the time we got in the car, shielded against the mild chill of the LA evening breeze and any eavesdropping paparazzi, I'd called Lloyd, furious but also desperately simpering, trying to get out of him any information that might help change the tide against me. Of course, he'd been reeling drunk by then, and I couldn't control my anger.

"They're gonna fire me," I interrupted his angry tirade of

what he thought he deserved.

"SHIPWRECK's gonna tank if they have to rewrite your storyline. Trust me. They need us, and I keep telling them, it doesn't cost them nothing to give me a producer credit—"

He was wrong. So wrong.

My whole life was falling apart, but to keep calm I told myself how this was the moment I truly understood I was smarter and more capable than a fifty-year-old man. Or anyone else who might handle me.

"Do not ever negotiate anything for me again," I said. "I'll get you your money, but your role as my manager is over."

I hung up the phone, staring through the windshield into the parking lot and beyond that, the alley and twinkling lights of Hollywood.

You're my golden goose, Lloyd had said as I pulled the phone away from my ear. That thin veneer of pity washing off, showing his true, slimy colors. *You're gonna lay and lay until I get mine.*

Could I leave? My mother had signed the contract because I'd been a minor, but I was eighteen now, so maybe I could find a way to break it. That would involve lawyers, which would put me further in debt. But it might be worth it to at least consult one. Might even be better to take on the debt than be tied to Lloyd.

...but as long as he was in my mother's life, I'd have to find a way to get along. She would pressure me to take him back. Painful as it was to admit even to myself, no matter how I tried to patch it up with my mother, the price of cutting of Lloyd might be losing her.

"Hey, sounds like you made the right choice," Chance said, leveling those green-blue eyes at me from the driver's seat. "He's gonna weigh you down."

He cleared his throat, awkward, thumbing the side of his phone. "I, uh. I'm getting texts from Don, and my agent. I think maybe your...um, your Lloyd guy. I think maybe Don will talk about writing a new contract for you to come back for a few guest appearances, but it's not looking good for a full contract to come back next season. They loved you. It's just, you know. Feathers got ruffled."

In my lap, my hand became a fist.

"I owe him," I said quietly. Not because I wanted Chance to feel sorry for me. I just needed him to know I wasn't stupid. I was trapped. "Forty thousand. Minus what I earned on SHIPWRECK this year. Plus whatever he tacks on. Interest. Expenses."

At the bewilderment on Chance's face, I gestured to my perfect jawline as if it were the grand prize on some game show. His expression cooled and he nodded slowly.

I turned the slightest bit away so I could blink back tears. I could see it now; Lloyd was exactly the kind of slime ball who'd keep me strung along, getting enough jobs to drag his sorry ass all around town, and then fuck everything up before I got enough traction to pay him off and free myself.

Chance said, "Listen, SHIPWRECK won't last forever. It's a show about high school and even on a desert island, I'll be a senior next season. What are they gonna do? Send me down the beach to SHIPWRECK college? Bring in a new class of freshmen on a capsized ferry?"

Gently he nudged me with his elbow until I looked at him. His expression nearly made me lose it. "Listen. They're gonna have to get rid of my class to keep the show going, or shutter it. Either way, I'll be out of a job. I've been talking to my agent about it for a while now. Don's talking like there's one, two more seasons left anyway."

I thought maybe he was trying to point out that even if I'd been re-signed, the job would've punked out soon enough anyway. "Easy for you to say. You still have a job."

"Come on Daphne. We're both actors. Staying in the public eye is the key to getting roles." He gave me the million-dollar movie star smile and wiggled his eyebrows. "I'm appealing to your sense of hustle."

It was as if Chance didn't understand he was made, that he was a legit B-list teenage heartthrob and could ride that cash wave for a few years at least. How could he not know his worth?

Another wave of rage at Lloyd. I had been so close to that level of security. But one season wasn't enough fandom, and anyone who might hire me now would wonder what happened to get me fired. Ugh, just thinking about it made me want to fall face-first into a pillow and scream.

Oblivious to my annoyance, Chance said, "So.... what if after SHIPWRECK ends, you and I do a show together?"

"That's sweet, Chance. But we can't. We don't own the characters. The show won't let us use them without permission."

"No, a reality show. As Daphne and Chance. Viewers will watch because they'll wanna know what happened with Vanessa and Leo. Especially if there's a little drama about you leaving the show. They know our relationship was cut short."

There it was. That glimmer of something. Hope. Reluctantly, I showed a little. "Yeah. OK. But what's the hook? What's the story?"

He leaned back in the car seat, grinning with this total unabashed happiness, like we were kids getting ready to pull the best prank ever. "We do what SHIPWRECK HIGH didn't get to. You and I get married."

FOUR

But then, instead of SHIPWRECK HIGH getting canceled, and Chance becoming another momentarily unemployed B-lister like me? He landed a part in a mother-fucking million dollar budget feature film. Here's how that shit went down:

Of course, I was at this half-skeevy laundromat downtown, folding my dryer fresh clothes when Daily Edition came on just above my head, on the cheap little flat-screen bolted to the wall, up too high to touch.

The laundry warden was watching the celebrity gossip shows, feet kicked up on her desk, making sure nobody cracked open the change machines or threw a dog in a dryer.

To be honest, celebrity gossip shows are half-considered legit news hours here in Los Angeles, since so many people are in the biz one way or another. I half-heard the *zing-zing-*

pow! sound effect to indicate some interesting tidbit was coming up.

But then the name "Chance Zak" perked my ears. Followed by catchphrases that meant someone's career was blowing up: *starring in... alongside such adored Hollywood icons as.... Long-awaited premiere...*

My stomach plummeted as what this meant for me sunk in. I took a deep breath to steady myself. It came out shaky and like half a sob.

You might wonder why I'd be bummed about Chance's success, like if I was jealous or something.

That wasn't it.

It was our reality show, the one we'd talked about that night in the car. We hadn't talked too much in person after that — I mean, he had the show, and I had this glamourous laundry folding life, but we'd hit a few texts back and forth, and his agent had reached out to let me know the business agenda of creating a reality show was still on track. And so while Chance's life continued as a normal sit-com star, I'd been waiting in the wings, trying to make it big on my own, but with the glimmering hope of our reality show tucked away, keeping me going.

And honestly, I knew it might fall apart. Deals go south in Hollywood all the time. And people get backstabbed all the time too.

But somehow I knew if it was up to Chance, we'd do that show. So I watched Season 4 of SHIPWRECK HIGH, even though I was bitter as a pill about getting written off the show.

In the season opener, Leo found Vanessa's boat capsized in the shallows offshore as if something bad had happened. On lonely nights, in my cluttered bedroom, I watched through my phone as the cast's desperate search to find

Vanessa dwindled near episode three, and a heartbroken Leo found love with that bitch Bethany Bimmel.

I'd booed at the screen when Bethany kissed Leo in front of the driftwood grave marker Leo had lovingly fashioned for Vanessa. And over dinner of a single boiled egg, I'd pulled up every fandom link I could to glory in the comments about how shitty Leo and Bethany's chemistry was, what a horrible mistake writing my character, Vanessa, off the show had been, how it was probably a nail in the series coffin.

I'd cackled at every mean comment. It was either that or get deeply depressed at how quickly I was running through the money I'd intended to use to pay off Lloyd. Gas was expensive. Rent was expensive. And I probably had a little mark next to my name with casting directors around town: *hard to work with,* or *has shit representation.*

Most of my days were all about going in for auditions, taking acting classes, or working out. But midway through SHIPWRECK's fourth season, the producers called to offer a one-time return to the show for the finale.

Ratings were indeed sagging with the Bethany/Leo romance subplot, and they wanted to know if I'd help them out. They could make it so Vanessa *hadn't* died, she'd been drawn out to sea by a riptide, *nearly* perished in the vast and tumultuous ocean... before being miraculously rescued by a passing cargo ship.

The plotline went like this: Unable to speak the crew's language and near-death by dehydration, Vanessa had to recover before she could convince the captain to radio for help. By then, of course, the location of Leo's island had been lost. Tragic!

The whole season closed with me as Vanessa, on a boat

searching resolutely for my lost classmates, and of course, for Leo.

The show didn't promise they'd bring me back, of course. Just that one episode, and I didn't even get to film with Chance or the rest of the cast. But the showrunners were giving me an opportunity to prove I could sign a freaking contract and show up for a call.

I'd signed the agreements myself, in secret, and slipped away from the house to film. There was no way to cut Lloyd out as my manager — he'd signed the original contract, so he'd always get his 10% off any SHIPWRECK work I got.

But I didn't tell him about it.

And of course, you know the episode was a big, schlocky, dramafest. All the old fans came screaming back over that last episode, giving SHIPWRECK HIGH a bump in social media interest. Me, looking out over the rail of a boat, became a meme for like two seconds.

Lloyd was NOT happy, even though the bum still got 10% for doing nothing.

"You think you're such a big shot?" he demanded when the show aired... which to be fair, was the moment he found out I'd gone behind his back and signed the contract without him. "Guess you don't need me to be looking out for your next lead."

He was trying to make me feel bad, but I felt the opposite. That one episode had gotten me $7000— more than double what I'd been paid per episode before.

Seven hundred went into Lloyd's pocket off the top. And that was just to be my manager, not paying down what I owed him. Taxes took almost half. Some of the cash I kept in my room disappeared, probably to my mother's drug habit. Groceries, gas, and insurance left me with a few bucks for my Fuck Lloyd & Acquire Freedom account.

But I knew my dreams of fame and fortune were about to become reality if I could just hold out a few more months: I'd get a contract for Season 5 of SHIPWRECK.

Or if they canceled the show, Chance would be out of a job and we could do our reality show. These were the promises I held onto when there was no food in our fridge and Mom disappeared for days. Or when it was just me and Lloyd in the house, and he made increasingly unpleasant 'jokes' about how I should be his girlfriend.

In the meantime, I'd gotten a job as a waitress, scheming endlessly over all the ways Chance and I could showcase all the pent-up chemistry between us. The fans were *still* talking out our fictionalized television romance, months after SHIPWRECK Season 4 had ended. I read their comments over, and over, bookmarked in my phone to keep my spirits up as I was getting my butt pinched at the diner.

Which was why I broke down crying when that stupid Daily Edition came on in the laundromat.

"You can't cry, sleep, or do that one other thing people try to do in here, hon. It's bad for business," the laundry warden called, half-sympathetic, half-bored.

"Got it." I sniffled quickly and got back to work folding.

The thing was, Chance was a good guy, but no actor who got fronted in a summer blockbuster would go back to doing TV. Especially not some rinky-dink, risky, small screen reality show.

Image in show business was key: you Photoshopped all your Instagram posts. You bought your face and your body. You didn't become America's Hottest Superhero Hunk and THEN do a reality show where all your warts and neck waddles showed the moment you stumbled into bad lighting.

OK, and total honesty: I'd been in two commercials since SHIPWRECK HIGH. They'd come through Lloyd.

"You owe rent," he'd said. "Either take the job or get out."

And that was how easily I'd fallen right back in business with the guy. Well, after I'd looked at apartment prices and realized I couldn't afford to pay a thousand bucks a month to share a one-bedroom with three roommates.

Now, folding the last of my laundry, I felt completely broken. This was exactly what my entire life was going to look like: struggling for work, always being an *almost-was* until I was old enough to be a *has-been*. I groaned with my mouth closed to keep the noise in. I just didn't get it. I was smart. I was doing my best. I had a good face and good skills and I wanted this sooooooo badly and—

My phone buzzed. Wiping a sniffle with the back of my hand, I picked up my phone.

Chance: *When you see the news*

I steeled myself for the official let down. Even though we were friendly, Chance was a busy guy. He usually only reached out with business stuff. I closed my eyes tight, exhaled slowly. Heard the chime go twice more before I was prepared for him to cancel on me.

Chance: *I didn't forget*

Chance: *We're still on for our show together.*

I SCREAMED. Like, unbelievable, cackling, wild laughter.

And promptly got kicked out of the laundromat. Apparently crying, sleeping and *screaming* are the three things you can't do there.

* * *

CHANCE: *Let's go shopping*

If we'd really been getting married, maybe it would've been bad luck to try on dress after dress with him.

("I love that one," he'd said offhandedly as I twirled in front of him. "The mermaid is more Vanessa's style, but that sheath is you.")

(I rejected that one immediately of course. We didn't go home until I stepped out in a dress that made him forget his phone.)

Or spend hours shopping for *Exactly the Right Ring*, which was loaned to the show by the jewelers in exchange for a clip of us deciding on the ring in their showroom. They also made me a cheap knockoff to wear for the rest of my days. Ah, romance!

Or sampling tiny pieces of exquisite cake from the most revered bakeries in Southern California, each vying for a sponsored spot on the show.

But none of it was real. And it was all in prep for launching our business together. And so we had the most fun I'd ever had in my life. It wouldn't be hard convincing the world I was a million percent in love with Chance Zak. Not when he made it so incredibly easy.

And the one piece of it that was very real? Chance's wedding gift, which came late in one evening as I lounged in my tiny bedroom:

Chance: *Hold out on your contract.*

Chance: *I remember your magic number. They'll tell you they can't do it, but they can, and they will. Promise.*

I understood in a hot second, sitting up in bed. Chance was talking about what I owed Lloyd for the surgery. Of course, now I had it paid down to just under $10,000, but the number I'd told Chance was...

Me: *40k for the season?*

There was a long pause. Maybe he'd made some terrible

predictive text error and had actually been trying to warn me there was no way they would give me that kind of money. Oh god, he was probably trying to figure out how to correct my misunderstanding as gently as possible. I hyperventilated a little and started to type, *Oops! fat fingered it, I meant—* when his text came through.

Chance: *Per episode.*

The phone slipped in my hand. That much money per episode? I could move out of my mother's house immediately. I could buy a new car that didn't threaten to shake apart pushing 45 mph merging onto the freeway.

Holy shit I love you!

I stopped dead, staring at the unsent text. Of course, people in Hollywood said that kind of thing all the time, every day. It was like a handshake, like a hello. But suddenly it seemed very dangerous to say. Maybe because I'd spent a lifetime getting *owing* someone and *loving* them mixed up in my head.

I deleted the text and sent him a thank you instead, palms sweaty. My life was risky. But you know I bow at the altar of my first two rules: get paid, be free. There was less than $10,000 left on my tab with Lloyd.

I asked for the money.

And got it.

FIVE

THE FIRST DAY of filming GOOD IN THE ZAK was also our wedding day.

The set: The backyard of Chance's Hollywood Hills mansion. All perfectly manicured lush subtropical Los Angeles greenery. Everything was landscaped to perfection to disguise the fact that no matter how big or magnificent, all these million-dollar homes were crammed together.

As the cast and crew set up sprays of flowers and a silken white fabric between the chairs, Chance and I hung out in his game room, which had been set up as the crew's home base.

The showrunner rushed in, barely glancing at us as we stood in our wedding duds: no sitting allowed for fear of wrinkles. We leaned against the wall, waiting. With a theatrical flourish, he landed the piece of paper on the table nearby.

The showrunner signed his name. "There. I'm your

witness. The pastor signed off. Now I just need your signatures here and...." He tapped the paper again. "Here."

Chance pushed off the wall. "You ready?"

A minute ago, we'd been playing rock-paper-scissors like this was any other day on set. Now, he looked nervous, which I would've chalked up to the fact that he was supposed to look that way — a groom on his wedding day. Except there was no one here to appreciate the acting.

Of course. He must've had doubts. His movie had blown past even the huge expectations. Chance was a big star. I was a nobody with a bad manager. And even though I'd signed the prenup that had come last week via registered mail, this marriage certificate was the real deal.

"We don't have to." I tried to assure him with a smile. "I mean, who'd know if we didn't do the paperwork?"

"Everybody," the showrunner cut in sharply. "You don't sign those papers and some tabloid will run a story on how you never filed, the marriage isn't legit. And you better believe— everybody knows reality shows are bullshit. Everybody. But the same people who know that will sure as shit be furious to be confronted with that fact. They will HATE you. Forever. So you sign, you sell the show, we all make money. But as far as you are concerned? From now until we wrap, you lovebirds are all about the magic of true freakin' love. Got it?"

I nodded sharply, blushing at the reprimand. I had only been trying to be nice. My mistake, and an amateur one. This was business.

Wordlessly, Chance flicked the pen across the paper, signing. He handed it to me and paced. My dress felt too tight. I couldn't breathe. He didn't want this. Something wasn't right. I gasped. My lips tingled as I went lightheaded at the rejection.

Holy shit, keep it together. You're a professional. Act like it.

Handshaking, I reached out for the paper.

CERTIFICATE OF MARRIAGE scrolled across the top. In the little boxes, my name had been typed under BRIDE. "Chance Zak" under GROOM. His real name, I realized then, not just some catchy stage handle. The fact I hadn't known for sure it was his real name made me question my judgment again.

Halfway down, the showrunner's signature under WITNESS, Chance's under GROOM'S SIGNATURE, the scrawl of the OFFICIANT. Blank under BRIDE'S SIGNATURE

That's you.

It's just a show, just business, you are in control, I soothed myself. But it was more than that. This was my chance to be on screen. To make it big. To pay Lloyd back and be free. I signed.

"Great. Congratulations. You two are married." The showrunner hurried out the door. "Call's in five. Be ready."

The last of the camera crew headed out for final check, leaving us alone.

Chance laughed. "We're not... we're not really married. Not yet."

"I think so. Officially anyway."

He sat down.

"Chance! Wrinkles!"

He laughed. "It'll be OK." Then. "We're married." And then a breathless chuckle. "Holy shit."

I'd thought he was angry, but now I saw he was about to faint. Relief washed over me. He was so ridiculous. Like, ridiculously handsome, and according to every magazine cover in the western world, the perfect guy. But also, flustered as a schoolboy, charmingly so.

"Relax," I rolled my eyes, softening it with a smile. "It's just a show. Not real."

Slowly, he nodded. My heart settled down, out of that strange, panicky place. I turned to the full-length three-way mirror set up in the corner, making sure everything looked right. Good. We could get through this. Just like we'd gotten through our season of SHIPWRECK HIGH; joking around on set, having a good time, enjoying the accolades and popularity. This was a perfect day because it was taking me exactly where I needed to go.

"But what if we make it real?" Chance asked.

"What?" I spun from the mirror to gawk at him. He had to be joking. He couldn't change the rules now. Not after I'd just signed my life away in show contracts and marriage contracts and—

The showrunner's assistant stood in the entry, breathless. "Come on. SHOWTIME!"

SIX

Hours later, Chance, carrying me in his arms, swung around and kicked the bedroom door closed. I said the line we'd practiced a few times before. "Omigod, what is THAT?" and on cue, Chance laughed.

"Annnnnnnd got it!" The camera guy said from beyond the door.

We stood in the bedroom, panting with the excitement of it. The energy of a great show, a live audience, the very real champagne toasts.

Beyond the bedroom door, the muffled sounds of the camera crew doing their last sound checks and a cut, someone asking whether they got the shot. A murmur of pleased agreement as they played it back.

I wiggled, and slowly, Chance relaxed. The arm hooked under my thighs carefully lowered, and I slid down his body until my toes touched. Under my dress, my thigh still naked from where he'd taken off my garter a half-hour before. To the jeers of the crowd, he hadn't tossed it but tucked it into his breast pocket and kissed me. Which of course turned the complaints into whoops and laughter.

The kiss had taken me by surprise. I'd expected the one when we'd said our vows, but I guess... my mind hadn't completely understood he'd be kissing me all the time. Whenever he wanted. Whenever I wanted. So long as it was on camera.

Standing in his darkened bedroom, waiting to see if the crew wanted us to do another take of him carrying me across the threshold, Chance held me close. I tried to breathe as shallowly as possible, aware of how each movement pressed me intimately against him.

The quiet became velvety thick, this bubble of only us. Chance reached for his tie, pulled it loose, unbuttoned the top collar. The cut of his Adam's apple at his throat, tan skin against the crisp white shirt. He wasn't on all those America's Sexiest lists for nothing.

"Should we..." I hesitated.

I hadn't thought this far ahead. Even though it was a show, the reality part meant the world saw us as married even when the cameras stopped rolling.

For a dizzy little moment, it felt like I might never completely know when I was his wife, and when I was off the clock and belonged only to myself. The small, feral part of me that only believed in those two gods of fame and freedom, panicked.

You chose this, I reassured myself. *You can't be mad at him if you agreed.*

Chance stood solemnly in his actual real bedroom... and what was technically to be our bedroom, for the show. How real was this for him? My pulse fluttered up a notch. When he'd carried me over the threshold, no one had hit the lights. The dimness of the room amped up the intimacy.

He put a finger to his mouth, half a smile on his lips.

I thought he was going to kiss me, even with no cameras

there. That somehow the slippery line between fantasy and reality had blurred. That this was our wedding night.

Part of me wanted it, wanted to keep pretending to be that fairy tale girl who'd gotten married today. Chance wrapped his free arm around me, hands slipping down the back of my dress, searching.

And turned off my microphone battery. He pointed at his waist, lifting his suit jacket. I obliged, understanding.

"OK, we're clear." He grinned. "You wanna get out of these duds and go have a real party?"

"I gotta pee like you wouldn't believe." As soon as the words were out of my mouth, I was horrified. Something about Chance just got under my radar, like I could say anything to him.

"Bathroom's all yours." He pulled at his tie, moving away from me, dissolving the sense that we were anything more than business partners. I let myself watch him move across the room, distracted. God, he was good looking. Since he'd taken that superhero role and was working out with a trainer, just... chiseled. I knew it wouldn't last; nobody can keep themselves in that state of perfection forever, but I kinda wanted a sneak peek of him taking that shirt off.

He must've felt my eyes on him, because he turned, a questioning expression on his face. Oh yeah, I was supposed to be dashing for the bathroom.

"Do you need help?" he said, hands going still. "Getting out of the dress, I mean? I can call someone up."

"You could do it," I offered. The back of the dress looked like it was pearl buttons all the way down, but like everything else in this town..."It's just a zipper, hidden under the fabric."

"Sure," he murmured, and I turned to present my back

to him, sweeping my hair across my shoulder and bending my neck.

We stood so close we almost touched. Through the floor, the distant sounds of the crew partying downstairs. Then the brush of his fingers at the nape of my neck, the warmth of his breath on my skin as he found the hidden zipper and tugged it smoothly down.

I felt it everywhere. The dress that had been so securely molded to my frame came loose, becoming heavy without the support, sliding down my shoulders. Reflexively, I clutched the fabric to my chest so it wouldn't fall.

The zipper was undone, but he hadn't moved.

"The dress," I said.

When I looked over my shoulder at him, my breath caught. His eyes smoldered, necktie undone, shirt buttons open. It would be so, so easy to let go. The dress was so heavy it would be at my feet in a whisper.

I liked having this kind of control over him, knowing I could have him. I mean, there was no doubt. But sometimes knowing you can have someone is even better than actually having them. Especially if you have to work with that person for the foreseeable future. Especially when your feral insides are already having problems sorting out what's real and what's not.

"Will you hold the dress while I step out of it? So it doesn't get crumpled on the floor?"

"Um. Sure?"

I could tell he didn't know exactly what I wanted him to do. I liked this even more.

"OK, so um, hold the bustier here." I moved my hands to show him were. The warmth of his hands again, against my skin where the dress opened. "Got it?"

His answer was a flutter of breath against my naked back.

"OK, now help me lower it, and when I step out, pull it back up off the ground so it doesn't get rumpled."

Inch by inch, the dress came down, his hands trailing along to the small of my back, across my panties, down my thighs. He was crouched, practically kneeling. I turned, and using his shoulder for balance, stepped out of the dress in nothing but panties and my heels.

"Just lay the dress out on the bed flat!" I called as he stood. "I really gotta pee. So I'll see you down there!" And then I dashed into his en suite bathroom before he could turn and catch more than a glimpse of either me...or that feral part of me that crackled with absolute joy over toying with Chance, at the satisfaction of being in control. Way better than the risky prospects of falling into bed with him.

* * *

DOWNSTAIRS, both of us in sweatpants, Chance and I weaved through the remaining cast, headed for the kitchen.

We ate wedding cake in front of his massive fridge, looking out the window at the after-party happening on his back lawn. No cameras in sight. That meant everything that happened was real, there was no other reason to act or say anything other than because a person felt it.

Even so, things overlapped. Like, we'd hired the actress who'd played Bethany Bimmel on SHIPWRECK HIGH to be my maid of honor. In our new reality show, she was supposed to act half-sour grapes jealous and flirt with Chance every time I was off-screen. In real life, she was half-jealous since it could've been her reality show if Chance had asked her instead of me.

And in real life, it thrilled me to no end that Chance was contractually obligated to turn her down every time she tried to seduce him away. At least, on camera. But I didn't have to worry tonight; Bethany was slow dancing on the patio with some guy I didn't recognize.

My mother and Lloyd were slow dancing too, out by the pool. I hadn't had time to see Mom during the taping.

"I'll be right back, husband." I winked at Chance and headed out towards my mother. She was humming softly when I tapped her back, head resting on Lloyd's shoulder.

"Well if it isn't the bride," Lloyd smirked.

"Hi, Lloyd." I gave him a neutral tone. "Hi Mom," I added in a warmer one.

"Oh honey." She laughed, letting go of Lloyd to half fall into my arms for a hug. It shocked me how light she felt like she had bird bones instead of human ones. "You did real good. Realllll good with that boy. They interviewed me!"

"I know! I saw!" I squeezed her.

That had been the only part of the contract I'd lobbied for: Mom would get screen time on the first episode, complete with a little banner underneath, proclaiming her as HEATHER, Child Star & Daphne's Mom. I hoped it made her and Lloyd both happy and showed Lloyd we could stay on good terms even when I severed ties with him as my manager. Plus, Mom would get royalties, plus extra if the show got syndicated.

I'd assured Chance it would be important for my image on the show— Chance and I had been closer to equals when we'd agreed to do GOOD IN THE ZAK, but since his movie star status had skyrocketed, I needed a little extra backstory to make me something more than The Girl Who Got Zakked. I didn't want to look like a gold digger, and being from Old Hollywood stock made me more... reputable, I guess.

Now, hugging her, feeling her excitement about the clip, I felt the most joy I had the whole day.

"I can feel it," she added, hugging me tighter instead of letting me go. I patted her back, laughing to let her know it was time to separate. "You are going to ride this boy's coattails all the way to your own star."

Ride his coattails. I went cold. She probably hadn't meant it unkindly, just misspoke. She'd had a few, I could smell up close. "Mom." I patted her arms to get her to break the hug.

"Let her loose," Lloyd said to her. "Don't get all sloppy now."

At his order, she did. Still standing close, she smiled into my face. "You are gonna make it all the way, honey. I can feel it."

The wider her smile, the more Lloyd soured, scuffing his shoe into Chance's immaculate lawn.

"You're gonna be in a huge mansion, with a driver and a chef, and go to all the award shows, and make them all stand up and clap for you," she breathed, eyes glassy. "And Lloyd here will tell all the guys how you were his million-dollar baby for forty grand. Before you wised up and dropped him. Isn't that what you said, honey? She's almost paid up everything."

Mom laughed, hitting Lloyd with the back of her hand like she was teasing, like she couldn't see his temper rise.

"Mom, I'm glad you came." I hugged her again to get her to stop talking. "Lloyd, could you take her home?"

He scratched the bridge of his nose and muttered something surely.

"What?" I asked, but that was a mistake. I should've known better than to give him any kind of spotlight.

"I said you ain't dropping me."

The couple closest to us had gotten quiet. Of course. People loved drama. Especially a bride with her drunk mother on the wedding day. Didn't matter that the wedding wasn't real. Sometimes people can't look past the white dress and the vows. Throw talk of money and a pissed off stepfather-type, and I could see I needed to shut this whole thing down immediately.

"We'll talk later. Time to go," I said.

But instead of taking my mother's arm, he grabbed mine and pulled me close to hiss in my ear. "You wouldn't be in this shit mansion if it weren't for me. Remember that."

"Let go," I warned quietly. He squeezed tighter, but the pain was nothing compared to my fear of people knowing I owed him. That behind closed doors, I had been owned by him.

"Let's not get out of hand now," Mom soothed. "Lloyd, take me home. I think I've had too much to drink."

Lloyd squeezed harder for a moment. I knew he didn't have the stones to do anything, he was just trying to make me flinch. I didn't give him the satisfaction.

"Hey, hands off." Chance came out of nowhere, suddenly so close his arm brushed mine, his palm against my wrist to let me know he was there.

Lloyd startled, letting go, stepping back. A shit-eating grin appeared on his face. He gestured at me as if he'd never touched me, as if there wasn't a ring of red fingerprints still circling my upper arm.

"This one was just telling me all about you, what a great boss you are."

"I'm not her boss," Chance said. I didn't have to look to know he wasn't smiling.

"Well, you know what I mean. Coworker. But you got her the job, she'd be unemployed if it weren't for this." Lloyd rubbed his nose with his thumb again, gazing anywhere but us. Like he was trying to stop himself from saying shitty things and just couldn't.

"No, I don't know what you mean," Chance said. I did take his hand then.

"Oh, you boys!" Mom tinkled lilting, nervous laughter. More people turned to watch. Mom couldn't help it, everything she did was tuned to attract attention. She'd been in the biz since she was three; being a star and being a person were all mixed up. "Daphne, good luck. I'll speak with you soon. Lloyd? Take me home honey. Weddings always put me in a romantic mood."

Oh gross.

Lloyd gave us a parting sneer and slunk off into the darkness with my mother in his clutches.

"What was that about?" Chance asked when they were gone.

"Nothing!" I said, brushing off my sour feelings. This, after all, was our GOOD IN THE ZAK first episode party and I wasn't gonna waste it on Lloyd. "Did you save me any cake? Because I. Am. Starving."

SEVEN

Hours later, Chance's massive house fell silent, our coworkers and friends either gone home or passed out on various pieces of furniture.

"Well, thanks for a great wedding," I said as we surveyed the wreckage. Someone had stacked the white wedding lawn chairs into a pyramid, all the pretty satin bows that had decorated them strewn about the house. You could not see the kitchen counter for all the plates and cups on it.

"You are helping clean this place up tomorrow, right?" he asked.

Tomorrow.

"Yeah, of course. I don't. Uh. I think my purse and clothes and stuff are up in the bedroom," I said. We'd started prepping for the show at 11 that morning. It had to be passed one a.m. now.

He rubbed his eye with a fist, like a little kid. "We'll find it in the morning," he said agreeably.

"Well, my keys are in there. I figured, you know..."

This was awkward. He hadn't technically invited me to stay over. In all the bridesmaid dress color combos and veil choices, we had never really talked about what our lives would look like now that the show had started. I mean, sure, we had the basic agreement that we were going to pretend to be married.

Relax, I told myself.

There was plenty of time to hammer out the details – the show wouldn't air for months, and somewhere along the way, we would have to decide whether we lived together all the time for the sake of making it look real, or only while the cameras were rolling.

But for now, we were free as birds.

But I wanted to stay.

"What? Keys? Don't be ridiculous, it's crazy late," Chance said, halfway yawning. "And how am I gonna trust you won't weasel out of cleaning if you leave now? Take the guest room. Come on."

"OK. Thanks." I followed him up the stairs.

But when we got to the first bedroom, by the embarrassingly loud and rhythmic thumping, it became very clear that not *all* the guests were asleep or gone.

"Do... do you hear that?" He leaned in closer, a shocked smile on his face.

"Chance!" I slapped his forearm. "That's so rude."

"Who do you think is in there? I'm guessing.... your Aunt Sally and that camera guy, Alex."

I grabbed Chance, pulling him away, totally mortified on behalf of whoever inhabited the bedroom. The guests were apparently undeterred. Behind the closed door, the bedsprings continued to squeak like they were full of mice.

"I don't have an Aunt Sally. Come on. You've got to have another bedroom in this place." I dragged him down the hallway.

"The one with the... green and pink..." he swirled a

finger above his head to indicate one of those British fascinators.

"That's the producer's ex. She brought their kids. One of them was our flower girl."

"Oh. She must've been joking." I realized Chance was either completely exhausted or maybe a wee bit drunk. I pushed open the next door. The room was dark inside.

"Occupied!" a guy sleep-mumbled.

"Beau?" Chance said it like he was running into an old high school friend at the airport.

A lamp came on in the room. A guy curled up on top of the covers blinked, squinting at us. "Chance? Aww, man. Great wedding! Too bad Minnie couldn't make it."

Something changed in Chance at her name. His shoulders rounded, head tilted down. It caught me totally by surprise, but this little flame of jealousy lit in the pit of my stomach. Whoever Minnie was, she meant something to him.

Oh, get over yourself. This isn't even a real sham marriage. It's a TV show.

"Hey B, sorry to do this to you, but can I move you to the couch downstairs?" Chance said softly.

"Sure." Beau slowly pushed himself upright.

"No, no," I said, mortified. "Don't do that. Go back to sleep." I couldn't kick a guy out of his own bed.

"S'okay," Beau mumbled, still trying to sit up. "Couch."

I hurried to his bedside and gently pushed Beau back in, drawing the covers up over him.

"Sorry we woke you," I whispered. "Thanks for coming."

I had this absurd notion to kiss his brow. Not in a romantic way, just ... you know a lot about a guy who'll get up from a dead sleep to give you the bed he's sleeping in.

It made me weirdly emotional. Probably the exhaustion

of the day, and the upset with Lloyd, but knowing Chance had friends like that, that if I stuck around, Beau might be my friend too? It felt weird. Like maybe there were other things out there besides becoming the most famous actor in town, or the highest paid.

Probably just getting mushy because I got married, and even knowing it was a total dog-n-pony show, sometimes when you go through the motions of a fake thing, real feelings get drawn up. Which was also a great way to explain away that weird jealousy I'd experienced over the girl they'd mentioned.

"Got any other bedrooms?" I whispered to Chance. No way he didn't. This place was huge.

"Well sure. But... that's the last bed. The others are storage or office space. Couches downstairs, but if the guest rooms are taken, I bet those have people on them too."

A breath of silent debate between us. *Maybe I should just head home.*

"Sleep in my room." He pointed down the hallway towards the master bedroom. Then he took a few steps down the hall in the opposite direction. He was leaving me up here.

"Wait!"

"I'm just gonna get some extra blankets," he said softly. "I'll take the floor."

He returned, comforters piled high in his arms, and together, we went back to his bedroom. Talk about awkward.

A massive bed in the center of the room. Someone had taken the dress, probably the costume designer. Now the bed was pristine: White comforters like clouds, stacked and piled with pillows. A surfboard in the corner had scuffed the soft green wall paint.

When I'd darted into the bathroom, leaving Chance holding the dress, I'd felt in control. Now, alone in his bedroom, it felt like I risked losing it.

Chance began making a nest on the floor with his comforters. I wondered if this was how the Sexiest Man in America envisioned spending his first night as a married man: on the floor of his own bedroom in a pile of blankets.

Was it how you *thought you'd spend your first night as a wife?*

No. But that was hardly a fair question. I'd never planned on getting married.

He said, "Want me to leave a little light on in the bathroom? In case you need it in the night?"

"You sound like a mother hen." I thought I saw him blush, but it was hard to tell in the dark. "No, I don't need a nightlight. And just sleep up here. The bed's huge and I won't try anything if you don't," I added, nudging him with my knee. He stood.

"Deal. What side you want?" He nodded at the bed and started pulling his shirt off. A glimpse of perfectly toned abs, flexing biceps as he moved. He stopped, poked his head out the neck hole, seemed to think better of undressing, pulled the shirt back on.

"It's OK," I said, but my throat had gone a little dry. The bed, which had been so huge when I made the offer for us both to sleep there, now seemed intimately close quarters.

I reminded myself this was Chance. We'd worked together for a whole season of SHIPWRECK HIGH, got along fine, always had great chemistry. I could trust him. I tried not to think about how I'd almost texted him *I love you!*

Or why I hadn't been able to.

"Oh, hey." He reached for the pile of fluffy comforters

he'd brought in and pulled out a toothbrush, still in its packaging, along with a trial size of toothpaste. They looked like toys in his big hand. "You want this?"

"Omigod, you really are a mother hen, aren't you?" I laughed, taking the toiletries. "Bespoke toothbrush? I should marry you for real."

He shrugged. "Some of my best memories are sleepovers when I was a kid. Beau, that guy we talked to? I lived at his place for like three summers, and his mom always had extra stuff if I forgot. His dad made pancakes every Saturday."

It made me wonder how many times Chance had shown up at sleepovers needing a toothbrush.

"That's like the opposite of me," I said. "I was always trying to grow up, trying to get away from being a kid."

I thought of making boxed mac-n-cheese for dinner in the empty apartment. The things people couldn't see? Mom let those parts slide.

He headed for the bathroom.

"For the record," he called over his shoulder, "I'm also the house that gives away full-sized candy bars on Halloween."

I followed him. Two sinks, a soaking bathtub, and a steam shower, a very expensive looking scale. Without a word, he grabbed his own toothbrush and got down to business. I did the same.

Again, that first date nervousness, the strange intimacy of seeing him in private, the casualness of his bare forearm, muscled and slightly hairy, moving the brush around in his mouth, spitting out foam. Different from standing in front of a cast and crew, reciting vows and exchanging rings. It struck me then, how we were really alone.

Your husband.

Those two words refused to stop haunting me, no matter how untrue they were.

I caught a flash of his eyes through the mirror. He'd been watching me, but now he busied himself, rinsing his mouth, tossing his toothbrush into its holder with a little *clink*, and then wiping water spots off the counter. He was nervous.

"Come on," I went back to the bedroom. He hesitated at the threshold, watching me. It made me bold. "You choose your side. And we'll keep it our whole married life," I joked.

"I definitely like the right." He moved to that side of the bed and pulled the covers back. The smell of fresh linen, the soft sound of a down comforter folding.

It would never not be weird to get into bed with him. So I just sucked it up and did it.

Chance Zak's bed was AMAZING. Like falling into a marshmallow dream. As soon as I was in, Chance got in too and pulled the comforter over us. It floated down, warming almost instantly. I snuggled it under my chin, sighing with exhaustion and delight.

"Night, Wife." He sounded almost unconscious already. No wonder the guy looked so great. He had beauty sleep nailed. Still, I felt a little needle of disappointment.

EIGHT

I THOUGHT I'D FALL ASLEEP LIKE TURNING OFF A LIGHT, I was so tired.

But as great as the bed was, as happy as I was we'd made it through filming, as blissfully far away as I was from Lloyd or the strange anger/pity I had for my mother, I couldn't sleep.

My sweats felt scratchy, uncomfortable, and a little hot. I thought about making a deal with Chance that we could both take off one item of clothes for the sake of comfort. But that seemed like a come on.

Instead, I stared at the darkened ceiling, thinking about how close I was to paying Lloyd off. Technically, I'd completed an episode of GOOD IN THE ZAK, which meant I had plenty enough money coming to pay him off the four thousand six hundred dollars I owed with tons to spare. That was my happy place, and I snuggled into the bed thinking of how good it was going to feel to be completely my own. Maybe I'd even hire a fancy, real manager. Someone I could trust to know what they were doing. Someone who'd be loyal to me.

"You awake?" he whispered. Like a kid at a sleepover. It made me laugh.

"Yeah."

"That guy with your mom."

"Lloyd. Boyfriend."

"Hers?"

"Yeah. He's also my manager, the one..." I gestured to my face.

Chance didn't say anything, but I could tell by his breathing he was still awake. I turned to look at him, my eyes adjusting to the dim room so I could see him in shades of shadow and line.

He studied me like a therapist might, that unblinking assessment as if trying to see something I wasn't sure I wanted him to know. Then it hit me. Maybe Chance thought Lloyd was MY boyfriend. With the way Lloyd had been grabbing me, I kind of understood Chance's confusion. Still.

"Eww. Definitely her boyfriend," I clarified.

"What were you talking about? When he had your arm?"

I fidgeted. It was easy to say too much in a bed. Like fake-getting-married, this intimacy crept up on you, even if it wasn't real.

"You still owe him money?"

"It's my business. And anyway, I've got it taken care of as soon as my first check clears."

"And then he'll be out of your life?"

It was a complicated question. I had no love for Lloyd, but he was my mother's boyfriend. And knowing both of them as I did, it seemed like as long as she was in my life, he would be as well. And that there would be some sort of grift attached.

Tonight, on the lawn, Chance hadn't thrown Lloyd out on his ass, but I'd felt the weight and power of my fake husband as he stood next to me, his authority so natural Lloyd had immediately bent to it. I didn't want Chance to know my deal with Lloyd cost me more than money, or see Chance's face when he discovered all the worms and centipedes under my pretty rock.

"OK, now you, husband." I flashed him my television smile, bright and practiced, and when I said that word, *husband*, I laughed for real at the surprise on his face. "Tell me something."

"OK, what?" He didn't seem tired now, snuggled into his pillow, his breath ruffling across the back of my hand as I held the covers under my chin.

"Who's Minnie?"

His easy smile faded. Uh-oh. He cleared his throat. "Well, when I was a kid, she was the one I thought would be up there at the altar with me." As soon as the words were out of his mouth, he shook his head. "Not that I'm not glad it was you."

"This is just business anyway." My words, in a rush to get out, trampled over his.

"Yeah, right, exactly." Chance nodded with relief.

But then we stared at each other, in bed together, really married on our wedding night. A snicker escaped.

"Very business-like," I managed.

"I hold all my meetings this way," he laughed.

When we'd wound down into sighs, he said, "I said that badly. Beau has been my best friend since way back. My mom was a typical Momager, showing me the ropes on auditions, acting classes, had me in plays and out of regular school by sixth grade. Beau's house was like my first memories, before I got in the biz, just being a normal kid. You know?"

"I don't. I'm second-generation Hollywood. My first gig was as a newborn on a soap opera."

The closest thing I knew to the life Chance was talking about was the stuff I'd seen on TV.

"Yeah, well, always thought I'd grow up and marry Minnie and... I dunno." His eyes went distant.

I didn't feel jealousy exactly. More like envy. In his voice, I could hear what it must've been like to have a secret safe place, a touchstone to go back to. I would never be Minnie; that safe place didn't live inside me. But I understood what was so attractive to Chance about that life.

He smiled somewhat apologetically. "I always thought Beau and I would play poker on weekends like Beau's dad did, and she and I would live in that house, and I'd... I don't know what I thought. Mostly I just imagined mowing the lawn and coming home from a regular job, and the house would smell like cookies. Sounds pretty stupid when I say it out loud."

"I dunno. Everyone wants the fantasy, right? Meanwhile, some guy mowing his lawn is dreaming about being a movie star." I shrugged. "Why didn't you? Marry the girl."

He inhaled sharply, as if he'd never asked himself this question, as if somehow he was just now realizing that he'd missed his opportunity to fulfill some childhood dream.

I wanted to tell him he hadn't. I would be gone eventually, and he could go live his small-town fantasy. But I stopped short. Was I really going to comfort this guy about his opportunity to divorce me someday?

His answer caught me by surprise. "I guess I was waiting until I was good enough for her."

"Um, excuse me?" I half sat up in the bed. "Don't tell me I married an idiot."

"Hey!"

I waived an arm about the darkened room. "You're America's Sexiest Movie Star. Whaddidya make this year? No, don't give me that look. You know what I'm making."

He was a producer on GOOD IN THE ZAK. Hell, he had told me to ask for 40K an episode.

"Two point five."

"What'd you sign for the sequel?"

"...Six."

"So you're a millionaire with a bomb-ass eight pack, gorgeous, and young. How are you worried some girl in your Podunk hometown isn't going to want you?" He was definitely blushing. Even in the darkness, I could tell. "You could have the best girl in the world," I started. *What's so special about this Minnie?*

But before I could ask that part, he leaned across the bed and kissed me on the mouth. "And I did." He grinned, easing back. "I married you."

The minty taste of him on my mouth, the pressure of his lips. New and exciting and gone before I really knew what it felt like, other than good. The impulse to lean in and really kiss him back was only stopped by my sternest of internal reprimands:

You are in a bed. You start something, better be ready to have things get realllll confusing with your new work buddy.

"Don't be smart," I said.

A knot grew in the pit of my stomach. He'd hired me to play the role of a virginal, goofy, slapstick beauty of a wife. That end episode line in the bedroom? All that had been scripted.

Now the parallels between this Minnie and my role

struck me, uncomfortably so. I was playing the good girl next door she really was.

"You.... you know I'm not like her, right?" I asked. "I'm not that feel-good safe place, waiting in the wings until you come home. Maybe in the show, but that's not who—"

"I know."

He was so attractive— the wide shoulders, muscles bulging as he slipped an arm under his pillow. Belatedly, it struck me that if he loved this Minnie, if he was just waiting to make enough money or be famous enough, or a good enough person, or whatever his personal metric for winning her over, that I was a placeholder, a guaranteed divorce. It stung.

Why do you even care? I scolded myself. *This is business.*

"But you could try," he said after a moment. "We could try."

"Just so you know. I like to fuck around."

I said it super harsh on purpose. Because for one thing, it was true. Maybe some people would try to slut-shame me over it, but this was my body and no one else's. But more than that, I wanted him to know in the bluntest way possible I was the very opposite of whatever it was he saw in that other girl, so he would never again make the mistake of trying to make me live in her shadow.

He pulled back into the bed. He was seeing me now, that was for sure.

Love me anyway, this crazy thought came out of nowhere.

"Daphne, you can't do that. Neither of us can. The show has to be real, at least for the audience. While it's running, we have to really act married."

"Are you going to cut Minnie out of your life then?"

He exhaled hard, nostrils flaring.

"Oh, so you get to keep your life how it was, but I have to change mine?" I laughed, feeling myself flying off the handle. But that's the thing about handles— once you lose your grip, they're gone. The bruises Lloyd had left circling my arm suddenly felt tender, a brand from earlier in the night. "What do you think this is— a *real* marriage? You don't own me."

Chance sat up, comforter pooling around his lap, and swung his legs out of the bed. "Look, we've both had long days. We can talk tomorrow."

"Where are you going? There's nowhere else to sleep."

"Goodnight, Wife," he muttered under his breath.

But I wasn't, I told myself over and over, tears leaking out from behind closed lids as I tossed and turned in the huge bed until I finally fell asleep.

I wasn't his wife. Not really.

* * *

THE FIRST THING I felt when I woke the next morning was joy, snuggled in the best bed ever, my body feeling as though I'd slept a week, my brain lighting to the fact I was filming a TV series.

Then I remembered the fight with Chance. By morning light, remorse seeped in.

Beefs with coworkers are just part of life, I soothed myself.

Actors were a high-strung bunch, and that worked in my favor this morning. I'd simply apologize, make nice, and Chance and I could let get on with our lives. He'd understand.

I stretched from fingers to toes, working on my play-nice-professional-actor game plan.

My traitor brain insisted I think about how Chance had invited Minnie to our wedding. What if she'd shown up? I'd thought his nervousness at the marriage certificate had been about the two of us. But maybe his thoughts had been about her.

I thought of the softness in Chance's face when he talked about her. No wonder. I mean, I barely knew Beau, and he was the kind of guy you could wake from a dead sleep and he'd offer to give you the bed. Nobody was that nice.

Not in my family, anyway. I mean, I loved her, but my mom would push you out of bed with her foot if you tried to crawl in with her and ask you to go put on coffee.

Probably Beau and Minnie came from some stupid-perfect family, with a dog and a cat, and they walked to school each day from their adorable cottage. Of course Chance would want to be part of that. I bet Minnie *did* smell like cookies.

I hated her.

I mean, how boring, right? What kind of life was that? Cookies? Mowing the lawn? Sounded as exciting as fucking a couch cushion.

Plus, Minnie was probably pretty, but no way was she a match for my *structurally engineered for maximum knock out* features. Feeling smug that was way better than admitting how a part of me had been falling for Chance, or that somehow, I'd lost him without even knowing it.

Even as I was pep talking myself on how none of this mattered anyway, because I was about to live my movie star dreams, and I was getting paid bank, and in a matter of weeks, a check would direct deposit and I'd have my FU money for Lloyd....

... part of me was also trying to remember if I'd ever heard Beau's last name so I could google this lame ass Minnie rival.

I grabbed the pillow on his side and pressed it to my face, smelling Chance on it. Why hadn't Minnie shown up to the wedding? Probably she loved my new husband like crazy and her heart was breaking somewhere. Probably she hated me.

I laughed and dragged myself out of bed, deciding I would track her down and get a good hard look at my competition. When I was satisfied that she was no match for me, that I was a better person in every possible way, I'd very generously let her know she had nothing to be jealous of.

Chance didn't want me. He loved her.

NINE

"So in this scene, Daphne, you want to make a home-cooked meal for Chance. You know, live out your girlish housewife fantasies. But of course, you can't cook. We're going to do a montage, classic newbie in the kitchen kind of slapstick. I want you to really lean into it. You've never been in a kitchen in your life. But also, really hit those emotional notes— what it's like to live with someone for the first time. You're desperate to impress. Remember kids, you're in love, and you're both beautiful. So you can act as dumb as cans of beans and nobody will doubt it."

We were all sitting around the pool in Chance's back yard, the showrunner talking about the film schedule for the week. I closed my eyes against the perfect SoCal morning— a gentle breeze, all the blossoming things twisted with the faint scent of the ocean, the gritty underbelly smell of traffic run by burning ancient dinosaur sludge.

I tilted my head back, snuggled in a terrycloth bathrobe to keep my outfit pristine for filming. Inside the pocket, my phone vibrated. Discretely, I pulled it out, looked at it under the table.

Lloyd: *Answer my texts.*

Before I could drop the phone back in my pocket, it buzzed again.

Lloyd: *Don't think you can skipjack into that pretty new life and ignore me. Answer ASAP.*

LOL, fuck you, Lloyd, I smirked. *I am going to skip right out of your life.*

I might technically owe him a little more money, but that was *all* I owed, and I wasn't going to give him any more chances to take 'interest' as he called it out of my hide. The phone buzzed in my hand but I let it slip into my pocket. It buzzed again like an angry wasp, trapped there. It made me smile.

"The B story will be Chance sneaking around to plan a surprise getaway for the two of you. So make sure when he's secretive, play into that, drum up a little drama and suspicion. Newlyweds don't know each other that well, and there's lots to dig into with vulnerability and trust. What's he doing, right Daph?"

"Got it," I said. "Where are we going for the getaway?"

The showrunner wagged his finger. "The surprise is what makes it reality TV."

Chance leaned over and whispered, "Hot air balloon ride."

The showrunner hit Chance playfully on the thigh. "Be fun!"

I smiled, tingling at Chance's friendliness, wondering if I was forgiven as easily as that. "It's OK. I'm an actor. I think I can handle it."

"All right people, check in with makeup, we're in the living room for our first scene, say... in twenty." The showrunner clapped his hands once, a dismissal.

As everyone got up, I leaned over to Chance. "Hey,

sorry about our... about not seeing eye to eye the other night."

With easy good nature, he said, "Hey, no. That was on me. I can see how we got crossed up, and I don't want to be crossed up with you."

My shoulders came down. He was certainly easier to deal with than Lloyd.

"Thanks," I said.

It made sense by light of day— we'd both fallen into the regular pattern for a scripted show with life ending at 'cut' without thinking about the beyond-the-camera issues.

Chance flashed a grin, showing off the not-quite-dimples that would only deepen into those rugged lines handsome men got with age. "Great. Let's set a time to go over the rules."

I sat up, not liking the sound of that. Rules? He didn't seem to understand we'd already started filming. He really couldn't make me *do* anything. But I put on a guileless smile and patted the seat next to mine. "Now's as good a time as any."

"Here's how I see it: We're selling the American dream. The drama's got to be us against the world for both of our careers to come out looking good. That means a Happily Ever After. No cheating, no cruelty, just romance, the kind of fights where the drama's about whether two good people can make the connection."

My pocket buzzed. Lloyd again. He probably wanted me to flash my tits one last time to get him free access to a club or sit in his lap at some Hollywood party so everyone thought he was a big deal. Just one paycheck and I'd never have to answer his calls again.

"Really?" I laughed, extending my neck, brushing my hair back, knowing I looked good. Chance's eyes lingered everywhere I wanted them to, a subtle change in his breathing. Chance Zak might be a big-time star, but I had him right where I wanted him.

And being totally honest, I remembered what he'd said right before our vows, about making it real. I wasn't sure if I wanted to try that, but I wanted him to say it again, to know that no matter what else was going on, he wanted more from me, that I had an edge.

With the warmth of his gaze still on me, I said, "Are you sure you want to be celibate so long? I mean, what if the show makes it five years? Are you willing to go without a partner, without dating, without even going out to dinner with someone? Are you going to ask that girl back home to put her life on hold while we play house? Because I don't think anyone would wait *years*."

He shook his head like he'd lost his train of thought. "I'm saying the rules apply to both of us. Me. You. And I'm not saying either of us has to be alone. I'm saying our show depends on no cheating, cruelty, or bitterness getting into the public eye. It's for both of us. For the show."

He stood. The sun glittered off the pool, so that Chance became a silhouette of lean muscle and perfect proportions. I squinted, trying to understand him.

What was he getting out of this? His movie franchise made him a much bigger star than me, and it was rare for someone who'd made it to that level of celebrity to risk sinking back into the world of dinky reality shows.

I could admire it as a daring move that might slingshot Chance into super celebrity, the way George Clooney had rallied fans by going back for the series finale of E.R.

They said that was how George did went supernova; remembering the people who had loved him when he was small time. Maybe Chance had the same game plan, showing his sitcom fans he hadn't gotten too important to show up again, goofy but lovable, for them.

But still... he didn't need me for any of this. That gave me a cold chill, but I had to face the facts. If I didn't play by his rules, I supposed he could replace me with his other love interest from SHIPWRECK HIGH, the actress who'd played Bethany Bimmel.

Except he hadn't done that. And if he'd merely wanted to help me, he could've put me up for a role in some other project. So I had to assume there was some part I didn't yet understand. But the end result was the same: for some reason, he thought he needed me for this.

"Break it off with the girl," I said, because I knew he wouldn't. Not the way his face had gone so stupidly soft talking about her last night.

To make sure he refused, I aimed to hurt: "If you haven't told her you love her in all this time, you were never gonna have the guts. If you want me to follow the rules, you have to too."

His voice hardened. "That's different."

I gave him my prettiest *fuck you* smile. "Is it? Or is it exactly the same thing? Because a tabloid about you all goofy-faced with your childhood sweetheart seems like it would blow up our show."

"No, it won't. It's a non-story. She's a friend, and I'm not going to mess things—"

"So we're settled then," I interrupted, standing. "You get to keep her, and I get to keep whoever I want, and we'll trust each other's judgment to keep it out of the news."

Very, very satisfying to hear his grunt of aggravation, that he had no words to contradict me. Painful to know it was because he wouldn't let her go.

* * *

TWENTY MINUTES LATER, I pretended to check on a pot roast that had been pre-burnt in props and waited alongside a piece of dry ice, so when I opened the oven door, fake smoke billowed out.

And when I squealed in distress, "Baby! I need you!" Chance was right there to grab an oven mitt and yank the roast out like the superhero he was.

And like I was so new on earth he must've unboxed me himself.

Chance tossed the pan on the top of the stove and laughed, first chuckles and then brays. I knew enough about Chance by then to tell when he was acting.

If I could tell, others would.

I didn't have to think about it; seeing something go south happens in your gut more than your brain. Second episode in, and the chemistry between us had gone rancid.

I was supposed to throw my arms around him and he was supposed to offer to take me out to a fancy restaurant, which the show might cut to later, depending on how long the episode came in, time-wise.

But I didn't do what I was supposed to. No peal of laugher, no high energy, no I Love Lucy.

"I ruined dinner," I said softly.

But what I kind of meant was that I'd ruined the start of our show. Or we'd ruined it together because we'd fought.

He did a double-take. That's the great thing about acting; you tell the truth when you're lying. He knew what I was doing. I could feel that connection between us instantly light up: we were back in that fight, but now we could use our characters to be brave.

"No. No, hon, it looks great. You did a great job," he said, more tender than the joking bit of zany comedy that was supposed to end the scene. But also ridiculous. The fake roast fake smoldered.

No one sees in a reality show how you are surrounded by cameras and lights and mics, and it's all so pretend you cannot slip for a moment into believing it's real... until you see it on TV yourself. But even though we were surrounded, somehow it *was* real.

That's when it hit me: I liked him *more* because he wouldn't ditch Minnie. And of course, I still wanted to hurt him for the very same reasons.

No one in my life would do that for me. For sure not Lloyd, he'd sell me for a five-dollar profit. Not my mother either. The night of our wedding, I'd seen understanding flit across her face about what Lloyd was doing to me, the calculation in her eyes. I'd never be truly rid of Lloyd so long as she let him weasel into her life. All these things were fresh and stirred up.

I sobbed. Shoulders shaking and careful not to hide my face with my hands so the camera could catch all my real tears and Botox-free forehead wrinkles. "I just wa-wanted to be a good wife."

Chance went perfectly still, like I was some kind of explosive device he'd stumbled upon, my clock at 15 seconds and counting rapidly down to his doom. To be fair, this scene was supposed to end on a laugh and a squeal.

He cleared his throat. "Um..."

Christ, he was going to ruin this shot.

"You've got to..." My sobs hitched. "You've got to hug me and... and tell me I'm good." Because that was true. I didn't care what else happened. I needed him to make up with me.

He wrapped his arms around me so completely I was nothing more than a head popping out from his massive embrace, the weight and strength and body heat of him immobilizing me, holding me snuggled against him, pressing all of him against all of me.

"Of course," he whispered in my ear.

Peeking out from over the top of his biceps I saw as the camera guy spun slowly around us, getting one of those cinematic shots. I pinched my eyes closed so I wouldn't mess up the image.

Inside Chance's arms, even his words were muffled by his bulk, nothing louder than his heart, thudding with this slow surety. I let my knees go. He held me like I was weightless as a security blanket held to his chest.

Safe, I thought.

The first time I'd felt safe since before the surgery, back before my jaw had changed, when everybody had thought I had the talent and skills to make it all by myself.

Chance shifted, uncovering my ear, and I could hear him clearly again. "You're a good wife." He kissed my temple.

I pushed against his massive chest and he let me get a tiny bit away so I could look him in the eye. "You promise?"

Somberly he nodded. "Yeah. Promise."

He kissed me again, lips soft against my tear-puffy mouth. A gentle apology, trying to console me. The first kiss I'd gotten that didn't want to take something, but give it.

In a flash, I was completely on fire for him. Whatever he was offering, I needed it in my life. Or to be more specific, in my body. Hard and fast and completely and over and over until I was sick of it.

I wrapped my arms around his shoulders, deepening the kiss. The only thing that kept me from tugging his clothes off was the fact we were surrounded by camera crews. Still, my hand slipped around his waist, under the waistband of his jeans in the back, everything inside me throbbing at the curve of his ass beneath my fingers.

"Take me to bed," I whispered.

Chance responded immediately in ways I hoped were not caught on camera. He pulled back the slightest bit, both of us breathless.

"Annnndddd CUT! Absolutely fantastic!" The showrunner became a one-man standing ovation. The camera guys ignored him and us, checking their equipment.

Not all of Chance had been acting. The proof pressed against me.

"This!" The showrunner pointed at us. "This is exactly what's going to sell it. Daphne, I love what you did. Try to keep to the script, but if you get an improv idea as good as this one? Go with it, you understand? And Chance! I bought the whole thing. Beautiful. Absolutely beautiful."

He turned away from us, his enthusiasm cutting the vibe, shining professionalism on the secret of whatever mad passion had gone on between me and Chance.

"OK people. That's a wrap. Let's set up for Episode 3, in which Daphne buys expensive shoes and Chance doesn't like the price tag!"

Chance stepped away, disappearing in the swirl of moving people and equipment. And like that, the spell between us felt broken.

TEN

THE NEXT DAY, I ASKED AROUND SET FOR BEAU'S FULL name.

"Uh... Williams? I think. Why?" The showrunner's assistant answered over his clipboard.

Because I'm going to jump him and every other guy in a fifty-mile radius. I've decided to do it by alphabetical order, I did not say, but wondered if that was the assistant's concern, like maybe they'd been warned to keep an eye on me. Probably just my nerves.

"I wanted to write him a thank you note for being the best man at our wedding," I said sweetly.

Three minutes later, I was locked in Chance's upstairs bathroom, googling Minnie Williams. Search results "Minnie Williams" claimed she was

a) seduced and murdered by the infamous serial killer H.H. Holmes back in 1893

b) also murdered by the "Demon of the Belfry" Theo Durrant, also at the turn of the century.

So c) pretty easy to find the Minnie I was looking for

since not too many parents had been daring enough to name their kid after two old-timey murder victims.

My Minnie— or rather Chance's— was instantly recognizable as everything Chance had got moon-eyed over. Tagged in a dozen photos with Chance, their arms wrapped casually around each other, Minnie Williams was pretty and athletic.

Wide, honest smile and big, dark eyes, easy in her own skin. A college student according to the photos of her playing soccer on her intermural team back east. In the action shot, her leg muscles cut with definition, perfect.

I had a G.E.D.

Minnie was no match for me in terms of sheer facial symmetry and classic good looks, but somehow in every photo posted on the internet, her smile came across warm, like she was looking right through the screen to share an inside joke with you.

A good girl. You recognize them instantly, right? You knew you could tell her a secret and she'd pinky swear. The kind of girl who'd run off crying if you were mean, instead of trying to kick your ass for you.

I don't know why I kept searching for information on her, hunting for an Instagram, any new clues that would open her up for me. Since she wasn't a public persona, she had no reason to brand anything with her real name. Probably had all kinds of goofy handles I could never track down. I told myself to let it go.

But it became like one of those obsessive mindless games you play on your phone in the downtime. Whenever I was bored, sitting in the make-up chair, I'd find myself googling Minnie. And like those games, it felt as though I got a fix every time I uncovered something new about her. I don't know why. I didn't hate her. I was just curious. But in the way like... maybe if I could figure out what it was about her that hooked Chance, I could steal it for myself.

But maybe her specialness was I couldn't sense through the internet. Maybe it had to do with the scent you caught when she pressed up against you in that innocent way good girls did, like they were too pure to notice their breast brushing against your arm. Or how they stood so close, you could kiss them if you wanted.

I looked up Beau too, cross-referencing his stuff to anything I knew about Minnie, studying his followers, trying to figure out who might be Minnie in disguise. Every link might lead me to the treasure trove of what was so amazing about her that Chance would ruin our fake marriage to keep her.

You might think I'd feel guilty about stalking some poor girl. But honestly, I was living in Hollywood, where people got stalked all the time. My mother had 23 guys in various prisons who regularly sent her stuff through the mail. Prison officials were supposed to notify her when any of them made parole.

Chance had a fan club, which was not too different, except it wasn't populated by criminals... I hoped anyway. If someone had asked me if I felt weird about what I was doing with Minnie, I would've known the correct answer was a blush and a shrug: *Maybe, yeah.*

But when it was just me and my phone? I didn't feel bad at all. I mean, she did seem like a nice person. And that was pretty rare. I wanted to study her.

And if she made a few surprise appearances in my *not-so-good-girl* dreams? Well, that was because Chance was teasing me all the time, making me want him. With our shooting schedule and his rules, there was no way to work that frustration out of my system.

And frankly, I was pretty annoyed about it.

But I did follow his rules, and I tried to trust that no matter how anxious and frustrated it made me feel, I could work under the constraints of Chance's plan.

* * *

"SPORKS!" A guy shouted at me as we got out of the limo.

That's the moment I knew we were really going to make it. Not just the flash of cameras and sea of rectangular phones, or the impressive crown waiting for us. Not the smell of excitement in the air. For me, it was some dude beyond the carpet's roping, wildly laugh-screaming, "Hands ARE motherfucking sporks holding sporks!"

Something I'd said on a reality show, repeated back to us in reality.

Chance cinched an arm around my waist. Of course, he was devastating in a tailored dark blue shirt unbuttoned at the collar and dark pants, and he could not take his eyes off my dress— a skimpy muted yellow sheath that made my hair look like blonde fire. It felt like even the crowds and what they meant couldn't tear his attention from me.

In theory, we were merely going out to dinner. But GOOD IN THE ZAK had premiered five days ago, and so really this was a test to see if the internet hype was real.

I mean, sure, GITZ had trended on Twitter, and there was already a gif of me kissing Chance under the LOVE dropdown. But all that can be manufactured by bots and a few stealth, determined PR people. Sometimes PR won't tell you what they're responsible for, because they know if you believe your own hype, others will too.

As Chance and I hurried into Night Bar, flashing our best for the cameras, I DID believe the hype. Because for the first time, they were calling my name too. Not just Chance's. That thing about sporks? I said that!

"You heard that, right?" Chance leaned in to whisper as we were seated inside the exclusive bar. I nodded, deliriously happy. He grabbed my hand across the table and brought it to his lips, kissing my knuckles. Definitely for any insiders to later report to the tabs. "They love us, Daph."

"Hey! Did you see the crowd! Wild! This is gonna be huge." The showrunner pulled up a chair, sitting next to us. "Let's toast!" He waved his hand excitedly, flagging down a waiter. "Something nice! To share! Champagne!"

Moments later, a bottle of champagne between us.

"To the bride and groom!" The showrunner announced, followed by a cheer from the tables around us. This weird shiver went through me. Sure, the tables right around us were sprinkled with the crew from our show. But there were other movie stars and TV stars here, producers I recognized, just out on the town at a bar I was now notable enough to get into.

That shiver again as my attention expanded from my own joy at bathing in everyone's praise. I watched people admire Chance Zak. I was glad for him, to see his success, our success. Which was a weird feeling, to not be jealous of sharing the spotlight.

Chance added, "To the whole crew in this amazing marriage."

People laughed, toasting. I knew we were gonna get plastered. It was OK, a limo waited to take us home.

Chance's home. The season was over. Now the real roommate situation had begun.

If the show had tanked, it probably wouldn't matter much if we'd lived together. I mean, I guess the few followers would be dissolution to see a paparazzi snap of us living separate lives, but who could sell it? Nobody, unless the audience cared.

While we'd been filming, I'd stayed over at Chance's maybe half the time. Especially if we wrapped late or had an early morning call. But usually, that meant crashing in the guest room. Once, I'd fallen asleep on his couch and woken up to find he'd brought a comforter down and put it over me.

With my check from GOOD IN THE ZAK, I had planned on moving into my own apartment, away from Lloyd and my mother. But the truth was, with the filming schedule, I hadn't had time to move. So sometimes I went there and crashed, or took a shower.

A tense stalemate between Lloyd and I had grown, in which he didn't quite dare ask me if I was dumping him as a manager. Filming gave me half an excuse for ignoring him.

I hadn't yet told Lloyd I could pay him off, because I knew once we had that confrontation, he'd probably get real mad. I'd probably need to get any stuff I had out of that house during the same conversation, and maybe in a hurry.

With the stress of this whole thing with Chance, I just wasn't ready to pull the trigger yet. And to be completely honest, I was still preparing for my mom's reaction when I fired Lloyd, how she might cry and hug me, but ultimately tell me I couldn't come back until I made peace with him.

But I pulled up my bank account at least once a day and looked at the number, refreshing and refreshing to make sure it stayed. I was free. I kept telling myself I could leave any time I wanted. All I needed was a free moment to grab my stuff and break the news.

But now GOOD IN THE ZAK had social proof. From tonight on out, Chance and I would be living together.

I wasn't going to fight it. This was what we owed the show.

* * *

Much later, as the crowd separated, Chance and I strolled out the back door of Night Bar. Our limo waited in the less than glamorous alley so as not to give the paparazzi before and after shots of our exhausted, tipsy asses. I slid my arm through Chance's to steady myself. After months of working together, it felt like an easy thing to do. The crisp newness of his shirt, the faint smell of laundry and champagne.

"So, I know the rules change now," I said carefully to him, so as not to slur my words even the tiniest bit, although it seemed like being so careful made me sound drunker than I was. "I surrender to the rules. We have to live like married folks."

He exhaled like it had been weighing on his mind, this fight we'd never fully completed since we started filming. His arm flexed, holding mine securely to him. "I get living with me wasn't your fantasy, but—"

"What?" I pulled away, surprised. "That wasn't why."

In the thrill of becoming a minted rising television star, it was a little hard to remember exactly why I'd been so pissed at him.

The chauffeur opened the limo door and I slipped in. Chance followed close behind, and a moment later, the limo crept down the alley to the main drive.

Neon lit up the night sky, laughter from the crowded sidewalks. For a second, I was in two places in time: At once some struggling kid out on the street, broke and desperate to be noticed, to make it, enviously watching a limo go by, wondering if someone famous was inside. The other part of me sitting next to Chance, knowing we were those someones.

Chance waited for an answer.

The limo could hold eight passengers, but somehow he and I were nestled together on the bench seat. Probably because it was the easiest to get to. The warm weight of his thigh against mine should have been familiar after months of filming, but now it was all I could think about.

The heaviness of his body rocking against mine as the limo cornered, the twinges across my nipples when our hands brushed. The impulse to slowly move my hand closer to his, until we touched completely, until he knew I wanted him.

"Daphne?"

I shrugged, eyes still drawn out the window, so I didn't have to look at him.

"I guess," I took a deep breath. "You know some of how it was for me, with Lloyd. For a long time, I couldn't get away from him."

I couldn't quite say the other part; the thing I was most afraid of: When I finally got up the nerve to fire Lloyd, when I took away his income and cut him out of my life, I was pretty sure he would force my mother to choose between us. Because a guy like Lloyd couldn't end things nicely. I knew Mom loved me. I was also pretty sure she'd go with him.

"What do you mean?" he asked softly.

I guess I'd half expected Chance to yell at me, make me choose or GTFO. I shrugged, pressing my lips together hard to keep my feelings contained.

"I just can't..." I exhaled slowly, trying to understand myself enough to tell him. "Because of that whole... lots of things. I can't ever depend on only one person. It's too risky."

"Daph, it's just a show. That's all I'm asking from you right now."

But I had to make him understand. Already Chance was the best thing that had ever happened to me. When I moved in, we'd want to make our roles on the TV show real life. There was too much chemistry between us, and already the lines were blurred.

If I let my guard down even a little, I knew I would fall for him harder than anyone before. And little by little, he'd see I wasn't the good girl he'd scripted me to play. I could see the end of us from here if I didn't do the smart thing now.

My face burned. But Chance needed to know the truth if we were actually going to pull off this fake marriage. Every word made me seem like the worst version of myself. But I said them all because I am a lot of things, but a coward isn't one of them.

"Chance, If I like someone, I sleep with them, and I don't feel bad about it. Because if I'm in control of what I do, then it's not a big deal." I swallowed nervously. "You know how this job can be, getting a part. It becomes a handshake. A hug."

The subtle change in his body, the way he seemed to relax when I'd been expecting him to tense up and get angry, made me finally look at him.

I said, "So when you asked me not to sleep around, it took away the thing I use to make sure I'm OK. I need to be a hundred percent in control of what I do with my body. Sometimes I need that part of my life to mean *nothing*, and...."

"Daphne, I know what a casting couch is. You're not on mine."

It surprised a little laugh out of me. Of course he did. I mean, who didn't? But it embarrassed me that he'd name the part of our deal that I couldn't. I was about to roll my eyes, close off to him, when he said, "How do you think I got where we are? The couch isn't only for women."

Suddenly, he seemed very real to me, more real than anything.

I wanted to ask him when, and who. But then he might ask me those questions back. Better to leave those memories locked in the basement, knowing they were there, but never ever taking them out to examine again.

"Really?"

He nodded and looked out his window like I had done before.

I wanted to tell him I loved him.

Maybe not true fairy tale love, but the love you have in rehab, when you see someone get really fucking brave and you just want to cross the circle of chairs, throw your arms around them, and tell them you love them in all the ways that maybe they don't know how to love themselves. Not just because of what Chance said, but because he made me feel really fucking brave, like I was the one in the chair, owning my shit too.

I nestled into him, not talking, just listening to his heartbeat, fast but steady. He laughed under his breath.

"What?"

"I thought you didn't like me, that was why you didn't want to move in. You wanted me to know you were sleeping with other people so I'd back off."

"Chance!" I lightly slapped his leg before nuzzling back into the comfy spot against his chest. I was getting makeup on his shirt. Proof we had been this close, even if no one saw it but whoever did Chance Zak's laundry.

"Say you like me."

I sighed. "I like you. And as long as you understand why I do what I do, we could fake this marriage pretty well."

"You'll move in with me?" He murmured it just right, into that hollow at my neck, more touch than sound.

Yes. I nodded against him. I couldn't resist. I tilted my head and kissed his jawline.

And then we were kissing. His hands in my hair, lips down my throat. I slung my leg across his thighs, needing to be closer to him. He shifted, and I felt the power of him, the strength of his body as he moved against me. He was lean but bulk, and I felt helpless against the raw sex appeal the guy had.

My phone buzzed in my purse, but everything would have to wait until I was done with Chance Zak. I fumbled with the buttons of his shirt, needing the clothes off him, needing his skin against mine.

Four angry buzzes until the phone went to voicemail. Then started up again. On the second buzz, Chance half cursed, half laughed against my skin, "Who actually calls anymore?"

"Hold on." I dug the wretched thing out of my purse to silence it. But grabbing the phone stopped me cold. Lloyd.

Always, this late at night, the small fear something had happened to Mom. OD. A car accident. A fight. I glanced at the texts as they rolled in.

Lloyd: *They want to schedule a meeting TOMORROW.*
Lloyd: *GET BACK TO ME.*

"Everything OK?" Chance murmured, thumb brushing a circle on my hip.

Didn't sound like a medical emergency, but the spell I'd

fallen under with Chance broke. What was I doing? Hadn't I decided the smart move was to keep Chance at 'business friendly'?

I shook my head, sitting up a little straighter. "It's just Lloyd."

"He's still up?"

I nodded.

"Hey, let's swing by, get your stuff. What's the address?"

"Honestly, it can wait until morning."

The phone buzzed again, even as I spoke. Lloyd. Chance saw.

"What's the address?" he asked.

I told the chauffeur. Why not, right? If Lloyd was getting so demanding, it probably meant he was drunk or high, which completely dovetailed with it being the middle of the night.

Maybe now was as good a time as ever to let him know we'd be going our separate ways. I could pack a bag, and get it entirely over with, send him a check by mail in the morning. Of course, I dreaded what would happen between me and my mother when I fired Lloyd, but there was no getting around that part.

ELEVEN

WE ARRIVED AT THE CONDO COMPLEX A FEW MINUTES later. Chance inspected the freeway soot speckled stucco walls as I unlocked the dated art deco gate at the property where the once-great Heather Conover had ended up. I lifted my head, daring him to say anything. My family might be down on its luck, but we were still Hollywood old school. Chance couldn't say that.

I led him around the old, green-tinged pool to our house. The lights were on inside. I let myself in.

Lloyd was up, rooting around in the fridge like a man-sized raccoon, wearing expensive duds wrinkled and pit stained and smelling like too many people's cologne.

"Well this is a surprise!" he said. "Chance? Hey buddy! Want a beer?"

He held out a bottle from the fridge. Chance took it with a polite smile.

"Here to talk? I tried to raise you half a dozen times."

"Yeah," I said.

"Great! Look, I got something lined up for you, it's gonna blow your—"

"Lloyd, we have to go our separate ways," I said.

Wow. I had imagined breaking with him a thousand times, but it had never gone down like this.

Lloyd shut the fridge, slow at first, then suddenly hard at the end, so the old thing rocked at the abuse. He laughed. "You're kidding."

He did not look like he thought I was kidding, only like he was giving me a chance to take it back before things got out of hand.

I shook my head, trying to stay as quiet as possible.

"Think you're some hot shit reality show star and now you're too good for me?" Lloyd cracked open his beer and drank half of it.

"I'll drop off a check for what I owe tomorrow" That was a lie. I'd send it through the mail. I was suddenly quite sure I never wanted to see Lloyd again. "First thing. You know, I appreciate you lent me the money for surgery. I don't know what would've happened if you didn't step in." ... *but I would've figured it out somehow,* I didn't add. "So I'm gonna throw ten thousand on top. A goodbye bonus."

He wiped his lips with the back of his hand. "Doesn't work that way."

"Yeah, it works exactly like that," I snapped before I could stop myself. "I pay you back, plus interest, plus rent, plus—"

I managed to shut my mouth before I lost it to anger. This asshole was into me for far more than $40K, and I'd paid every dime back, so sure as shit he was letting me go now.

"You owing me money was a separate deal. You paid back for the cash I fronted for your surgery. Fine. But our agreement making me your manager still holds."

"No it— there's nothing like that in the contract."

"YOU THINK YOU CAN USE ME?!" He whipped the bottle hard and fast into the floor, where it exploded beer and foam and skidding glass. Everything went blurry with tears.

Lest you think I was some damsel in distress, I was only near crying because I was thinking about how angry I was, and how easy it would be to kill him, because I'm hella smart and LA's a great town to dispose of a body. But the fact I couldn't brain Lloyd with one of his own stupid beer bottles because Chance was there was literally making me cry. Because holy shit, I wanted Lloyd out of my life.

"HEY." Chance strode through the beer pond and got in Lloyd's face. "Settle down."

My mother's boyfriend shrunk about three inches, but that sleazy smug grin stayed on his face.

"Back off, man," he half-pleaded, half-commanded. Chance only moved closer. Lloyd stumbled back, knocked against a kitchen chair, and put himself in it.

He pointed a finger at me. "I invested time and money in your career, you can't cut me out of our partnership the minute money starts rolling in. You owe back taxes from all the work I put in that's just now starting to show itself."

"I'll go out tomorrow and get a lawyer—" *who'll wipe his ass with you,* I wanted to say.

He laughed, greasy and hateful. "You wanna roll the dice that way? I'll burn you to the ground. I know half the players in Hollywood. They'll get an earful, how you got drug problems, an unreliable pain in the ass. You wanna lawyer up? I'll take your ass to court. Might get one of those Hollywood judges who'd see you for the gold digger you are. You should take a note there, Chance. What she's doing to me, she'll do to you."

"Look, I'll pay what I owe, plus ten grand. Don't make

this a big deal." I tried another tack. "People part ways with their managers all the time."

Lloyd sneered. "You still don't get it? By the time I get done, it won't matter who won. Nobody will remember anything about you except how you went bankrupt mudslinging with the guy you hired to look out for you. If I don't get mine, you sure as hell don't get yours."

"How much?" Chance didn't seem at all like the easy-going guy I knew, the big puppy I'd felt so safe with. Now he seemed huge, all muscle and testosterone, hulking over Lloyd, fists clenched. Lloyd shrank into the seat.

"Wh... what?"

"For you to take money, shut the fuck up, and disappear forever unless she reaches out to you?"

Lloyd licked his lips, considering.

What was he saying? "Chance, no. Don't—"

"A million dollars," Lloyd said, shaky, looking like he might puke.

"Done." Chance put his hand out for Lloyd, and Lloyd hissed away like a scalded cat. Then realized Chance was trying to shake his hand.

"No. You can't do this. I can pay him. I have the money, let me handle this." I paid him, and then we were done. That had been the deal.

Lloyd gave me one final, smug sneer, and put out his hand. They shook once. Chance let go like he'd shaken hands with a pile of dog shit.

"Chance, you can't—"

Lloyd laughed as though my anger was the most amusing thing he'd experienced in a while. "Good riddance. That money tomorrow, or deal's off."

Chance turned from him like Lloyd ceased to exist. To me, he said, "Get your stuff, Daph. Let's get out of here."

* * *

It all happened so fast. I turned to go to my old room, wondering where my mom was. As I passed by her bedroom on the way to mine, I saw it was empty. Probably they'd fought and she'd left. I hoped, anyway.

In my room, everything once familiar now looked fake and distant as if I were watching some wobbly camcorder movie of my life. I threw clothes in a duffle bag until it was too full to zip closed. Then checked for my jewelry box. Anything remotely valuable was gone.

Which, admittedly, wasn't much. Some earrings my mother wore on the set of her most well-known movie, earrings that were only valuable because of the film. A little sapphire and gold ring she'd bought me for my 10th birthday. I looked around. My laptop was gone too.

Maybe he hadn't even taken them tonight. Maybe I'd been spending so much time becoming Daphne Zak, I'd let my past eat Daphne Conover.

I still had a closet full of memorabilia from all the small jobs I'd had, but that was too heavy and disorganized, and somehow it felt like it belonged to my mother more than me. Or maybe I hoped it was a way some part of me could stay with her, in her home. On my way back to the kitchen, I went to the hall bathroom, grabbed my meds and toothbrush.

"Contract's not broke until my check clears," Lloyd was saying.

"*I'll* pay you what *I* owe tomorrow," I said. "Not a dime more."

Lloyd laughed and threw a nicotine-stained finger at Chance. "He set your price. I get a million from somebody or I take you to court. And you better know by now I'll be just as satisfied to see you lose a million trying to fend me off."

"Shut up," Chance said to Lloyd. He held out his hand to me and took the heavy duffel bag. "You ready?" he asked in a much more gentle tone.

I needed to GTFO before I brained Lloyd with a brick or something.

"She'll fuck you like she fucked me, boy," Lloyd called as we left. "Enjoy the ride."

I climbed gracelessly into the back of the limo and crawled to a seat far, far away from Chance. My whole brain felt like fire. I had been so close to being free. And this white knight asshole had just put me back in debt to the tune of *a million fucking dollars.*

Until I could pay him back, Chance Zak owned me.

"You gonna say something about that back there?" he prompted, face set to scowl.

"No," I snapped. Then, "Yes. Actually. Nobody asked you to do that."

"Are you kidding me? That guy looked ready to beat you into next week. What would've happened if I hadn't been there?"

"The same thing that's happened all those times you WEREN'T there, Chance. I told you, stay out of my business."

"Was he right?" Chance demanded. "Are you gonna use me?" He didn't say, *like you used him,* but I felt the sting of it.

I didn't give a flying fuck what Chance thought of my romantic life, but an accusation tarnishing my business reputation stung like he'd sucker-punched me. I mean, I could be a slut six ways to Sunday in this town, but being a bad investment business-wise was what killed my mother's career.

"I didn't ask you to throw away a million dollars on something I could've taken care of with ten grand and pocket change!" I screamed.

"My million dollars!" He yelled right back. "My reality show. My reputation on the line. Why do you think I'm so goddamn desperate to save you?"

"Save me or own me?" I didn't yell that part. I didn't have to. The cold in my voice could've given him frostbite. "I would've been free."

The power shifted between us. Now it was Chance looking punched in the guts.

"That's... that's not how I meant it. I wanted you free from him. And I knew I could do it, he'd take the first offer I made. Because all he sees is money. He doesn't..."

Chance looked at his balled fists as if they weren't his and he didn't know how they'd come to be in his lap. Under his fitted shirt, his muscles bulging, adrenaline making him flexed and ready for a fight.

"He doesn't what?" I asked.

"He doesn't realize you're worth dropping a million on easy. That you're gonna make so much more, be so much more than that." When Chance looked up, his expression was closed to me. "He's a fool."

That kind of offering, at the altar of the gods I serve, channeled all my anger into something different. I could paint it in some romantic notions, but fights turn to fucking on a dime, and in an instant, I crawled across the seats to get right in his face.

"You gonna let me go free and clear, an act of chivalry? Or do I owe you a million dollars?" I breathed against his throat, his collar still undone from earlier.

He didn't answer, except for the bob of his Adam's apple, his otherwise absolute stillness, like I was some venomous snake in his lap. It made me smile. He was right to be afraid of me.

"Save me or own me?" I taunted, nuzzling his neck.

"Save you," he said after a moment.

"So I'm free?" I knew the answer, but even at the slim hope he might say yes, my heart raced.

Slowly, guilty, he shook his head: *No.*

I knew it. That was the real rub between him and me. Underneath it all, he wanted the part of me I wanted most for myself. On his second slow headshake, I leaned in and kissed him.

He kissed me back hard, pulling me close. I hiked my dress skirt up so I could straddle him, and in a second I was in his lap. Only thin nylon underpants separating, the part of me calling the shots from getting chafed on his zipper.

I slung my arms around his neck, pulling him into me, the scratch of the little sequins on my dress like nails dragging against his shirt. He tried to kiss me again, but I moved just out of reach, teasing him, staring him down as I tilted my hips to get a better feel of him.

"Is this what you want?" I murmured, moving again, turned on as much by the feel of him as the expression on his face, the answer undeniable.

He squeezed my ass, grinding me into him, stealing my breath away.

"Say it," I warned.

"I want you." His voice was so ragged, I thought maybe I was breaking him.

Good. That's what he got for trying to hold on to me.

I reached between us, lifting up slightly to run my hand

along the tent of his pants, enjoying him groan into my neck as I found the button of his fly.

"I want," I said as I moved my hand over him. "This."

And I did. He'd broken the rules, and now I was going to do whatever I wanted.

"I want every part of you." The barest scratch of five o'clock shadow, bristly and thick, against my neck.

"But everything I told you holds," I said.

His pants button came loose and I pulled the fabric until the zipper gave way, tooth by tooth, to let me inside.

Chance went still, so I knew he'd heard me, understood me. I'd bang him like a screen door in a hurricane, I wanted him so bad. But there was too much at stake here for me to get lost in what my body wanted. Maybe some girls could, but I was going to rule Hollywood someday, and that would never happen unless I had complete control over my fate.

His panting breaths let me know how bad he wanted me, and although underwear still hampered my full understanding of his anatomy, I knew enough to already be aching. But I could feel the resistance settle into him in the way his kisses on my neck slowed, the press of his body against mine became more thoughtful, less frantic.

"You're the same, no?" I whispered the words into his ear. "In love with your best friend's sister, even though you're here, with me, now. You understand."

I rolled my hips, and it wasn't an act. His thigh muscles flexed, lifting him and me both. My breath caught.

"Daphne, you're killing me."

I kissed him, desperate to get his clothes off. As long as he knew the rules. As long as he knew them. As long as he—

The limo slowed to a stop. Not to Chance's yet, but off the freeway, making our way through the grid of surface streets. Definitely not enough time to do all the things I wanted to do to him. But still enough time to torment him.

I slid off his lap until I knelt in front of him, in the floor space of the limo. Like the best present under the tree, I unwrapped Chance's pants. Hot and thick and heavy, his cock sprung from his pants. I gave him my best batted eyelashes and leaned forward.

Hands on my shoulders stopped me. Impatient, I wiggled past them, bending to touch him with my tongue.

"Daphne, stop."

I froze. No one had ever told me to stop before. But I did, because more than once I'd said that word, and I knew what it meant. Even if some people didn't.

It must've been too close to home, or he was too close. God, I hoped he wasn't too close.

"You're right."

He pulled me up into his lap, so we were eye to eye, the dress and nothing else between me and him. I squirmed, needing more contact.

"I have feelings for someone else, and that's been with me almost as long as I can remember. But I'm falling for you. I feel like you could break my heart, Daph," he said. I swallowed hard. "I love that you're honest, that you tell me what you want."

I shook my head, denying what Chance said. I was only honest so I didn't get hurt, not out of any personal awesomeness. He was mistaking me for a good girl.

"I want to keep spending time with you," he said. "But we have to go slow. It's complicated."

I kissed him to shut him up. He was getting it all wrong, but I'd teach him. This was an 'I want you *and*' situation, not some 'I can't have you *because*' nonsense, and I was gonna teach him that the hard way. As I kissed him, I rocked my hips, grinding my ass into his lap.

He groaned, flexing his hips into me, making sure I felt what I was doing to him. Taking his hand, I slipped it into the front of my dress, over my breast, holding his palm to me, squeezing my own nipple to show him how I liked it. He was a quick study.

"It *is* complicated," I murmured. "While you figure your end out, I'm going to be living mine exactly the way I want."

The car stopped and the driver killed the engine. We were home. Or at least to Chance's home, my TV set.

The limo rocked as the chauffeur got out, came around to our door. Like waking from a dream, Chance and I straightened ourselves. The door opened and Chance got out, waited at the car door, and extended a hand for me.

Maybe only because it was polite, or he knew getting out of a limo in a dress was an awkward endeavor, but knowing what I was about to do to him? To our working relationship? When I took his hand, it felt like bungee jumping off the edge of a bridge; excitement and bravery and the real possibility this whole experience might be the end of me.

But at least I'd die doing something awesome.

TWELVE

THE HOUSE, USUALLY FILLED BY DAY WITH THE REALITY show crew, now stood empty. Cleaners and a laundry service kept the property looking correct as a TV set and venue for placement product. But now, it was silent as a library.

He sauntered over like he was going to kiss me. Eyes, hypnotic. I could feel everything; the brush of skirt against my thighs, the dampness in my panties from being so turned on in the car, nipples poking against my top, demanding attention.

He bent.... and picked up the bag of my things. Hefting it on his shoulder, his eyes lingered on the front of my dress, daring me to touch him first. We were so close I could barely catch my breath. The electricity between us razzed my skin, but I couldn't quite get up the nerve to make the first move. He had the home-field advantage, he had told me in the car we had to go slow. Now it felt like he was toying with me.

"Follow me," he said.

I knew from spending every day here there were

twenty-two steps, but going up the staircase in the dark and quiet, it seemed as if there were at least a hundred. What was I doing?

He was my business partner. No, it wasn't even that equal. He was a producer on the show. If Lloyd decided to smear my name a little just for fun, this might be the last work I got for a while. Holy shit, that didn't even cover how Chance had shaken his head in the limo when I'd asked him if I was free and clear. No, he'd indicated. I was a million dollars in debt.

At the top of the stairs, he reached for my hand. I swallowed nervously. The way he'd said he still loved Minnie—that sounded classic player, the kind of game a guy would run so later, he could blow you off and point to how he'd always told you he wasn't serious. My heart thumped unevenly.

I'd thought I could take this guy with no regrets. I almost had taken him on the ride here. But now, I felt powerless. His house, his show, his money over my head, his rules, his other girl.

I squeezed his hand in the darkened hallway. To the left, the master bedroom. To the right, the guest rooms. He leaned in for a kiss. I knew he felt me slipping away.

"Don't. Stay." He kissed me.

"You were right. In the car," I broke the kiss and whispered into his shirt. I doubted he would see the logic of all the business stuff; men in power tended to be blind to how their power can fuck those without. So I pressed an issue I didn't care about to make him care about my side. "It's complicated. What about your other girl? Childhood sweetheart? Owner of Chance Zak's heart?"

At least, I hadn't thought I cared. Until he went still against me, then pulled back a little. Touched his forehead to mine. I could feel how much he wanted me in the way all parts of him leaned into me.

Yet somehow, he said, "You're right. I can't make this decision tonight."

My body was on fire. But I nodded and let him take my bag to the guest bedroom, my brains completely scrambled.

I'd thought I'd want the upper hand with him, coercing him to do as I wanted. Instead of feeling victorious, it made me want to scream, punch his retreating back, tell him I hated his guts.

What had I wanted from him? Had I expected Chance Zak to declare undying love, absolve me of the million-dollar price tag he'd put on me? Had I wanted him to beg me to get into bed, promise that there would be no other for him but me?

Yes. Holy shit. Yes, I had.

Well, Chance having qualms about cheating on his long lost childhood sweetheart solved my business problem, but my needing to get fucked problem was still raging.

This kind of bullshit was exactly why I could never, ever depend on just one person. Because they could change their mind and leave you any old time they felt like it.

I texted the chauffeur to wait in the drive. As soon as the light went off under Chance's bedroom door, I crept down to the laundry room and found my jeans in a hamper. Inside, a phone number. I dialed.

"Where are you?" I asked when she picked up. She named a club I knew. "I'll call you back when I'm outside."

WHEN THE LIMO pulled up in front of the club, I texted.

"Meet me back here in an hour," I told the driver when she came out, and slid out the door in my soft yellow dress.

Out on the street downtown, I knew how eye-catching I looked, wearing the same clothes as when the paparazzi had covered me just hours before. Lots of those guys trolled downtown after hours and probably made just as much money with blackmail photos as things they could legit sell to the magazines. This was dangerous.

But when Audrey saw me, I didn't care. Her whole body glowed with excitement, and immediately she came right over and stood so close our bodies brushed as we moved.

"I was hoping you'd call," she said. Minty breath, like she'd gotten ready, her eyes all over me. "I saw you on TV. I couldn't stop watching, thinking about how we'd met."

"Come to the alley with me," I moved even closer, so there was no way she'd mistake this meeting as anything other than it was. She nodded quickly, looking up and down the crowded street, and grabbed my hand.

I didn't look. The thrill that we might be caught by paparazzi only made me more frantic to have her. But there was more to it. This was what Chance was most afraid of, and he'd hurt me. My inner bad girl was completely triggered.

I had to have Audrey in the worst way possible, and the most dangerous way too. After all, Chance was breaking the rules keeping Minnie, he was just doing it so the only person who got hurt was me.

In the semidarkness of the alley, I said, "Kiss me."

Instantly, her mouth on mine. Sweet and soft and wanting to please. I kissed her back, teasing her, pressing my body against hers.

"Come back to my place," she whispered.

"Here."

She turned her head, checking out the main street, the people walking by. I wondered if I was throwing everything away, if this was exactly what Chance had predicted. Wearing the same outfit as the one I'd been photographed earlier in would only make the sleazy candids more convincing.

What the fuck was I doing? Trying to ruin everything?

Maybe Lloyd was exactly right about me. Maybe I was exactly like my mother— screwing my career with my uncontrolled desperation for affection, for getting love in all the wrong places.

Nothing below my neck cared. If anything, the fear only turned me on more.

Audrey pressed her hand between my thighs, tugging the hem of my dress, crawling it upwards by inches. I put my hand on hers, stopping her.

"Touch yourself."

In the dimness, her face so close to mine, breathing fast. Her eyes on me. I slid my hand down my thigh to the hem of my dress, under, into my panties. I kissed Audrey, pulling her so close I could feel the jog of her hand between her legs.

I was so swollen down there from all the teasing Chance had put me through, but it still shocked me how slippery I was, so sensitive the first touch made my knees go weak. I kissed Audrey again.

"Tell me when you're close," I whispered.

"I'm so close," she said immediately.

"Stop."

She whimpered, hand slowing, not completely still. Every stroke she made, I did too. I started going faster, watching her face. Her eyes closed, her mouth falling open. She sped up too.

"I said stop," I told her.

"I can't." Her arm moved in that jagged, furious way of someone going over the edge despite themselves.

It got me. I came by surprise, caught up in her. I knew I was going to make noise, so I kissed her again to cover it. She pressed against me, movements slowing as she panted against me.

"Holy shit," she said. "Holy shit, what was that?"

I kissed her again, nuzzling into her. Audrey. I didn't even know her last name.

I knew what most people would think, that there was something wrong with me. There probably was. But I knew that by doing this, whatever hold Chance Zak had been trying to have over me was weakened.

I could go back to his house now, and pretend to be his wife, and know that he owned me until I paid a million freaking dollars back, and I could keep my cool. I wouldn't feel so trapped and desperate. If I was attracted to him, I'd know it wasn't Stockholm Syndrome. I'd know who I belonged to. Only myself.

I dropped the hem of my dress but kept kissing her, not wanting it to end quite yet. "Holy shit," she said for maybe the hundredth time. "You're Daphne Zak." Her eyes were all shiny with excitement.

I made a, *yeah, that's true,* face.

"I would do anything for your number," she said, hand coming out of her pants and trailing from my hip, up to my belly and ribcage, outlining the curve of my breast.

"I have yours." I kissed her again in half an apology, mostly enjoying the fact I held all the cards in whatever this was. "You hungry?" I asked. "Let's go get something to eat."

THIRTEEN

I woke the next morning in Chance's guest room, everything coming back in pieces. My duffel bag on the floor, Chance in the limo, Audrey in the alley.

Audrey under the bright florescent lights of an all-night donut shop off the strip, how she'd been funny, easy to talk to. How I'd shifted and the scent of Chance's skin had caught in my nose as she'd come, the way her face had changed.

I stretched in the bed, waiting to feel guilty. I mean, I had to admit he was right— I had to get my fucksilly impulses under control. The success of GITZ depended on the public seeing me as a virginal, infatuated bride. My behavior last night had unnerved me. It was stupid. But even so, thinking about it made my pulse race, alive with the risk of getting caught.

And recognizing Chance had my best business interests at heart didn't change my resentment about his personal choices. When the cameras were gone, he had decided not to get together with me because he had feelings for someone else. So on a personal level, I didn't feel guilty for starting up with someone else. Chance and I weren't together.

As I snuggled into his clean bedsheets, I understood the reason I was mad. Part of Chance was using the business argument to try and control more of my life than what the cameras saw. He wanted me, but he wasn't willing to give up the fantasy of some other girl. Maybe with time, he'd understand being bound to one person was too tight, too close.

If I could have two, I could be faithful, the smartass who lived in my head remarked. *Maybe arraignment that would take the stick out of Chance's butt as well.*

But only if they both loved me most. Like Audrey. She would never, ever turn her eye away from me... unless someone more famous came along. But I understood that. And the way Audrey made me the center of her universe? I'd booty called and she'd dropped her whole world to be standing outside that club waiting? That was how I wanted my life to be. Maybe that was how I *needed* it.

I grabbed my phone to check the time. What I saw made me jump out of bed and get dressed.

* * *

"Morning," Chance said when the juicer shut off.

He was making one of those green blended things. I knew it tasted like ass, but watching him make it nearly sold me on how good it would be; the guy would've killed in commercial work.

"Want one?" He poured himself a glass.

"Hey, I have news." I cozied up on a barstool at the immense kitchen island. Boobs nudged up by the counter, spine lengthened, all my tricks second nature.

He didn't say anything, but it hung between us that I'd gone out last night.

And that he knew I'd gone out.

And as the silence stretched out? That he knew I knew he knew.

It wasn't a secret. I'd had to key the alarm to get out and get back in, plus the chauffeur had driven, racking up a couple more billable hours than planned.

Still, this push-tug unspoken argument thickened the air between us, daring one of us to call it out.

Other parts of me felt the pull differently, like this ESP from the flex of his muscles and the set of his face, and maybe even the smell of him, that let me know however pissed off he was, the part between his legs was definitely still interested.

I'd like to say it made me feel powerful and in control. Instead, it made me feel a little quivery and skittish like he'd have the upper hand with one flick of his tongue... anywhere on my body.

But I was an actor, so I ignored all that and raised an eyebrow: *Say it or get over it.*

He grunted, poured the rest of his *green whatever* into his glass, gulped it down in a few swallows. "I have news too. We're on Honeymoon Thursday."

"What?"

"Promo." He rinsed his glass out in the sink before putting it in the dishwasher.

"Oh. Well, guess what?" I didn't wait for an answer. "Last night, before we saw Lloyd and... and all that? He sent me a bunch of texts that I didn't look at until this morning." I inhaled hugely, grinning, and let it all out in a gush. "Chance, DeltaStar made an offer. A feature film. They want to schedule a meeting."

A major motion picture studio. And not something straight to streaming, or some low budget indie. This was big time.

"ALL RIGHT!" Chance whooped, sliding into full bro mode. "Daphne! That's awesome! Who's attached? Did they say?"

Phone in my hand, I hesitated. Of course, Lloyd hadn't given me any of that information, or who he'd been contacted by, or how I could reach anyone. Since I'd cut him out of negotiations with the last SHIPWRECK contract, he'd gotten pretty wise about not telling me enough to do the deal myself.

Chance cleared his throat. "I know some people at DeltaStar. I could ask around, see if we can backchannel the deal."

Are you doing this as my friend or my new manager? I was afraid to ask. Asking would make it real, and pretending I didn't see the difference might help me later if this went south. A million dollars. He had me for a million more dollars. It made me lightheaded, how everything I'd worked for had been stolen so easily.

"Yeah. Yeah, make the calls," the breathlessness came through.

He already had his phone scooped out of his back pocket, scrolling. "If DeltaStar is calling, you know the fix is in. We're huge."

He was right. The revelation made me go even more lightheaded, until I had to lean against the counter for real, not merely boob propping. If DeltaStar was calling because of the heat from GOOD IN THE ZAK, this might be my trampoline to bounce right into the big time.

Chance had said.... what? Two point five million dollars for his first movie? But he'd started out a bigger star than I was now. And he was a man, and that factored in. But still, it didn't seem crazy I could ask for a million. Maybe high hundred thousands.

This could be it.

This could be my ticket to being totally and completely—

FOURTEEN

"OK," I said when we'd been seated in The Lilly's exclusive patio dining area.

Chance had insisted we have lunch after I met with DeltaStar. Although he'd reached out to his contacts, after he'd gotten a response about who was interested in me, Chance had airdropped me their contact info and told me they were waiting for my call.

I hoped he didn't think that cut him in for a manager's percentage. But I also reluctantly had to admit that if he did, the guy had made his money helping me out, then backed out unobtrusively. I would've paid a stranger to manage me like that.

"They want me," I said, unable to contain my excitement.

I rocked in my chair a little from sheer happiness. Chance leaned across the table and took my hand, probably to keep me anchored so I didn't truly squeal with excitement.

Of course, we were also fishing for the opportunity to make some of the tabloids. Me, shrieking while making the human equivalent of googly eyes? Not part of our highly curated newlywed look.

I squeezed back, throwing both my hands in the mix just for something strong to hold on to.

"OK, breathe," Chance laughed.

I did. Like... once. "Shooting starts in two and a half weeks. It's an adventure romance. They're filming on the Yucatan Peninsula. Chance, I've never been farther into Mexico than Tijuana."

He asked me everything. Directors, script, costars, what they had said and what I had said. The whole time, his eyes stayed on me, like if I kept talking the whole rest of the day, he'd be eagerly along for the ride. I didn't hold anything back. I mean, he laughed when he was supposed to laugh, and he asked all these clever questions, some stuff I hadn't even thought about.

This little alarm kept flashing in the back of my head, how dangerous it was not to hold things back, how this was inviting him so deep into my life, that this information was sensitive, and I was trusting him not to hurt me, or fuck it up like Lloyd had.

But I kept talking, because... I didn't know why. I guess I trusted him. Not with my heart. But he hadn't hurt me yet in business. The truth was, even though I hated what Chance'd done about Lloyd, I was breathing easier just from not having to deal with my mom's boyfriend anymore. Chance was a million times better quasi-manager to have. He was actually a decent guy most of the time, and smart too.

So I risked it.

"So it sounds like after we shoot our honeymoon, we'll go our separate ways for a while," he said.

"No." I shook my head, but even as I did, came the

unpleasantly cold splash of reality. "You could come with me," I added, even though I knew it wasn't true.

And what the hell was wrong with me, asking that? I was a big girl. We weren't really married, it wasn't like we had to travel together.

He shook his head, saying the thing I knew. "I gotta call in Canada next month." The second installment of his superhero franchise. That had been scheduled since around the time we'd married. And unlike my little five-week adventure, his was for months.

"Hey, Daph." He leaned across the table. "It's OK. This is good. This is exactly what we wanted, right?"

But all I could think was how, despite all my tantrums and plotting, somehow I was in this place where Chance felt like the very center of my world. And just like I'd known would happen, I was about to be left alone.

"But we should also come up with a plan to be on the same page for our image. Blowing up like this means the stakes are high for both of us. The TV show is taking off, and that's gonna be our broadest reach. We cannot afford to tarnish that arm of our empire, right?"

He grinned, and I knew he was on purpose making it sound like we were on the same side, like we were soooo big and famous we could take over the world. The guy knew me well enough by now to know what made me tick.

"I've been talking to my people. They say, especially in a... *new business relationship*," he said these words like code for *marriage*. "It really helps to have a buddy. On-location filming is great and exciting. And also boring and lonely. I think you should take a friend, someone who can keep you—"

"On the straight and narrow?" Just so he knew I wasn't falling for his tender wording. They say the first fight you have as a married couple is the fight you have for the rest of your marriage. And in this case, the saying was certainly proving true.

"Yes. Both of us," he said.

That answer was an unexpected sucker punch. Was he already looking at other people? Or at the perfect vision of childhood sweethearts?

"Fine. Who's your entourage?" I sniffed, glancing away.

"Beau. He's going as my personal assistant, keeping me on my workout schedule. He even cooks so I stay right for the camera."

"And Minnie? Will she be coming to visit her brother while you all are freezing your asses off in Canada?"

He might've looked guilty. Or maybe it was just surprise. I was definitely studying him, but I couldn't tell. "No. Well, I guess I hadn't thought about it."

"I have a friend, Audrey. She can come." Oh, she would be coming all right.

"OK. Get her name and deets to Beau, he can set it up so she gets paid for her time, we can expense her travel and board."

"Fine." It felt like a standoff. "She can stay in my room with me."

Chance's eyes narrowed. "...OK. Audrey can go, but I want you to take someone else, someone trained to do the sort of chores Beau will be doing for me. Someone—"

"To spy on me?" I hated him right then.

"To protect my investment."

Did he mean me and the million?! The show? Was I a thing to him now, as I had been to Lloyd? I could feel emotions bubbling over in my facial expression. I pushed away from the table.

"You get to go up to Canada and have Beau, who for all

I know you're fucking, and full access to Minnie coming up there any time you want, and I've got some warden I don't even pick myself? How the fuck is that fair?"

"Relax."

"Don't tell me to—"

"I'll send Minnie with you. You'll know where she is, and you'll know it isn't with me."

I opened my mouth, but absolutely no words came.

"And for what it's worth," he added, "Beau and I have always kept it in the friendzone."

FIFTEEN

Hollywood is a weird beast. And so Chance and I ended up going on our honeymoon after the first season of GOOD IN THE ZAK had completely filmed and started to air.

The reason for this was the same as for everything in this town— publicity.

As viewers watched us get married on television, they saw 'news' photos of us honeymooning, which was a great way to keep our faces in the tabloids and create the illusion that the audience was watching something as it happened.

We honeymooned on the beach in Santa Barbara, a mere ninety minutes north of Los Angeles, so that even the lowest brow paparazzi who could afford a tank of gas could get candid photos.

The show rented out the honeymoon suite of the Barcara Hotel— a corner set of rooms overlooking the green grass courtyard and beyond that, the beach. An on-the-beach room was key because while the tony hotel security would keep most of the paparazzi out, the beach in California was public space. Photographers wouldn't even need a fancy zoom lens, which meant we could scoop up those amateur shots. Nobody loved posting to social media more than people on vacation who've seen a star.

A big part of our job was to stand out on the balcony, in our bathrobes, looking sexified, or having a lover's spat, or chilling with a glass of champagne. Whatever we thought would sell images.

"That suite's $2250 a night, so you two lovebirds are gonna share the room," the showrunner had told us over the phone that morning. "But don't worry, there's a sitting area with a couch. I'm all for equality, so I suggest you flip a coin for the bed. You'll have to share a bathroom, but I assume that's a reasonable request?"

He probably had to get our OK for legal work-related sexual harassment reasons or whatever. But clearly, he thought it ridiculous he had to ask.

* * *

OUT ON THE beach in front of our room, someone left a note, WE LOVE YOU in stones and sea flotsam the day we checked in.

"That has to be GITZ props, right?" I asked Chance as we stood out on the balcony overlooking the amazing view. The room was plush ivory and dusty blue décor, posh and yet slightly mildewed with damp ocean air and sea salt in that way that conveyed how all human endeavors would eventually surrender to nature. Chance stood behind me, his arms around my waist.

We'd been standing out there twenty minutes, for the second time that day. I was quickly feeling like the wooden figurines that pop out of cuckoo clocks at the top of every hour and do their little mechanized dance.

"Photographer," he murmured in my ear.

I glanced up along the line of beach, catching the black glint of a telescopic photo lens, the blank face of a man staring at us with no intention of interacting. By the size of his lens, he could probably see if my eyeliner was on smooth.

Chance nuzzled my neck and I tilted my head back, making for a better angle. I also took the opportunity to nudge my butt against his crotch, do a little reconnaissance about my new husband. He growled softly.

"All part of the show," I breathed.

"You gonna miss me in Mexico?" His hands slipped to my hip, pulling me tight against him.

"Nope." Not because it was true, but just to remind him I wasn't his good girl.

"Yeah, you will."

The strong hands around my midsection turned to curious fingers... and then to tickles digging into my ribcage. I screamed laughter, trying to squirm away, but he held me to him, tickling me unmercifully.

"Stop!" I squealed, gasping. "Stop it!" I hit his forearms, but it was useless. "Stop! I'm mak— I'm making— the ugly— laugh!" I begged him.

He paused but didn't let go. I could really feel him then, how turned on he was, his heart thumping against my back, his breath a little ragged. *I was going to miss him.*

The thought made me uncomfortable. Three more days of our honeymoon. And then I would go away to Mexico, and for the first time in months, I wouldn't see Chance every day, wouldn't get to talk to him about our plans. Wouldn't have to put up with his goofiness between scenes, or the taste of whatever mint and spinach and cucumber juice thing he made on his lips when he kissed me. The secure way he held me, so I could totally relax against him.

Don't get sidetracked, I told myself. I would never be like that. That was something my mother would do. You take your eyes off the prize and you get taken down by all the careless things your heart might want. Drugs. Parties. Men who told you they loved you but turned out not to be worth a damn.

"All part of the show," Chance said in my ear.

As we both caught our breath, rocking gently from side to side, allowing the photographer to get his fill of shots, Chance said, "I bet the crew put that sign down there for us. But look at that."

He pointed down to the beach before tucking his arm back around my sore ribcage, snuggling me tight. The cool Pacific breeze chilled my skin, and his body was warm and strong and comforting.

Below, a girl and her mom stood near the sign, reading it and pointing to it. The girl turned toward the hotel and spotted us. I could see the exact moment she realized who we were, the shocked happiness like when you give someone a gift for no reason. She shrieked, this thin noise carried up to us on the ocean breeze, whipped out her phone and aimed it at us.

"Wave, Mrs. Zak," he said.

I did. The girl cheered.

* * *

THE SHOWRUNNER FILLED every day with honeymoon photo op adventures; a bike ride down to the pier where Chance bought me flowers at a local shop that paid a moderate amount to have their storefront in our show, the end credits scene we shot of us signing autographs for all their workers.

A hot air balloon ride at dawn, which might've been romantic except for the GITZ cameraman and sound guy accompanying us, getting footage to show as little 'extras' for social media. Chance and I kissed romantically as the balloon guy monitored the flame for safety and the crew crouched in the wicker basket, hooting and making catcalls to try and make us break character as the drone circled for cinematic shots.

We hiked the trails in the foothills above the ocean and sat down to romantic dinners on State Street or in Montecito. All trailed by small-time paparazzi, looking to sell a photo for a couple hundred bucks.

Chance brought them donuts and told them when he and I would be out on the balcony, scantily clad, during a fight (Saturday midmorning), Chance making frowny-faces alone (Saturday evening) or with him painting my toenails in apology (Sunday morning) and rounding out the week with a TV14 photo op of us making out with implication of partial nudity as I sat balanced on the balcony's rail, my bathrobe slipping off to reveal my topless back (Sunday).

Bit by bit, people added more stuff to the beach below our window. Flowers and art made of rocks and driftwood. Too much and too weird to be only GITZ producers sneaking down there to glorify our show. Sometimes, teenage girls would be down there when we came out, and immediately scream when Chance walked out the doors.

And at night, there would be this awkward pause. The couch pulled out to a sofa bed (I guess even fancy honeymoon suite decorators understood marriage wasn't always what it was chalked up to be), and Chance would pace around nervously in his boxers or sweatpants, even on those days when we were exhausted from obligations. He would prowl.

I could feel him, wanting to make a move, or be cast out to the couch.

Each night, instead of doing either of those things, I would crawl into my designated side of the bed, wearing the thinnest of T-shirts and skimpiest of panties.

Like an asteroid pulled into my orbit, or like a starving wolf circling a bear trap laden with fresh meat, Chance would approach the bed and get in.

I could feel the tension coming from the other side of the bed, knowing once we fell asleep, our bodies would gravitate towards each other. I would wake in the darkness snuggled into the crook of his arm.

Or to him spooning me, garden cucumber pressed at the crevice of my bottom, reflexively stretching, nudging his whole body against mine until we both woke and became motionless, fully aware of the situation.

In that awkward silence, I'd swallowed nervously, throat dry even though other parts of me were definitely... not dry.

It was all I could do not to squirm against his lap. Even staying perfectly still, every place we touched felt like a brand. His cock nestling snugly in the pocket where my ass cheeks met my thighs, where my thighs touched each other. The smallest tilt of my hips and I would feel the head of his cock sliding against my most sensitive parts, nudging toward that entrance he was so close to.

It was also incredibly embarrassing. I couldn't stop that, but I did my best to keep silent, so maybe he wouldn't notice.

His even inhales and exhales sent tingles racing across my skin, zinging my nipples, making me bite my lip. Was he awake? I should've been thinking of a smooth way to get out of the situation, to separate out, to dodge into the bathroom for a cold shower.

He kissed my shoulder, warmth as his tongue darted out to taste my skin. The muscles in my lower back clenched on their own, arching, allowing him access.

It made me gasp. I couldn't control it.

His hand slid over my hip, up across my belly, making everything inside jump, half ticklish. Sliding up my ribcage, over my breast.

I made that noise again, and he moved, his mouth grazing from my shoulder to my neck, his other arm burrowing between me and the mattress, pressing his palm against my belly, fingers so so close, brushing the edge of my panties. He hugged me from behind, and I ground my ass into him.

His hand slipped between my thighs, on top of my panties, the barest skim of fingers along the place where my thighs pressed together. He slowed, tracing, mapping out the feel of me through the thin fabric. His breathing uneven.

I tried to slip my hand between us, to touch him like he was touching me. But he refused to separate even an inch from where my butt cradled his cock.

Frustrated, I squirmed against him, reaching for his ass instead, slipping my hand under the waistband of his boxers. Every time he pressed himself against me, his ass cheek flexed, became stone under my hand. I could barely dig my fingernails into his flesh.

I needed him immediately, naked and inside me. Otherwise, I was embarrassingly close to losing control and coming like this, desperate as any groupie waiting in the back of a tour bus.

His hand slipped inside my panties. He nudged

between my thighs to the place where my lips met, exploring between them. When his fingers went from bare skin to where it got slippery and slick, he groaned in my ear.

I yanked at the waist of my panties, raking them down over my thighs, needing all my skin bare.

"Inside me," I commanded.

He left, whole body gone in the bed, and I cursed, rolling to chase after him.

He was on his side, leaning over the bedside table's drawer, no doubt searching for a condom. I pulled off my top and climbed on top of him, using my weight to try and press him onto his back. The muscles of his thigh between mine flexed. I loved feeling his naked skin there, against the most sensitive part of me.

I pushed on his shoulder. "Now."

"Jesus," he laughed under his breath. "Hold on."

He tore the condom packet and had a two-second lead on me unrolling as I straddled him.

All the desperate, thoughtless need to get him. And then he was, sliding inside, stretching me out.

On top of him, still feeling the stretch, that most-intimate reality of being in bed with someone? That's when I started to wonder if this was a good idea.

He flexed, socketing himself even deeper. I made the executive decision to worry later. Besides, I had already told him I liked to fuck around. He couldn't be confused as to what this was, if not me fucking around.

I started to ride him. "Come first and I will literally kill you."

He laughed, bucking me a little, making me gasp and then slap his chest. I was in no mood for pranks. I started moving on my own.

Although my public life was all about being sexy for

other people, when I'm in the bedroom, I'm selfish as hell. Every tilt of my hips, every jog of my ass, even bending down to nibble at his nipples until he groaned and sped up the pace? That was all for me. If Chance wanted to come along for the ride? All the better.

I didn't expect him to entirely stop, to hold me still, to wait like some freaking instructor until I quit squirming around.

"What?" I rubbed my nipples against him, anything to get him moving again.

"I wanna watch you come."

Those seascape eyes. That iconic half-smirk a million horny housewives had as screen-savers. That was the guy on the pillow below me.

"Then make me."

He secured my hips more firmly, keeping me lifted just enough not to fully get where I wanted to go. He didn't move that much inside me, just these rocking thrusts as he put his hand firmly against my belly, his thumb stroking me. If I moved or tried to egg him on, he'd go perfectly still again. It got so I felt almost hypnotized, trying to get the most out of each movement, watching him for any sign of weakness.

The whole time as I watched him, he watched me. Studying me. He'd let me go, increasingly frantic, until I was right there, ready to explode... and then he'd slow down, going still, his thumb on my clit like he was taking my pulse.

Motherfucker was edging me into submission. How was he not about jet seed all over the place? I could feel how massive he was inside me, his balls hard as walnuts. The more he had control of me, the more I needed to come, the more I resisted.

I was not going to become some mewling, desperate

fuck puppet. Even as I rocked, desperate and breathless, I turned my mind to all the ways I might unravel this guy. It seemed desperately important that I had the upper hand, that I came only as I was riding as fast as I could, trying to beat this guy as he chased me in utter, helpless abandon.

I leaned into him, kissing him. His thumb slid over me and I almost came from the barest movement, the dual combo of him moving down there and his tongue against mine.

"I'm gonna come," I breathed against his mouth.

I didn't know if I was warning him or trying to dirty talk him, only that it was true. My hips were going on their own. He groaned, all that restraint gone in an instant, thrusting inside me like he had to fuck me or die trying. *Fucking finally.*

Everything inside me exploded, so built up it shocked me. He kept kissing me, the taste of him branding how it felt, like kissing him after this would bring me back to this moment. Like *he* had branded me.

It felt too out of control, not just a roller coaster, but like being on a roller coaster that had flown off the tracks, hurdling through the air, where it wasn't just a ride anymore. Like that feeling you might die.

But he kept kissing me, and he kept his thumb fluttering there, and thinking how scared I was, he made me come again.

SIXTEEN

After, we were practically stuck together with dried sweat, Chance's arm slung around my shoulders. He breathed like he was deeply relaxed. Even so, when I tried to roll away, to get some clarity outside the mesmerizing guy-sex-smell of him, he pulled me back closer.

My body felt completely at odds. All my muscles easy and warm, stupid sex hormones making me sleepy and satisfied, like the best thing in the world would be to lay around here until Chance woke up again so we could screw until I couldn't remember my own name.

My heart was still thudding so strong that when I looked down at my chest, my boobs tremored a little with it, nipples pulled tight, sensitive, insisting I curl up and press them against his skin. Like my dumb ass was trying to get imprinted on him or something.

All of which I was fairly confident were caused by those hormones your brain doped you out on to make you bond with others. I was pretty sure all those good feelings in my body were most likely come-drugs trying to mess with me.

It was tempting to let them. I mean... drugs are fun. For a while anyway.

But underneath that, fear.

No, worse. Dread — that I was in danger of losing myself, of losing those two things my whole life was centered upon, losing my very identity. That I would be as lost as my mother— poor and faded to obscurity, my happiness determined by someone else's whims.

Luckily for me, escape was written into my script. In two days, I'd get on a plane to Mexico.

"I like you," he sighed, arms flexing to keep me close. In that same sleepy, relaxed tone, he added, "I know about Audrey. The chauffeur."

"Keeping tabs on me?"

He grunted. "You were gone for several billable hours. Of course I had follow-up questions."

I stretched, pressing key parts of my body against him. "Look, don't act like I'm in trouble. I was straight with you from the get-go. If you have a problem—"

"I don't mind if you screw around." He shifted in the bed. "It made me angry, at first. I guess because my upbringing just assumed... I dunno. That I wasn't a real man if I didn't get jealous or expect monogamy. But then, I thought about it."

He opened one eye to squint at me for a moment. "Most people in my life assume I have a side piece at all times. Why is OK for me and not you?"

His fingers thoughtlessly traced abstracts across my skin. "I like that you're different, that you don't pretend otherwise."

I thought of all the women under our balcony calling for him, even as I stood at his side, promoting a freaking show about how we were married. I also thought about the casting couch, and what he'd said. Maybe Chance understood the same way I did that it was dangerous to put too much value in something that could be taken so easily from you.

He scrubbed his hair with his free hand. "Putting all my cards out, we both know I'm taking the bigger risk with this show."

I must've made a noise, because he added, "That's just facts. Moving back from films to do a TV show with you already makes me look a little whipped. It would knee-cap my sex symbol status to have my wife caught cheating our first year married. And frankly, you'd come out looking rough as well."

When he put it that way, his rules seemed sensible, and I sounded like a spoiled brat. I tried to keep my body relaxed against his as I worked out how he was trapping me. Because there was a trap in his argument, I could feel it.

"So you're fine with me living my life in private, just so long as it doesn't make the news?" I clarified, because it seemed even murkier now that we'd slept together.

He kissed my temple. "Yeah."

"So you trust me?"

I felt more than saw his nod. "Yeah, I want that."

"Then you won't send Minnie to watch over me?"

Again, I felt his answer before he said it, in the tension that ran through him, making him stiff in every place except where it would do me good.

He exhaled. "Nah. I can't do that. You're leaving in two days. She took the money, she changed her plans. She thinks she's going with you to maybe get a part on GITZ next season."

"*Does* she have a part on GITZ?"

He shrugged. "Maybe. Look, I thought it might be fun, you two would like each other. She's my family, and for however long this show lasts, you're my family too. Does that make me a bad guy, wanting to line up money and opportunities for the people I care about? Make some kind of..."

"Is that what you did for me?" The pieces were all fitting together now. "Agreed to do this show so I could have a job? So you could collect me, the way you keep your other childhood friends around?"

He shifted so he could get a better look at me. "Yeah, Daph. You're rare, and kind of amazing, and brave as hell. I want that in my life. If I can create a world where we all make money and get famous by banding together for projects, where you and I get to laugh and play and share memories with our friends until we all dodder off into old age? Yeah, I want that."

"You want control," I murmured. The trap he'd set in that beautiful pillow talk of a promise. "You think you're easy, all carefree. But you *have* set up this whole world. It's all about the way you want it. You say you don't care if I screw around, but you've set up everything so I can't. You think you're not the bad guy, it's optics. But you could've given me a role in any kind of project."

He shifted, seeming uncomfortable. "No. Newlyweds was a natural extension of what we had on SHIPWRECK—"

I had him right where I wanted him, and he was about to get called on all his bullshit.

"We could've done any kind of show together. You could've put me up as an extra on your film. If you just wanted to help me out of the goodness of your heart, to lift me up? You could've chosen any kind of way to do it. Don't act like being married isn't exactly what you wanted from the start. You said it yourself. You wanted a family. And for whatever reason, you didn't go back to Minnie. So you wrote a script for her, and you put me in it."

"No, that's not—"

"Fucking Frankenstein!" I laughed triumphantly, slapping him lightly on the chest. "Putting me and her together like this."

Chance grunted in aggravation. I pounced, throwing my thigh across his legs and straddling him again. Fighting or not, the part of him pressed between my legs showed immediate interest.

"You know what?" I put my hands down on his arms and leaned, pinning him against the bed. "You were sooooo open-minded to accept me screwing around. So in turn, I'm willing to give you some grace on being a secret control freak with some fucked up girl issues. But don't lie to me anymore. Or yourself."

I'd grievously misjudged his strength.

In a flash, I was on the mattress and he was on me, and he seemed a little less amused about being called out on his bullshit. Lloyd flashed through my head — the pinches and snide remarks, the ways he tried to get over on me to keep me in line. What would Chance do?

I had too much practice being scared to let it show on my face. Even as he stared down at me, inches away. He was rock hard against my inner thigh and I waited to see which way this was gonna go.

"OK," he said. I let out a breath I hadn't realized I was holding. "Maybe it's the way you say. It must be, because all I can think about is how bad I want to be inside you."

"I'll fuck whoever I want the minute I get to Mexico."

If anything, his cock only throbbed, even heavier against me. *He likes that about me,* the thought sizzled through me, setting everything on fire. *He doesn't want to like it, but he does.*

"OK," he said it like surrender, kissing me, nudging against my hips. It turned me on even worse to have that power over him, to know that no matter what game he thought he was playing about making me his good girl, the real thing he wanted was the fact I was anything but. "Let me in."

I butterflied underneath him, bare legs brushing under the weight of his heavily muscled ones, my pelvis tilting to provide him access. For a moment, he was right there, about to be inside me, heavy, warm, spongy head prodding just enough to make me gasp. Then, gone. He reached for a condom.

That's when I understood Chance Zak, right there, in that moment I had to think before every part of me devolved into getting edged insanity: He wanted to be in control.

That might be a red flag for some people, but game recognized game as the saying goes. I couldn't hold his control-freak tendencies against him because I understood them completely.

They say knowing is half the battle.

The other half, of course, is bending the opposition to your will.

PART TWO

SEVENTEEN

Two days later, I sat in LAX. Even though I could still smell Chance on my clothes and skin almost as if the ghost of that life with him still clung to me, I was technically free as a bird.

Chance and I had come to an understanding. I was traveling to an exotic locale to complete my first feature film. And just this morning, I'd gotten my first payment for the film— after taxes, a sweet two hundred thousand dollars in my bank account, with two more installments coming as I completed my work.

That meant although I couldn't pay Chance back quite yet, true freedom was within my grasp. How awesome was life when you are in spitting distance of all your life goals?

Slouched in the lounge seats at the terminal, surrounded by a few familiar GITZ camera guys and some unfamiliar film crew and actors, everything felt beautiful: the dusty windows overlooking the tarmac, all my new coworkers, bored and drinking coffee or scrolling their phones, the news anchors on the overhead TVs with predictions of perfect Los Angeles weather. I couldn't stop smiling.

Which was when I first saw her.

She hadn't spotted our group yet, her eyes drawn to the terminal gate numbers, that anxious vibe of a lost tourist. I'd spent so much time studying the images I'd found on the internet, recognizing her in real life gave me a little thrill, as if she were the famous movie star and I was the fan.

I very pointedly ignored her, even when she came right up and in front of me with all her breathless good girl excitement and said, "Hi Daphne? I'm Minnie."

Simple ballet flats, sensible for travel. Gorgeous legs. A soft, easy midi skirt that came off with what must've been her signature *sexy but not trying to be* good girl style. Big smile, clearly a little nervous.

I tilted my head, showing off my best angles so she knew from the start that while she might be attractive, I was the movie star. And while she might think she was some old-fashioned chaperone paid to keep me proper, this was in fact the 21st century and I was going to do whatever the hell I wanted.

She grinned, all honest and open, as if she were my best friend, and made a little gesture to ask if she could sit next to me. At my nod, she perched with her perfect posture. I couldn't decide if she was going to drive me nuts or if my new favorite hobby was going to be tormenting her.

"Chance says you're my new best friend." My smile had an edge. How long would we play this game before she copped to the real reasons she'd been assigned to me.

She sat next to me, our knees brushing, sending this little thrill through me. Just after-effects from the thrill of spotting her in real life after all my months of study. Still, it unnerved me a little.

She was definitely cute in a way that didn't try to draw attention, but that would probably grow on you, until one day you realized she had been beautiful all along, or some cheesy made-for-TV nonsense. That's probably how she'd gotten Chance so twisted.

"Did you see the resort?" she asked, scrolling to photos of the beachfront complex where she and I would be roommates for the next few weeks. Like, in an instant, so friendly and talkative, as if we were going to be best friends. Did she think she was pulling one over on me? Like somehow I was in the dark about why Chance had hired her? Like the two of them were going to gang up on me?

It made me feel weirdly possessive of Chance.

"Why you?" I interrupted her scroll. Just testing her, you know? To see if she understood I was the movie star and Chance's wife, and she was.... nothing. "Why did Chance pick... you?"Minnie fidgeted, cheeks going pink, the truth unspoken about her assignment hanging between us. This was definitely I wanted her, where both of us were crystal clear on who was the boss. Just to toy with her, I asked, "You sleeping with him?"

"No!" she nearly tripped over herself. Honestly, good girls were so easy to trigger. "No, I've known Chance forever. My brother is his best friend."

I sighed, shoulders coming down. Minnie didn't seem like much of a threat. She'd do her little assignments, and I'd do whatever I wanted, and now she'd know to mind her own business, and everyone would be happy.

I got up dismissively and went over to sit with Audrey, who was waiting with the rest of the crew, wearing an expression like a puppy desperate for a pet.

Audrey tilted in her seat, so our heads were together. "Who's that?" she whispered.

"We hates her." I smiled, knocking my knee against Audrey's.

Audrey smiled that secret smile. "That sounds fun. What about him?"

She nodded over at my co-star, Rand Studebaker, who looked both like he was completely absorbed by his phone, and also like he was posing so hard he should've been in the middle of a movie shoot. I could feel him sneaking glances at everyone else under the cover of his thick, dark eyelashes.

"Don't know yet."

"Might be fun to find out," Audrey whispered, giggling like we were school girls.

"No." I slapped her lightly on the knee. "You're mine."

Across the seating area, Minnie frowned at us, pretty little forehead lined with displeasure. Pretending to check my phone as well, I tilted it enough to snap a photo. I sent it to Chance.

Me: *Guess who I just met.*

A few minutes later:

Chance: *What'd you do? She looks unhappy.*

This little twinge inside me. I couldn't tell if I missed him or I was mad he'd asked about her.

"Hey, take a selfie with me," I told Audrey. We duck-faced the hell out of it. Audrey went all breathless with excitement when she saw me send it to Chance.

Me: *I'm making her earn her money.*

Chance: *Come on, be nice.*

Me: *No promises.*

EIGHTEEN

So here's what I learned about on-location shoots: They were *grueling*.

After months of the easy familiarity of Chance's house, the same crew every day, and the ease of having Chance there, familiar and soothing? Now everything was upside down.

Filming was no vacation, despite the balmy weather, amazing scenery, and all the new and exciting things that caught your eye. Our schedule went all day, sometimes late into the night. We woke at 3 a.m. to be in full make-up and costumes for sunrise shots.

Everyone was new to me except Audrey, and to be honest, I barely knew her. The cast had real names and their film names. Every day we were memorizing lines, and then filming the pieces of the script out of order. I loved it all.

But I'd be lying if I said there was any semblance of normal. Days and nights snowballed into each other until everything began to feel like a fever dream.

That's how I actually began to be glad for Minnie. At

first, it was purely physical: she was there. All the time. There on the set, there in our little condo with its beach-front views of the Caribbean, the familiar hum of her as I went to the master bedroom at the end of the day and she went to the guest bedroom facing the gardens.

Whether I liked the reason or not, Minnie was there only for me, to make sure I was OK. Sometimes I'd look out from the scene we were shooting, and everything would just start getting to me; I'd forget a line, or accidentally call Rand by his real name instead of his character's while film rolled. This anxiety would claw at me, this fear that I'd get fired, or that I couldn't do it.

When that happened, I found myself searching the small group of people beyond the lighting, for her.

Not that she meant anything, or was cheering me on or anything like that. Half the time she was scrolling her phone, not even paying attention. But Minnie was this connection to Chance, and he had been a big part of my normal world. Seeing Minnie there reminded me of the world I'd get to go back to once this was over. It was enough to get me to start breathing again.

Also, it sounded so dumb I couldn't bear to say it out loud, but I loved that Minnie got up every morning and made me breakfast. She'd pack me a little lunch for the set. She'd make me dinner. All these simple things off a list someone must've sent her, but foods I liked, things that felt normal.

Sometimes, I'd walk past the crafts table, with all its fresh-baked muffins and energy bars and coffee, and I'd think of how physically bad I'd feel if I was eating stuff I scrounged things for myself, and how connected I felt to have food homemade for me. I got on the scale every morning and sighed with relief at staying the same weight. I might be the worst actress ever, or forget my lines, but Hollywood could forgive all that in a way they wouldn't forgive me gaining ten pounds over a film.

One day, she caught me studying her. I wanted to get into her skin, understand what it was like to be someone like her.

"What?" She blushed. "What are you doing?"

"What are you doing?" I mimicked, using all my skills to steal her face. The recognition in Minnie's sent shivers all across my body. I could see them on her arms. I liked doing that to her. Thanks to my face, I knew what it felt like to be seen, and I loved the power of giving Minnie those feelings too.

"Ew! I see it!" Audrey came out of nowhere, breaking my concentration. "Fucking superpower!"

Audrey squished right up against me. *Wow, she's getting territorial.* And on the heels of that, what Audrey had picked up on that goody-two-shoes over there definitely didn't have the kink to catch: I was into Minnie.

I got what Chance saw in her. She was like this totem, this safe place.

At first, I figured this for the stupidest thought that had ever passed through my head. But the thing was, everyone gravitated toward me and Chance because we were physically attractive. It kind of made strange sense that maybe Minnie wasn't beautiful, but there was something about her that made people feel good.

I'd think about her late at night, hearing the movements in her bedroom as I lay in the master bed. Did it feel fucking awesome all the time to be Minnie? I'd always assumed 'good girl' meant proper and not mean or sexualized or... or real. That good girl was what other people wanted you to be. But now, late at night, I wondered if the 'good' part meant you felt good, like low-level buzz all day just from being yourself.

That's when I got, too, why Chance had never made a move on her... I liked having Minnie around. What if I did something to fuck it up?

* * *

CHANCE: *I miss you. Canada's cold as a snowman's balls.*

His text came alongside an update the filming schedule had changed; they were shooting some of Rand's scenes they hadn't quite completed yesterday. I was still in bed, the sounds of Minnie rummaging around in the kitchen. Even with the air conditioning on, the slanting morning sun warmed up the room. I threw off the covers, stretching, thinking of Chance. Kind of missing him, to be honest. My phone chimed again.

Chance: *I dreamed last night I snuck out on an early flight to go home and see you.*

My heart thudded in my chest. Like that, I was missing him so bad I could barely breathe.

Chance: *But of course you weren't at home. I was bummed.*

Not love, just exhaustion, I told myself. We'd been working a hectic schedule in an unfamiliar place where everything was new and strange to keep me busy. Now, I had half a day off out of nowhere. Just enough time to get a little homesick, to think about how I'd left things with Chance.

And just because Chance was homesick didn't mean I was, I reassured myself, even though my insides felt hollowed out and frazzled. I wished then I'd thought to bring one of his shirts. Or that pillow off his bed. Something

I could put my face in and breathe until I felt more at ease. Probably Chance was feeling the same way. Actors had a well-earned reputation for being neurotic. We were both just living up to the stereotype.

Me: *That's seriously the cutest thing anyone has ever said to me.*

Chance: *Really? You need more love in your life.*

I thought of sending him a tits pic but rejected the idea almost immediately. Mostly because I wasn't that great of a photographer, and there was no way I'd send something that might eventually get into circulation. I had nothing against my boobs being splashed across the internet... as long as I looked amazing. Sending Chance an improv nude would be the ultimate in doing something stupid to impress some guy. No way.

But I did have the morning free. And now I had a project.

Me: OK, *hold on to your frozen Canadian butt and I'll have something to return the favor by tonight.*

I crawled out of bed and went to the kitchen. Minnie barely looked at me, and when she did, her cheeks went a little pink. I wondered if Chance was acting like a control freak in her texts. If he was missing me, maybe he was turning her screws to get more information.

Maybe that kind of thought should've pissed me off, but actors are mostly exhibitionists anyway, and I liked the idea they were both spying on me in their own ways. I liked being the center of their attentions. Which was exactly why I now had my morning filled with plans to mess with both of them.

"Come lay out with me," I said. When she hesitated, I added, "They moved all of Rand's action shots to this morning. I'm not in until this afternoon. Come on, please?

Pleaaaaassse? It's been a million years since I had a chance to relax. Don't make me sit at the pool by myself."

Minnie gave me a reluctant, doubtful look. "What about Audrey?"

It got me somewhere right below my bellybutton— this strange ticklish feeling. Minnie suspected me and Audrey? It almost made me laugh right there. How proud she must be, to have figured out what probably everyone on set could've told her.

Minnie narrowed her eyes. She'd be no actress at all; everything she thought glimmered across her face. And right now she was definitely feeling superior. But the joke was on her; I was having all the fun, and she was just a repressed horndog and paid tattletale.

"Oh, I'm sure she'll show," I ignored her soft rejection.

It was Minnie's job to watch over me, after all, even if she couldn't do anything about what I did. She had to come.

"Wear something cute. I hear one of the bodyguards out there is like... superhot. Not for me, silly!" I added, enjoying it as Minnie got angrier and angrier. "For you. So I can live vicariously through you now that I'm an old married woman."

"Chance is a really great guy," she scolded.

"Should I be jealous?" I smirked.

"No." She turned away, so pink I thought she might actually cry. Wow, something more complex was going on there. She looked heartbroken. "That's not what I meant."

Maybe that was the downside of being a good girl; it made naughty things all angst and guilt, and no fun.

"Come on." I'd meant to torment her a little, not really hurt her.

And anyway, I needed her for my project to torment Chance. Without thinking, I slapped her lightly on the butt.

If she knew the real story with me and Chance, she wouldn't be so despairing.

But I was hardly going to give her the upper hand since I quite disliked her judgy face. "I was teasing. Let's go out and have some fun."

I headed to the pool without her, skin warming under the bright morning sun. The sparkling aqua pool, the green lawn, and beyond, the Caribbean. I inhaled deeply and walked all the way to the sea wall.

There, I stood for a moment so the paparazzi could see was there, in my swimsuit, and likely to stay awhile. There were a couple, under a pitched tent, sitting on coolers. Without acknowledging them, I headed back and spread my towel over one of the poolside loungers.

Minnie came out in her swimsuit, and from behind the protection of my sunglasses, I admired her. Since she didn't have to be in film, she wasn't as thin, but she was clearly an athlete. The curve of her stomach, decidedly feminine, the cut of her legs, powerful. She took the lounger next to mine, at first seeming uncomfortable. I thought I'd pretend to sleep until she relaxed a little but accidentally dozed off for real.

When I fluttered back into consciousness, Minnie was snoring a little. Not like cartoon snores, but almost like a cat purring. At her hairline and in the valley between her breasts, little sparkles of beaded sweat, the faint, smell of her warm skin in the air.

I watched her, the evenness of her breathing, and wondered why she hadn't ever dated Chance. Obviously, he'd had feelings for her, still had them. And the way she defended him today, obviously she had feelings for him too.

My costar, Rand, was pretty famous for being a lady-killer. I'd seen him put on his slick, *Hey what's a girl like you doing on a set like this?* act for Minnie over the crafts table a few days ago. She hadn't given him the time of day. Which had made Rand scowl and me laugh, which had made him mad at me.

I'd had to console the guy for like fifteen minutes after that, telling Rand he just wasn't Minnie's type. He said getting shot down by some no-name girl had ruined him for the rest of the day.

Unfortunately, we still had to do a scene that afternoon, in which he was supposed to be seducing me. Stroking his ego had been boring as hell, but it had left me plenty of time to wonder what a girl like Minnie *did* go in for, if it wasn't just any guy who happened to be a hot-as-hell movie star.

Chance was probably on his movie set about now. And if texts could be believed, freezing his very well-muscled butt off, probably while wearing some spandex super-suit that left very little to the imagination. And likely eating nothing but chicken breasts, living with some very small percentage of body fat.

I glanced to make sure the paparazzi still lingered, rolled out of my lounger, and gently sat on the edge of Minnie's. On her other side, a pretty beach bag, and inside, I thought I could see the orange top of a sunblock bottle.

I leaned slowly over Minnie as if I might kiss her. Her mouth, slightly open, eyes closed. Where my hip touched hers, warm skin. Closer and closer, until the side of my belly pressed against hers. I swiped with one hand into her bag, lost my balance a little, pressed fully against her.

The little twinge in her belly muscles, the feel of them jumping against my stomach. Her eyes opened, huge and so dark brown they were almost purple as I stared into them. Shock, but no fight in her, just surprise.

I stayed there for a moment. Maybe she was a huge

prude who looked down her nose at me for screwing around. But that only made it seem like a challenge to make her want me.

"I was just looking for your sunblock. Didn't want to wake you."

I grabbed the bottle.

Something out at the beach caught her eye. Minnie flinched, starting to get away from me, but also making all the places where our bodies touched slide against each other.

"Shhh. Don't look at him. Look at me." When she understood it was paparazzi, I said, "Roll over, I'll get your back."

I could feel her on the cusp of not trusting me. I got that. I didn't know if I would've trusted her were the situation reversed. Cautiously she rolled over. Careful not to look at the photographers, I squirted sunblock into the palm of my hand and slid it across her shoulders, drawing her hair to one side to get the base of her neck.

She sighed, relaxing into the lounger. Impulsively, I tugged at the tie of her bikini.

She tensed up, but didn't object, didn't slap my hands away, didn't tell me to fuck off. I was pretty sure under all that pristine good girlishness and snootily defending Chance's honor, Minnie was attracted to me. Knowing this made me a little slippery.

Then, to make sure Chance got something to keep him warm at night, I pulled her bikini bottom away from her skin and lotioned the top of her ass.

Minnie squealed, perfectly goody-two-shoes.

"No lines, Silly!" I teased, lengthening my body for the best photos possible for ant paparazzi taking shots. "Hold still, I'll tie you back up."

Putting her clothes on wasn't half as intriguing as

taking them off, but I thought maybe she enjoyed that part a little more than she wanted to. I mean, I got it— I spent most of my life crafting how to be as sexually appealing as possible.

"I think it's important to Chance," she said as she straightened her suit. "Important to the publicity for GOOD IN THE ZAK, that it looks like you two are totally in love with each other, you know what I mean?"

You are so into me, I could have you in bed in two days... you know what I mean? I didn't quite say, but definitely thought in my own superior tone. I wondered how fast I could make her come if I caught her by surprise.

"I like you."

It surprised me to say it, and surprised me even more that it was true. She had a stick up her ass the size of a baseball bat, and she was clearly fighting some feelings about Chance even as she was scolding me about my wandering eye.

"Not at first." I caught her with my eyes to make sure we both understood each other. "Because I knew Chance must've sent you to keep tabs on me."

It was hard not to smile, watching her catch her breath like she'd been caught as some soviet era spy or something.

To take her anxiety down a notch, I added, "But you always make my breakfast perfect. And you're loyal. I can see why he adores you. So... We should definitely hang out more before we film the spot for GOOD IN THE ZAK. Maybe if you test well, we can get you a recurring spot or something."

It was the thing Audrey would've most wanted— an entry onto the show, and the opportunity to become one of the famous people. It made me feel like Willy Wonka, handing out golden tickets.

"Hey losers." Audrey slung her bag down next to us, breaking the spell. "Move over."

* * *

As soon as the photos started circulating online, I sent them to Chance.

Me: *These should warm you up.*

I left my phone on the bed and hit the shower. I was so twisted up, I should've called Audrey. Seeing the chemistry between Minnie and me caught on film? Knowing Chance was looking at them? It got me going in the worst way.

What was Chance doing to himself as he looked at those images? I ran it over and over in my head: sometimes he was a hundred percent into it, on my side, wanting us both.

Sometimes he was hard and taking himself in hand, even as he gritted his teeth with jealousy. That was even better. If I was missing him, I needed him to *ache* to be close to me.

If I texted Audrey, she'd be at the front door in two minutes, but I didn't I want that. Or more honestly, I didn't want Minnie to hear us.

The thing about good girls was they had lots of pain-in-the-ass Victorian Era rules about sex. But still... I thought if I played my cards right, I might get Minnie to get a little more affectionate with me.

Groaning with frustration, I stepped out of the shower, wrapping myself in a towel. The terrycloth scratched my oversensitive skin, aggravating and unpleasant.

That's when the stress of the whole trip caught up with me. The strange hours, the unfamiliar faces, the pressure of filming.

Still damp, I grabbed my favorite lotion and headed back into the master bedroom. Each scissor of my bare legs against each other agitating me a little, inflaming that little bud of nerves burning a low fever. Texts from Chance awaited me.

Chance: *Wow*

Chance: *You win. I AM totally crying. DAMN. Looks like you and Minnie are getting along.*

Chance: *I miss you.*

Chance: *Tell that swimsuit I said hi and I want to see it again real soon.*

Me: *What are you doing right now?*

Me: *To yourself.*

He didn't answer. I figured he'd gone before getting my messages, was doing a scene, perhaps out to dinner or even taking a quick nap.

I lay on the bed, replaying the night we'd had together in my mind, waiting for him to respond. After a few minutes, I stood in front of the mirror, studying my face as I thought about him in bed, noticing which expressions were the most attractive or compelling so I could roll these memories into my acting.

If I didn't come, I could think about him all night and blame my aching desire for him. If I did, and my thoughts cleared, and I still missed him? I might have to worry. It was one thing to be hard up and flirtatious, wanting someone so badly you couldn't think of anything else. It was another, much more pitiful thing, to be lonesome for someone, to need them around just to feel right.

It might start to feel like the La Brea Tar Pits, where you might believe you could pull yourself to safety, but an eon of history knew girls like you would only get more trapped the more you struggle. I couldn't afford to be like that. Not in this business.

To keep myself in line, I went out to the condo's main living space and prowled the kitchen space, agitated.

"Almonds on the counter," Minnie called from the couch.

Bless her heart, she'd set out a packet of proportioned almonds for me, all cute in a twee container. Nibbling on one, I flung myself down on the couch next to her.

She was a good companion— quiet, texting on her phone, not hogging the remote or talking. An American program was on, but neither of us had figured out how to turn off the Spanish captioning that scrolled in big block text at the bottom.

Minnie shifted next to me, calf brushing my shin as she re-crossed her legs. Immediately, all my attention was on her, pinpointed into a quick glance to check if she was making a pass at me. But she was deep in her phone, texting.

Half the time I watched the show, the other half, I snuck glances at her. Her pupils seemed large, making her eyes luminous and even darker than usual, chewing at her lip with concentration.

She barely moved, barely breathed as she read whatever response she got on her phone. I wondered who she was talking to, what her life was like outside this strange bubble of us living together.

Probably she had some steady, reliable boyfriend she'd met in college. Probably she'd agreed to marry him just so he wouldn't throw a fit about her taking this job from her childhood sweetheart.

Maybe she'd had to convince him, say stuff like, "Chance

Zak won't even be there. It'll be hopelessly boring. I'll be doling out 12 Almond packets for Chance's B-list gold digger *wife*, and when I come home, we'll wed at your family's ancestral home."

I entertained myself with thoughts of poor Mr. Minnie, who probably wore Dockers and parted his hair tight and straight on the right. Guy like him would be prissy in his jealousy. I wondered what a guy like him would think about me teasing out all of his future wife's repressed lesbian tendencies. I nibbled an almond, considering how maybe when Mr. Minnie got her back, she'd be less of a *good girl* and more of *a good in bed girl*.

When I glanced over again, it struck me that I had some competition. She was definitely pretty into whoever she kept texting.

She was so close. I pretended to shift, stretching, and snuck a peek at her text chain:

Chance: *I knew once you got out of college, you'd start up your life. I could feel it when*

All air? Gone. She was texting Chance.

I swallowed a couple times, feeling as though I'd been sucker-punched, tears hot in my eyes. I had sent him sexy photos, hoping he'd be jealous or mad, or at least horny and want me more.

He'd taken that energy, and instead of texting me back, he'd reached out to her.

Slowly, I got up off the couch, my legs shaky, went to the bedroom, and closed the door behind me. Turned on the TV in my room for noise.

I couldn't stop the feelings coming up, so I did the best I could to cover them: I grabbed a pillow from the bed and held it to my face, and fell face-first into the mattress, and screamed. And screamed. And screamed.

NINETEEN

I spent the next few days so sick to my stomach, I couldn't even handle lemon in my hot water without my insides churning like I'd throw up.

It was my own fault. I'd known better, and I'd let myself develop feelings for Chance anyway. I'd let myself be like good old Heather Conover; pitiful, vulnerable, willing to put any kind of fleeting attention ahead of all my goals. Stupid.

I couldn't even use my phone, because every time I went to it, texts from Chance piled at the top of my list of unread messages.

I knew they'd be a hundred percent nice and concerned, wondering why I hadn't responded, if I was OK. Of course— because Chance was a decent guy who'd helped me out by fake marrying me. He'd told me from the start he'd had feelings about Minnie. He'd done absolutely nothing wrong. I hated him.

Even more honestly, I'd never thought he'd pick her over me. I thought I'd always have the upper hand— whether I wanted him or not, I could always have Chance Zak. I was his wife. I was a movie star. He had given me a job and paid a million dollars to keep me.

I couldn't bear to look at Minnie now.

And yet, there she was, always in the background, watching me with those big glossy eyes. She had won, and she was such a fucking good girl she didn't even act smug about it, just kept on treating me like she always had. I bit the inside of my lip until blood seeped into my mouth, everything inside stinging wildly.

"Hey, you OK?" Audrey touched my arm the next morning in makeup chairs, concern in her tone.

I swallowed the hot coppery taste in my mouth, running my tongue over my teeth to make sure I looked right.

"Minnie's acting like my warden," I lied. "Do you mind... could you just distract her so I can have five minutes without her watching me? I feel like I'm in prison. Like, she's gonna ask me to squat and cough up in here."

"Sh... sure?" Audrey seemed doubtful, flicking a glance over at Minnie.

"Thanks."

"OK Daphne," the director said, catching me by surprise.

I'd been so wrapped up in my seething, I hadn't noticed him approach.

"This next part with you and Rand, I need to feel the connection between the two of you. He's saved you from the bad guys, and in this scene, you're gonna save him right back by trusting him with the treasure map you've been holding onto in secret. Now, the dialogue here is brief, so I need you two to carry the scene with chemistry."

"Got it," I said. He'd never pulled me aside like this

before. I hated myself for adding, "I've been good so far, right?"

"Christ, don't go all actor on me." He rolled his eyes. "Yes, yes, phenomenal. Fantastic. You've been everything I hoped for." He stepped closer and lowered his voice, "But between you and me? See that?"

We both casually turned. Rand, lanky and dripping with greasy sex appeal, was muttering to himself. Probably running his lines. His posture bad, he picked at his thumbnail. Halfway through whatever he was muttering, he got hung up, cursed, kicked some nonexistent pebbles across the floor.

"What's the deal?" I wasn't anyone's on-call therapist, but it made me nervous to see Rand having a hard time. The movie's success depended on us both selling star performances.

"The fuck knows? Actors are worse than cats. Present company excluded of course. Just..." He paced, agitated. "Please, please, please, make sure you do your absolute best, got it? Make them look at you today, not him."

I ran my tongue along the inside of my mouth, focusing on the ragged edge of flesh, the salt and sting. I knew I was about to do something necessary for my career. But also, terrible. I could feel it well up in me like a tide.

Chance wanted me to act like some chaste and perfect wife while he poured his heart out to Minnie, which is exactly what he'd promised not to do if I agreed to his rules. He had me under his million-dollar thumb.

Maybe he even assumed that because I'd slept with him and sent him some sappy texts that I'd fallen for him. Maybe he thought those things would keep me in line, letting him have it all while I pretended to be someone I wasn't. Letting my career founder because I put him first.

Audrey was talking to Minnie. I smirked, catching a glimpse of Minnie trying to sidestep her, and Audrey gamely dancing into her path.

I headed directly for Rand.

"Want this?" I asked. It felt amazing to not care what he said.

"Wh...what?" But I could tell by the way he changed posture, parts of him knew exactly what I meant.

"Limited time offer. Meet me outside. Ten minutes."

I was a fucking goddess. With one pass from me, Rand Studebaker morphed from an insecure, scrawny, twenty-something to being lit up with sex appeal and forbidden romance. He stood taller, flexed his muscles, that curling half-sneer marking up his face, even the subtle tilt of his pelvis, like if you got too close, he'd dry hump you. Exactly what the director had noticed missing.

The dodge into the empty parking lot. The fear of getting caught, of doing the one thing Chance didn't want me to. A quick glance around. No one, nothing. Practically jumping out of my skin with adrenaline, knowing it could change in a heartbeat.

And then he was there, his hands all over me, frantic with need. He shoved my skirt up, panties down. We'd spent weeks pretending to be in love, lighting up the screen, giving semis to the crew with the chemistry sizzling between us.

But out in the parking lot, where any intrepid paparazzi or crew with an iPhone and a dream of side hustle could have spotted us, sex felt exactly like everything else with Rand— like we were acting.

"Daphne Conover," he breathed in my ear as he took me from behind, like my own name was some erotic notion to me.

This is a mistake. Not a traumatizing one or anything. Just a misstep, something I'd learn from, so as not to make the same error again.

Getting caught in the scandal papers stepping out on my fake husband would hurt Chance, but I thought it probably wouldn't hurt me. Hollywood loved a bad girl, after all. And a sordid, dirty secret sex tape had launched more than one B-lister into ultra-fame in this town.

But as I waited for Rand to finish, all I could think was how this might've given my scene with Rand a shot in the arm, and therefore helped my career. But trying to hurt Chance didn't give me any satisfaction, and it didn't make me feel free.

It just made me feel like an asshole.

* * *

THE SCENE with Rand went really well; both of us exuding confidence and calm and a strange evolution of the connection that shimmered on screen.

"Your mom was my first crush," he told me over the crafts table the next day. Minnie had come down with a stomach bug and stayed back at the condo. Not wanting to catch whatever she had, I'd told her not to bother packing me any snacks for the day. As a result, I had been standing over the service table, trying to find something familiar when Rand sidled up next to me.

He didn't try to put hands on me or stand too close, but he did stick around like he wanted something from me. I murmured, "Hope you understand that was a one-off."

"Got it. Gift horse." He said it like we were buddies and I'd warned him not to steal the last glazed donut. Then he'd said the thing about crushing on my mom.

"What?" I had to look at him, trying not to laugh.

"Oh yeah." He nodded, stuffing popcorn in his mouth. "Actually my dad."

He pointed at himself, pausing to swallow all the popcorn. He was actually kind of dorkily sweet when he wasn't trying so hard to look good. "He grew up crushing on your mom. Still follows her career. My whole life, he had that picture of her from The Sunset Club."

Already, I was nodding. It was her most iconic cheese-cake photo. A million teen boys had that poster on their wall back in the day. "Yeah, in the swimsuit."

He let his knees buckle dramatically, took a stumbling step forward.

"Oh man, that swimsuit. All my life, that poster hung in the garage. Used to work on this old muscle car he had out there." Rand made this dopey love-struck face. "I mean, respect, she's your mom and all."

This was the kind of thing I was used to. I remembered how he'd said my name while we were having sex, how I was something special and also nothing at all. A collector's item. Still, sometimes the things that don't make us feel great are so familiar we gravitate to them.

"Call me when you're in LA, I'll see if you can stop by," I said. Which was exactly how fucked up Hollywood had been all my life— me, introducing a guy I'd fucked to my mother because he had a crush on her. It was hard to know what a healthy choice was in this town, but I did think it would make both of them happy.

I got out my phone, looked at all the unread texts from Chance, put my phone away without trying to text her about it. There were no other messages except his anyway. I'd reach out to her when I got back to the states.

Rand nodded like a little kid, eyes all shimmery with happiness. "Yeah, please."

* * *

I BARELY SAW Minnie when I got back to the condo that evening. She seemed distracted.

Must be busy texting Chance.

I wondered if he'd told Minnie how he actually felt about her. I could hear it all in my mind, even though I wanted it to stop: he'd had to explain that he didn't really care if I slept around. Because he didn't really love me. He loved her.

I couldn't sleep. It killed me, imagining the scenario over and over. Killed me worse thinking how they must be making plans to get together. Good old goody-two-shoes sweating the whole morality of it, whether her getting together with Chance was going to hurt me. Maybe hurt me twice because she'd felt the chemistry between me and her. Ugh. Embarrassing! I kicked a pillow off the bed. Small satisfaction as it hit the wall with a *poomf!*

The next morning, Minnie spilled hot water everywhere as I sat at the counter having breakfast.

"Minnie!" I snapped, enjoying how she jumped, face flushing. Had I looked like that when I'd thought about Chance? All dreamy and pitiful and sappy? Well, never again.

"Did I get you? You OK?" She wiped at the counter, scalding herself on the spilled steaming water. "Ouch! Darn it!"

"I'm fine," I told her, then stuck a needle in. "*You're* in a daze though. You in love or something?"

I watched, waiting for her to squirm, maybe defiantly

announce she'd stolen Chance out from under me. Maybe accuse me of sleeping with Audrey.

Instead, Minnie looked like she might start sobbing. Her palm where she'd burned it was beet red. Quickly, I put my cool breakfast bowl in her hand. Unnerved to have any gentle feelings for her at all, I busied myself getting a damp cloth for her.

"I'm OK, you don't need to..." she started, but it was either do something or maybe risk her seeing on my face that I knew she was in progress stealing Chance away from me, and how that was breaking me in unexpected ways. When I'd stalled all I could, I turned to face her, taking her hand and wrapping it.

"So who is it?" I couldn't stop myself from twisting the knife, even if the blade also cut me.

"Who is what?"

The same way as at the pool, I could feel the tension in her body, the way her breathing changed. Not about the question. But over my touch. I glanced at her, but she wouldn't meet my eye.

Chance might want her, and so I might lose him. But I thought maybe I could even the score in my own way.

"Is it me?"

She didn't even have to answer for me to see the truth in the way her breathing picked up, how she arched her back almost imperceptibly, in the way my body responded. Her face went a painful shade of red.

"It's OK. Everyone has a crush on me. I'm used to it." I laughed.

"I don't have a crush on you," she muttered, sullen, pulling away.

"Yeah, you do."

The guilty catch of her breath, the confusion in her

eyes, the faint goosebumps rising across the top of her cleavage. *I know all your secrets*, I let her know with a smug smirk.

"Thanks for the first aid." She practically stalked out of the room. At least she wasn't smugly thinking about running away with Chance now.

"Anytime," I smiled.

TWENTY

With a week and a half left on the feature film, the vibe around the resort shifted gears. The GITZ crew started taking up more of my downtime, shooting stuff for teasers and commercial spots.

The beauty of filming GITZ footage here, even if Chance wasn't around, was the cross-promo. Getting my makeup done for the movie made for another angle of 'realness' for GITZ — me 'not acting' behind the scenes for the film.

The double blur made everything seem fun like an office Christmas party where everyone got drunk, where there's always something interesting going on. The camera was always on, and every move I made was helping me get more and more famous.

I'd promised Audrey a spot on the show, and she'd been talking about it nonstop before the GITZ crew started filming. I didn't mind; she reminded me of myself— so ambitious. So single-minded. But it also unpleasantly reminded me that those qualities I had could be pretty annoying to other people.

One afternoon, I was in the makeup chair, Audrey lounging in the vacant spot next to me, making duck faces into the mirror, practicing her angles.

My shadow, Minnie, was there because *of course* she was. She was always there, watching me on Chance's orders. Except she wasn't really watching me at all. She was knee-deep in her phone.

I tried not to let jealousy get to me. She could be texting anyone.

The camera guys took shots, waiting for us to do something dramatic. There was no real plotline for promo work, and it seemed half likely if nothing interesting happened, it would end up on the cutting room floor; replaced by bloopers from when Chance and I filmed together, or possibly our footage would get edged out in favor of whatever hijinks Beau and Chance were up to in Canada.

Audrey probably guessed at least some of this, and I knew it for a fact. Minnie seemed oblivious.

"I honestly don't understand people like that." I nodded to indicate Minnie.

Audrey was immediately on my side, giving Minnie stink-eye. I didn't love Audrey or anything, but I felt the pinch of true affection for her. Probably because we were aligned with a single goal of getting face time on camera, Audrey had my back. When the cameras swung to catch Minnie, I blew Audrey a kiss.

It would've meant nothing had the cameras caught it. Or at least, nothing more than the kind of fan-fic fodder that drove a rabid fan base.

"We hates her?" Audrey purred.

I made a face like, *Maybe? Let's test the theory.*

On my phone, a dozen unread messages from Chance. It hurt too much to miss him and not have him here. I couldn't decide whether or not to tell him about Rand. Every time I thought I knew which way to jump on that, the reasons would flip-flop and I'd be sure it was smarter to go the other way.

My ego couldn't take being one-down right now, which was what got me into bed with Rand in the first place. Minnie had been withdrawn for days, and all these things had left me spoiling for a fight. Any excitement to keep me from thinking about how messed up my life was. Especially when I'd thought making a movie and being on a hit TV show would be the only things I needed to be happy.

"Go get 'em tiger," I murmured.

Audrey launched out of her seat and snatched Minnie's phone.

"Gimme!" she shrieked. "Who're you texting?"

I nearly died laughing, I was so surprised. Audrey had great comedic timing, all of us, including the camera guys, half-asleep in the balmy heat. She pounced Minnie like that phone was a prize.

The look on Minnie's good girl face was worth everything. Following Audrey's game plan, I put on my best mean girl expression, sure Minnie'd run off crying.

So it was even better when Minnie went surprise full-on brawler. Face red, teeth bared, she went after Audrey. And unlike Audrey's over-the-top real-fake drama inducing grab at the phone, it was a hundred percent clear that Minnie's reaction was completely authentic.

That kind of thing, where you see someone's mask slip? It's the most obsessively watched TV there is. I knew it was gonna be gold.

More than that, seeing the real Minnie for a moment, that wild fighter, her athlete's body come out swinging? It jolted my core with a single, shocking throb of attraction.

Probably not just me in the room, either. There's a reason gladiators and mud wrestling get cash money.

In the small room, the camera guys both backed up and bent closer to catch every second. Poor Audrey had clearly bitten off more than she could chew.

"Owww! BITCH!" she squealed, hands flapping, coming down in limp wristed slaps across Minnie's face and shoulders.

"GIVE IT." Minnie separated Audrey from the phone with one deft yank.

I couldn't help myself. I fucking LAUGHED. MY. ASS. OFF. I loved her in that moment. Maybe not fairy tale love, but like when someone surprise wins the day so thoroughly you fucking cheer their asses and buy them a drink, and if you run into them a decade later, and the memory still makes you laugh.

"Can we get one more?" The camera guy called.

Audrey wanted to be on TV, and I had to give her props for picking her beatcn ass off the ground and gamely leaning into a few catchphrases.

Holy shit, I can't wait to tell Chance.

And then, this dull hollow ache followed.

What if I just ignored all his unread texts and went straight to telling him this part? It had been days since we'd spoken. I sighed. My phone buzzed and I checked it out of habit.

Chance's message came up on the home screen for a moment before fading into the screen saver photo of the Caribbean I'd taken our first day here.

Chance: *I miss you.*

In a moment of weakness, I started scrolling back through his messages.

Chance: *I miss you.*

Chance: *In the gym with THE Kirk den Breejin RN. Will trade a photo for a photo of whatever you are up to.*

Chance: *I miss you.*

Chance: *Maple syrup is overrated. Fight me. I miss you.*

My heart hitched, this bittersweet need to save them, look at them slowly, so I could feel that electric current straight to my heart every time he had been out there, missing me when I'd been missing him. It gave me this feeling, like maybe it could work between us.

I hated becoming exactly the kind of stereotype of some dickwhipped fangirl over him, but when it was just me and the texts that couldn't judge me, I read his words over and over and over and—

And then, the whole world blew up.

TWENTY-ONE

We were taking a fifteen-minute break between scenes that had gone really smoothly. My one afternoon stand with Rand had definitely calmed the two of us down, and our shots were going really well, our chemistry easy and relaxed and natural.

Off set, too, Rand would come over and sit in the chair next to mine and bullshit me a little in quiet tones. I didn't think he was trying to get inside me again, just like we'd broken the ice and could be friends. He was actually kind of shy; he's sit down and it would take him like a full minute to work up to saying anything.

So I was kind of surprised he didn't sit down with me at the break. I looked around, but Minnie wasn't there either, which was also a little strange. But with the GITZ fight she'd had, I supposed maybe the crew had reeled her in for some confessional box stuff, or maybe to do some screen-shots to send to hair and make-up if Minnie made the cut for Season 2.

Bored, I rummaged around for my bottled water. I

mean, I wouldn't have said no to one of those snack packs Minnie sometimes slipped in my bag either.

Instead of all my familiar things, a few pages of printer paper, folded up haphazardly, like someone had mistaken my high-end bag for a trashcan.

Annoyed, I yanked it out, hoping to figure out who it belonged to so I could be rude about them leaving their shit in my shit.

D*APHNE*—

$5000 or I sell these to the paparazzi. I have video too, no doubt what you did.

You have one day before your pics are headline news. When you have the money

signal by

Here on the message, something had been erased and written over to say:

black socks with sandals. The whole day. Instagram it so I know you're serious.

M*Y* *HANDS WENT COLD.* Slowly, I folded the top of the blackmail note down to look at the second page. A cheap scan of a grainy photo, the black toner and shades of gray making it difficult to understand what I was looking at. Honestly, it felt like a Rorschach of whatever might scare you. In my case, it could've been a couple things.

Confusion... confusion... and then my eye made sense of it. A photo of Rand and me in the parking lot. Whoa. OK, it was a GRAPHIC photo of me and Rand.

Careful t not to draw any attention in the crowded room, I refolded the pages to hide them from view. As I did,

I cut my eyes around the room. Who was watching this? Was my blackmailer here?

Everyone looked as though they were going about their business. I didn't know if that made me feel better or worse.

By the time I'd casually stuffed the note back in my bag, icy waves of dread, the bad smell of my body going into overtime anxiety sweat: This was exactly what Chance had warned me not to do. He'd given me the whole world, and like some Bluebeard Horror story, he'd only ever asked me not to do one thing.

And here in my bag? The photographic evidence I'd done it.

* * *

I'D NEVER BEEN OUT-AND-OUT blackmailed before, but I'd spent time under Lloyd's thumb, and sure-as-shit had experiences with people trying to manipulate me into doing things not in my self-interest.

In fact, if it had just been my own ass on the line, I felt like I could've blown this blackmailer out of the water— for one thing, it was a terrible photo.

Too graphic and our faces barely recognizable, turned away. Not even the sleazy online place would post photos with actual dick-out-sex-act like this. Not in the same story as our famous names. Not enough viewers would click to make the lawsuit risk worth it.

Kind of the way everyone in Hollywood 'knew' that explicit sex videos that got 'leaked' had some kind of implicit permission from every single person on the tape. The way the laws were going these days with revenge porn, it seemed risky for any publication to post those photos without mine and Rand's permission.

But beyond that, it wasn't a great photo. There was no chemistry. You didn't get hot and bothered looking at the two of us. If anything, I was concerned if these photos did get out— say as a blind item— the lack of chemistry might hurt our movie sales.

Of course, this was probably one photo out of several, but I wondered why the blackmailer had chosen one where it appeared Rand was boning a mannequin.

Still, this was a big problem. The blackmailer might find a publication willing to risk a lawsuit, someone might ID us by our set clothes. And if that happened, I'd be ruined with Chance.

But the price they were asking? Five thousand dollars was laughable. They should be demanding a ton more money. If the blackmailer didn't know enough about my net worth or the price of a salable scandal photo to name a realistic price, it was a pretty ballsy move to shake me down. Five thousand wouldn't cover a lawyer's retainer fee if they got caught by police.

So what was I dealing with here? Someone was trying to hurt me, and just because they were being stupid about it didn't mean they couldn't.

My phone buzzed, a text. I grabbed it up, half afraid Chance would know already.

Chance: *Holy shit! That footage of Minnie slam dunking your friend Audrey! LOLOLOLOL*

I read it, read it again, still half-thinking I was caught. Finally, I understood. He was talking about the freelance GITZ promo I'd done at the pool.

Chance: *that's gold how did you not send me that immediately? How are you not sending me gifs and memes RIGHT NOW?*

You know that feeling when you smile to see someone's

texts even when it's a truly shitty day? The relief I was still OK with him, that I still had time to fix this. That's what was happening inside me.

Chance sent me a gif of Audrey's angry face, and I laughed, tears from the stress of the day swimming in my eyes.

Without thinking, I texted:

Me: *Oh man I need you here. That's perf.*

Chance: *Daph?*

Chance: *Hey, I'm glad you're texting again. It's good to see you.*

Chance: *Are you OK? Is everything OK?*

I was doing the ugly cry before his last text came in.

Chance: *Wanna facetime?*

Me: GOD NO.

Chance: *Facetime me.*

Me: *I'm crying from missing you. I don't want you to see me all gross.*

The FaceTime button came up: CHANCE. I declined, gasping a little from the horror of it. I would tell him everything if I talked to him now, the moment he saw my face. I knew it.

Me: *You sick fuck, you never get to see my ugly crying face.*

Chance: *Come on. I'm into it. It's my kink.*

I snort-laughed, my nose all stuffed up from the tears. Thank god he couldn't see this.

Chance: *What's going on?*

I considered the blackmail note. I almost told him.

Me: *Nothing. It's just end of the tour stress. Plus, someone's giving me a hard time.*

Chance: *They're fired. Gimme a name.*

Me: *I've got my big girl pants on. I'll handle it.*

Chance: *Wanna talk it out? I look good in a cheerleader skirt and can cheer with the best of them.*

I *did* think about it. But there was no way he wouldn't jump in and try to fix this. He'd be worried about the show, and about his reputation. And of course, he'd hate me. And Minnie-two-shoes was waiting in the wings.

Me: *How about I tell you everything when we get home?*

Bubbles on his side came and went. I wondered what I'd said to give him pause. That word, *home?* That I so casually referred to his as mine?

Maybe. Although it seemed fair enough I could be talking about all of Los Angeles. But... I did think of Chance's place as home. At my worst homesick moment, it was his fridge I wanted to go root around in, his couch I wanted to lay on for hours watching television, his bed I wanted to wake up in.

I'd tried so hard to keep everything simple between us, and now it was so, so complicated.

Chance: *If you need me, I can be there. A the end of next week, I can get away for a few days.*

Me: *Yes. I want that. I want to see you.*

Chance: *OK*

Me: *OK*

I wanted to talk all night, or call him up like in those old movies and just fall asleep with the phone line open, listening to him breathe.

How had I so stupidly stopped texting him? I felt better already. I wanted to tell him how goofy my blackmailer was — black socks? Was I being pranked by a kindergartner? Talking with him, the whole situation began to feel utterly ridiculous, easily beatable.

Me: *Hey, I lost a bet and have to put something really dumb up on my Insta. Will you cheer me on?*

Chance: *I can't wait to hear this story.*

Me: *When you get here, promise.*

I sighed, shaky. I hoped I could come clean then.

Me: *Gotta get some beauty rest.*

Chance: *OK, love you, sleep tight.*

Chance: *Shit.*

Chance: *OK, that was basically like calling the teacher Mom.*

I laughed out loud. Chance Zak embarrassed!

Me: *Am I... are you calling me your mom?*

Chance: *NO. Crap. I'm digging my own grave here.*

Chance: *Like you call the teacher Mom by accident and the whole class laughs. When you end a phone call and say I love you bye.*

Me: *You love me.*

Me: *Can't take it back.*

No bubbles on his side. I began to get anxious. Shit. I was more nervous about this than the blackmail situation. What was wrong with me?

Me: *OK, goodnight.*

I could feel him on the other side, waiting for me to ease the tension by telling him I loved him too.

Chance: *OK, sleep tight. See you soon. I'll send you the details when I get my tickets.*

I love you, I love you, I love you.

No matter how many times I said it in my head, my traitor fingers wouldn't type.

No bubbles. I kept waiting for them, hoping for them.

He was gone.

And then it was awkward.

TWENTY-TWO

I texted Audrey later and sent her on my errand, to keep up my end of the blackmailer's demands. She dropped off a six-pack of black men's socks, size small, at my balcony doors around midnight.

"Can I come in?" she held tight to the socks when I tried to take them from her hand.

"Another time."

"Who are these for?"

"I'm seeing a guy with very small feet and a sock fetish." I pushed the balcony doors open so she could see the room was empty. She peered over my shoulder. "What do I owe you for the socks?"

"A hundred bucks."

I wondered then if Audrey was my blackmailer. OK, wow, this WAS like a game. That tingle of suspicion, the process of eliminating suspects. She squinted at me.

"Fine. Fifty bucks, just stop looking at me like that." She shivered, overly dramatic. "You gotta pay me something for running errands in the middle of the night."

I went to the room safe and got her a hundred. "Thanks. I appreciate you doing this."

"If you really appreciated it, you'd invite me in."

Considering what fucking around was already costing me, I decided to pass. "Chance told me he loved your slap fight with Minnie."

The look on her face suggested this news was even better than us getting naked together. She sighed, blissful. "Am I gonna be famous?"

I shrugged. "Thanks for the socks."

* * *

"Daphne?" Minnie called through my door the next morning. "Time to get up. It's a little late..." She kept talking, but I tuned out the rest.

Last night, I'd read the blackmail note until the paper was no longer crisp and new, but almost like cloth. It still surprised me how unprofessional it was, like a kid's game. But maybe a kid's game involving a wild crocodile.

Today, I was definitely in the mood to play.

I paraded out of my room in a tight pink T-shirt, black shortie shorts, and absolutely hideous, cheap men's socks scratching my bare ankles. Just to be sassy, I'd added a pair of strappy sandals to highlight the look.

Minnie's eyes went straight to my feet, her face way too pale, two bright pink dots on her cheeks.

That was interesting. I mean, I kind of had Minnie sewn up as totally devoted to babysitting me. If she'd caught me in the parking lot with Rand, I would've expected nothing less than her shrieking like a fire alarm and immediately, tearfully bull horning the news to Chance. Like speed dialing from the parking lot. If Minnie was the blackmailer... well, that was unexpectedly devious.

I was really getting into this game.

Minnie practically crawled into the fridge to get away from me.

"How's Chance?" I asked, a little too close, just to see if she'd jump. Maybe she was just feeling guilty for trying to steal my husband.

"He said he was going to text you last night," I lied. Worth it: she practically flinched. "Didn't he get a hold of you?"

She nodded, guilty. But guilty of what? Talking to Chance? Blackmailing me? Staring at my boobs like a schoolboy? Biting her bottom lip like her thoughts were impure?

"Come on," I ordered, feeling weirdly... well honestly, weirdly turned on. I really liked the idea that hidden deep under her good girl façade, there was some sliver of bad girl I could bring to the surface— whether she wanted me to see it or not. "We'll be late."

She followed me like a puppy all morning, glowering as I did my lines in front of the camera, full-on scowling at everyone else, including her phone.

I started to wonder what would happen when Chance got here. But I did feel confident that once I figured out who the blackmailer was, I could find a way to come out of this on top.

"Annnnnd cut!" The director called. "OK, reset the lighting, and let's take it again from 'he was supposed to die' in five."

I heaved a sigh and slunk off set, flopping in my chair next to Minnie and digging through my bag for my phone. I half-expected my blackmailer had managed to send another note with Daphne here watching.

No note. Grabbing my phone as Minnie made small talk, I checked IG to make sure my black socks were public. Right now I needed to appear as compliant as possible.

There it was. In all its submissive, *I'll Do What You Say, Please Don't Hurt Me* blackmailee glory: Sock Selfie.

Chance had messaged me his post. What I saw unexpectedly donkey kicked me right in the feels: His huge feet. Black socks. Hideous sandals. Captioned, *I LOVE YOU BABE*.

I thought about how I hadn't been able to say it last night, how awkward it had felt, how I'd assumed we'd never speak of it again. Instead, this all caps declaration for the whole world. And yeah, part of it was probably for GITZ promo. But I knew some of it was a private thing between him and me, a double-dare. Maybe even an I-don't-care-I-love-you-anyway.

"WHAT?" Minnie demanded next to me.

I showed her, annoyingly braggy as people with baby photos or awards.

"I took a photo this morning and posted it on my..." It was ridiculous, trying to explain. "Anyway, I was getting teased. Isn't he the sweetest?"

"Yeah. Completely." Minnie sounded like I'd stuck an actual knife in her guts.

"You love him."

She laughed, pained. "Of course. Who doesn't?"

"You know what I mean, Minnie." I goaded her, loving the flush across her collarbone, how her eyelashes fluttered because she was too nervous to look me in the eye. The catch of her breath and flicker at her throat.

She'd thought about having Chance in ways I'd actually

had him. Because maybe the part of her crush on Chance that embarrassed Minnie the most was how underneath that, she had a bit of a crush on me.

How fucked up she must feel, bound so tightly in her perfect good girl role, to have feelings for both of us. I could definitely tell she hated the way I made her feel. I leaned in until my breast brushed against her arm. Same trick she'd pulled on me before.

She stood at the touch. "I'd do anything for Chance," she warned as she left.

I pressed my lips together to keep from laughing. Little Miss Righteous was definitely taking her job seriously.

* * *

THE NOTE WAS on my bed when I got back to the condo:
Bring money, all cash.
Tomorrow, 2 a.m., women's cabana below the pool.
Follow exactly, or photos go out.

* * *

THE THING about working so hard to be in control was that sometimes, being a little out of control was the most exciting feeling ever. I paced the bedroom, going over my plans.

I had the cash, but I'd decided not to bring all of it.

The more the blackmailer had to interact with me, the more clues I'd get about their identity. I kept trying to figure out, why $5000? Would they take less? Or did they have to pay a debt, or need that exact amount? If money was the motive, I could pay more to keep them quiet forever.

But mostly, it felt as though the note was almost... flirtatious somehow, this silly play pretend of a kid's game. There were so many ways to send money, who but a kid playing dress-up would demand I go to the cabana at two in the morning?

The idea I'd get kidnapped or raped crossed my mind. I mean, what read as playful in a note might just be a dimwitted thug with ill intent. A girl can't be too careful. I was bringing a knife and a phone.

The women's cabana was the 'public' bathroom and changing room for resort guests using the pool. There were outdoor showers for those just needing a quick rinse or coming off the beach, but the cabanas were below the pool, at the bottom of a winding staircase that probably situated them somewhere under the lounge chairs and dining tables set up around the pool.

Down there, it was cool and dark. No windows. Only one way in or out, with a door at the bottom of the stairs that dead-bolted. Inside, a vanity, a changing area with bathroom stalls, and a sitting area with a wicker couch and some fake potted plants; a silk orchid on a small table.

The clock crept closer and closer to our two a.m. meeting. I lay in bed, making my list of suspects. Audrey was probably number one. Minnie number two. I didn't think Rand was in on it; our rendezvous had been too spontaneous for him to tip someone off to photograph us.

A couple of guys in the crew were also suspects, but once I started considering people in the industry, I had to ask myself all those questions about how they wouldn't know the photos were mostly unsalable. The resort staff was also possible, especially with the last note being in my bedroom, but it seemed less likely because of the first note... unless the blackmailer had slipped it in my bag here at the condo and I'd only noticed while on set.

The thing you learn as an actor is that most everyone

has stage fright. Jitters about an upcoming show happen to the most confident stars among us. But you also figure out, or someone tells you, that your body really doesn't know the difference between nervousness and excitement. The feelings are the same: heart racing, senses heightened, too much energy. It's only your thoughts that determine what those feelings mean.

What you eventually figure out is that maybe your body doesn't even know the difference between anxiety and excitement and wanting to fuck, or fight, or run. And everyone knew you could get rid of some of those feelings by rubbing one out real quick.

I decided this was a good idea. I had to be calm about this. I slid my hand into my panties, closed my eyes, tried to focus on the physical touch.

My brain kept wanting to puzzle out who might be my blackmailer, but that wasn't exactly something I could get off to.

I thought of Audrey, how she'd looked that first night in the alley, her expression— lips pulled back, showing her teeth when she got really close. Would she be down there in the cabana? Would anyone be there? Or another note, instructing me to leave the money and get out?

I kicked my legs against the mattress. *Focus!* I ordered my brain.

The night got quieter and quieter, I heard Minnie, rustling about in her room. Nice or not, this condo's walls were pretty thin.

I looked at the clock. 1:55. I stroked myself soothingly, distracting myself. Minnie was also on my short list of suspects. I waited to hear if she'd sneak out. 1:57. Nothing. 1:59. Nothing. Maybe she was only a restless sleeper. Or an insomniac.

I couldn't quite concentrate enough to really get going, and now it seemed too late unless I went for my vibrator. But the telltale sound would give me away if Minnie could hear me as well as I could hear her.... but maybe after I'd figured this blackmail thing out, that might be another fun game to play with her.

At 2:04, Minnie was still in her room. So maybe she wasn't the blackmailer.

I got out of bed, unsatisfied. But it was too late to do anything about that now. From my dresser drawer, I took the knife I'd stolen from the kitchen, my phone, and the money, and put them in a small bag.

Carefully, I opened the balcony windows and looked out at the resort's pool area, watching for movement. The air smelled like sea salt and flowers and the tinge of pool cleaners. Maybe the blackmailer was already down there, but I hoped to catch them creeping down after me, assuming I'd be on time.

I watched for almost ten minutes. Nothing. I closed the balcony doors, rather than try to make my way over the rail and through the hedge.

As quietly as possible, I snuck out the front door.

TWENTY-THREE

I WIELDED THE KNIFE ALL THE WAY DOWN THE DARK
stairs. The fact that the light wasn't on down there made me
fear the blackmailer might intend to jump me in the
darkness.

But when I got inside, there was no one. Breathing
raggedly, I flicked on the light.

On the couch, a note, a strip of cloth.

No blackmailer. I checked the note.

Put on the blindfold.

Wow, this got gamier and gamier.

Nervous, I sat down, got up, sat down again. I slipped
the knife between the couch cushions, within easy reach.
OK, that was good. What about the phone?

There was a little table with a fake orchid on it, but
that seemed too easy to spot. I prowled the area, went to
the sinks. A cube-like metal container for Kleenex, a
spray-on deodorant, an extra bottle of soap in case the
wall dispenser ran out. A trash can under the sinks.I
turned on the video recording and placed my phone
behind the Kleenex box, so only the camera popped out.

This was risky; blackmailers in general probably did NOT like the tables being turned. And really, there was nothing I could do with the tape except know who they were.

Maybe with evidence, I could confront them. Get them to leave me alone. If they were smart, they'd realize I could hardly use tape of them blackmailing me without revealing how I was being blackmailed. If they had violent intentions, discovering my phone might make it a lot worse for me.

But I did it anyway. I'd come out of this situation on top. Or at least I'd go down swinging.

With one final sweep to make sure all my secret weapons were as unobtrusive as possible, I sat down on the couch and slid the bag under it. Then I took a deep breath, knife hidden at my side, reread the simple note. More evidence. I folded it and put it in my pocket.

Where the hell was my blackmailer?

I wondered then if perhaps they could see me, or sense in some way what I was up to. Shit. Well, too late now.

But it made me a lot more nervous as I slowly tied the blindfold around my eyes.

* * *

THIS WAS THE WORST PART: waiting, not knowing. Light seeped in around the blindfold, but somehow that was more claustrophobic than total darkness. The need to rip off the cloth, almost overwhelming.

Footsteps on the staircase and I couldn't catch my breath. They slowed, coming closer. I pressed a hand against the couch, feeling for the metal buried between the cushions. I told myself the worst they could do was murder me, and if that happened, I wouldn't be around to care anymore. I kept my eye on the prize: by the end of the night, I'd know who'd done this to me.

They were in the room. I focused on breathing slow, on the feel of the couch under my body, the solid floor under my feet, the cool, damp smell of the underground cabana, the faint smell of soap and cleaning products.

"It's OK," a static-laced, robotic voice announced. What the literal fuck?! "Daphne, I'm not going to hurt you, OK?"

OK, I was being shaken down by a Sci-Fi character, an electronic .... Oh, OK. I got it. They were disguising their voice with some kind of electronic. The choice of movie crew nerds, I felt sure.

Did that mean they were going to really hurt me and didn't want to leave evidence? My breath caught. Or... or maybe it meant I would recognize them.

"Is that the money?" The voice asked.

"It's *some* money." I laid out my trap. "I couldn't get that much out of the ATM, and the banks were closed. I can get you more. This is a sign of my compliance."

"OK, I'm going to take the money. Don't be alarmed."

No rage at me stiffing them on cash. No suspicion that I'd changed the rules. Instead, this blackmailer tried to console me. I'd been right earlier. This person was playing a game with me, they weren't dangerous. I mean, they could definitely hurt me with those photos. But it seemed as if they were almost going out of their way not to.

Still, they had started this.

"I need the note back too. From your pocket."

Uh oh. They had been watching me somehow. Guess I'd lose my phone. Damn.

But as I handed over the note, I realized the blackmailer FOR SURE should've taken the knife first. It was right there. Why didn't they disarm me? Something was wonky. How did they know about the pocket and not the knife?

Well, the note was gone. Maybe it was just a lucky guess it was in my pocket.

"What are you going to do about the photos?" I asked.

That electronic buzz: "Are you gonna screw around anymore?"

OK, could this be Chance? I mean, that would have to be an elaborate freaking prank, but who besides him.... "Why do you care?"

"You wanna be humiliated in the tabloids? How much money did you bring?" The blackmailer demanded. Angry. Ha, I'd hit a nerve.

"I can get you the rest easy."

I held the note close to my stomach, making the black-mailer lean in closer, to get a better sense of them, a whiff of their smell, anything. Their pants brushed my legs. Soft cotton.

I dropped the note in my lap. As the blackmailer moved to snatch it, I grabbed at them. Blindfolded, I wasn't as accu-rate. Peering down toward the bottom of the blindfold, I thought I saw a feminine hand.

Who in the world would play this childish game with me, not want to hurt me, and care if I was fucking around? Minnie, possibly Audrey. Time to mess with them a little.

"I could make up the difference."

I tried to sound scared, but it was hard to suppress the smile. This problem was turning into cotton candy, evapo-rating in my mouth. Bold, I reached out and slid my hand around the back of her thighs, caressing a little circle with my fingertips. If it was Minnie, a thousand dollars said she ran, squealing.

"The money. Or I send out the photos and your marriage is over."

Ooh, the balls on this one! My blackmailer thought she could keep me in a chastity belt with threats? Well, she was about to get very caught up in my messing cheating situation.

"I'd rather pay this way." I slid my hand farther up the back of her thigh, grabbed her ass, and pulled her toward me. Burying my face against the vee of her legs, I exhaled from my mouth, knowing how the warm, damp air would prickle through those sweatpants, against her skin.

Her gasp, not contorted by the electronics. She jerked as if I'd shocked her. But she didn't exactly pull away.

"No, this is wrong." Pretty sure Audrey would *not* say that.

My blackmailer could've broken away, but when I tensed the arm around her, she almost immediately gave up, letting me keep my face buried against her.

"I'm pretty sure I know who you are," I whispered.

My adrenaline was off the charts. Like the way going to a horror movie always makes you a little sexualized towards the person sitting next to you— all the electricity and tension, the way you grab for their arm, feeling them grab you back.

If this *was* Audrey? I'd already had her and Chance knew. I wasn't committing any kind of extra sins. And if this was Minnie...

This swirl of feelings came over me, too complicated to pull apart. Jealousy and envy and wanting her, or maybe wanting what Chance wanted. He had everything and Minnie was the one person he'd never quite had the nerve to ask for.

Or maybe just that she was a good girl, and at this moment, she was very, very naughty. All of it made me squirm wanting her, wanting to see how far I could push it before she broke and bolted for the stairs, crying like a good girl would.

If I'm being honest, maybe I liked not knowing yet.

Grazing my nails lightly across her skin, I tugged the band of her sweatpants down, revealing her bellybutton, the inch of skin below it. Her breath, shaky, body trembling. She put a hand on my shoulder as if to stop me.

"One of these comes off," I said. "My blindfold or your pants."

Her gasp made me clench my thighs, her legs between mine.

"Why?" she asked.

"Because right now, I don't feel dead inside. And it's been a long time since I've felt... anything." Saying that surprised me. I wasn't even sure if it was true, but it came out of nowhere. Holy shit. I thought maybe I'd accidentally told her the truth.

"Give me the note," she demanded, using the digitized voice, startling me.

Her flickering tries for control were like a fish pulling at the end of the line; I felt in control, but she was definitely keeping my interest. The note sat in my lap.

"You know where it is. You get it."

"You wanna pay this way, do it." Electronic and harsh.

Who was this? I had to know. I tugged her pants down her thighs. This time, she didn't try and stop me. The strange swirl of her talking like the boss and acting like I was turned me on even more. Like she was fooling herself. Like she didn't even know how bad she must want me. Definitely like she thought she was a good girl when actually she was anything but. Or maybe like she thought she was a bad girl when really she was good.

"You're not a man," I toyed with her, running the tip of my nose against her panties. The blackmail photos were hetero. I was married to a guy. I shrugged, teasing, wondering what she'd do. "I don't really know how to..."

"I saw you with Audrey too."

Minnie. And wow, what a streak of bad girl she had running through her after all. Blackmailer, voyeur, secret hots for the wife of her childhood sweetheart? This kinky bitch.

"If I make you come, will you destroy the photos?" It surprised me how everything inside me clenched saying that. I wanted her. I wanted her prissy little good girl ass totally corrupted. Did good girls come harder when they were behaving so badly? I was desperate to find out.

Her little ragged exhale. She was definitely in over her head. My biggest fear was she'd chicken out. I felt true anxiety at the idea, that I'd be so close to having her and she'd slip away. She might give the photos to Chance — that was actually a huge threat.

But she could do that no matter what happened here tonight.

"I'll send them out of you don't." She said it.

My core throbbed. I'd broken her. She wanted me more than she was afraid, and she'd never give out those photos once I had this to hold over her head, and my own video to prove it. She was trying to control me and completely losing control instead.

I tugged her panties down, catching the sweatpants band and taking those down her legs as well. At her knees, they dropped to the floor. She stepped out of them.

I could feel the almost-flutter of air around her, as if she were trembling everywhere. Within my reach, the part of her Chance had dreamed about.

I leaned in, afraid if I moved too fast, she'd lose her nerve. I had one chance to get her where she couldn't leave, and I couldn't see what I was doing. The only sound was her hitching breaths. It felt like at any moment she might change her mind, realize what she was doing and end it.

I darted my tongue out like licking frosting off a cupcake, catching just on the underside of her labia, sliding in between them. Salty and sweet. I penetrated a little further, feeling for that bud of nerve endings.

Instead of bolting, she nudged herself against me, hands coming up to grab my hair and hold me in place. Her muffled, soft moan, as if she were helpless to do anything but, electrified me. Maybe I'd expected the most I'd get out of her was some reluctant virgin routine, but was she so fucking horny. The pebble of her clit made it obvious the creature living between her legs was calling the shots.

She thrust her hips against my face, kind of awkward at first, needy and unskilled. I lost all control, running my tongue over her like I'd want to be fucked.

"Slow," she panted, but she was already there even if she didn't recognize it.

In the next breath she whimpered, bucking her hips against me. The taste of her seared my brain. I kept rolling my tongue over her, trying to get a sense of it, something about it I could almost name.

Triumph surged through me. My jealousy over her and Chance satisfied, fears about the photos a distant spec on the horizon.

Breathing hard as she came out of it, I felt her tense against me. A thread of nervousness — what if she pulled up her pants and left? What if she'd just used me, and I'd been so swept up in the moment, I hadn't seen it coming?

A small pop and suddenly, complete dark behind the blindfold.

"What was that?" I asked. Shit, maybe I'd read this whole situation totally wrong.

"Light's on a timer." She was back to a robot voice.

My shoulders came down and I breathed again, not realizing how much I'd tensed up until she explained why it had gone dark. What had I thought— that she had left? That she was gonna kill me for knowing her secrets? I was too keyed up.

She said, "Daphne, I'm sorry. I'm—" And here was the Good Girl bolt, fleeing up the stairs in horror over a sexual good time. Only, if she'd wanted to pull that off, she would've had to run *before* I made her come.

"You're not leaving me like this, are you?" The fuck, right?

"You want me to leave?" She whispered, sounding frightened.

The tension in my body eased a little bit more. OK, maybe she wasn't going to fuck and run. Maybe she was just inexperienced. Time to educate her on how she might think she was in charge, but now I held almost all the cards.

"I want what's fair. So now it's your turn. Either you get me off, or..." I reached up to touch the blindfold, going slowly so she could feel my movements in the dark. With a gasp, she grabbed my wrist.

Whatever lies she was telling herself, she couldn't tell me. I wanted to feel her on me. Awkward, fumbling, virginal would-be blackmailer oral was gonna be my go-to fetish for a while after this, I could already tell. I thought of all the fluttery glances and angry stares, all the breakfasts, all the adamant insistence that she was in love with Chance. And all this time, she'd been fighting feelings for me. How that must scald her, to become the thing she was assigned to prevent.

I had to admit that was a big part of it— Chance thought she was such a good girl, and Minnie acted so holier-than-thou. I was definitely going to have to come all before either of us left this room.

"Come on," I pulled her down on the couch.

"Don't. I don't. I ummm."

She'd tried to blackmail me. She'd set this whole kinky game into motion. She'd threatened to send those photos out if I didn't make her come.

And then I was alone on the couch. She was gone. Fuck. FUCK. FUUUUUUUU

"Hold on, let me get the door," the robot voice called from the door. She only wanted privacy. I'd forgotten the door had been open. The *thunk* of the deadbolt. I shivered at the sound. I had her. I was going to have her.

"Do you really want this?" she asked.

I was already halfway out of my pants.

She leaned over me as I pulled off my shirt. Her breath on my bare skin, the sound of throw pillows hitting the floor as she moved over me.

"You should always be naked." Minnie's unaltered voice, soft and sweet and full of adoration. The skin at my belly rose with little goosebumps.

"Do what I say," I told her.

If this was her first time, I was going to brand her so the way she knew how to do things was exactly how I wanted.

Already, though, I wanted her back against my mouth. If this was her first time, I wanted to fuck her until she couldn't get out of bed tomorrow morning. Whatever happened after this, I wanted to be in her secret spank bank of orgasms. The one she might never be able to own up to but couldn't let go of.

I eased back on the couch and she sat, prim and proper, next to me. Even with the blindfold on, I could feel her looking at me. Guess if actors have a superpower, that's it. It tingled over my nipples and ribcage.

Slowly, I let my legs fall apart, listening to her little gasp. It made me smile. I could still taste her, I didn't know how she could act shocked. But it pleased me.

Her fingertip, on my stomach, over a tiny tattoo I had right above my pubic bone. "Are you sure?"

Without waiting for a reply, her lips against my thigh, soft naked breast against my knee.

"You've been stalking me since we got here." She wanted me, and it was time for her to let go of that innocent shy bullshit. "Invading my privacy. Watching me. Don't act gentle now."

She froze, but I was tired of her good girl games. She was the one who had tried to take advantage of me. "I'm going to come all over you whether you like it or not."

I reached for her. She caught my wrist and pinned it against the couch. She leaned in and put her mouth on me, not shy at all.

I had already been so turned on, and the shock of her tongue, warm and urgent, took me by surprise. I thought I'd have to talk her through, but in moments I could barely think, let alone give instruction.

It got away from me, so fast and hard I didn't even have time to warn her. She slid over my clit, and I couldn't stop myself. I came while she played with me. I bit my lip trying to be quiet because I didn't want her to know, because I didn't want her to stop.

Her hand squeezed my wrist, the restless twist of her body between my legs, the way she kept licking me so I kept coming, clenching under her, too selfish to tell her if it meant she might stop, if it might mean it was over between us.

As I came down, I scrambled away so I could reposition myself. I still wanted her in the worst way possible. "Do exactly what I do, understand?"But that was only so she wouldn't make me come so fast again, because I had to do things to this girl she wouldn't ever forget.

I crawled over her, mesmerized by the silkiness of her skin brushing against mine, the warm smell of her. I wanted to be inside her, run my tongue all over her, taste her. I drew her skin into my mouth, nibbling at her.

This time, it felt like a dance. As I moved, so did she, everything I did in mirror image. Her tongue against me was almost like licking a nine-volt battery, an undeniable electric buzz I felt everywhere until I couldn't think of anything else. Had I thought I was the boss here? I couldn't stop, I couldn't stop, I couldn't.

All I could do was adore her in every way possible as I came again, holding on to her desperately, kissing her over and over until she jerked against me, those uncontrollable motions, the clench of her opening against my fingers.

* * *

I came back to reality half collapsed on her. I had no idea what time it was, only that I wanted her again.

"You can take off the mask." She sounded defeated.

It stung. Had I disappointed her? Was it over between us?

I stretched, flexing my leg where it pressed against her

cheek, flirting, hoping she'd give me a kiss, start up with me again. But when she did, her lips were soft, almost reluctant.

"No, I don't think I will," I said.

I didn't need to take off the mask to know who she was. But after a moment's thought, it occurred to me this was probably a complicated thing for her, if she really had feelings for Chance.

I supposed I should feel guilty too, having slept with the person Chance had sent to make sure I didn't sleep with anyone. But I didn't. If anything, I felt like maybe there were possibilities here.

I knew I could never feel right in a monogamous relationship with Chance, especially not with the power dynamic between us being so off. But I did want to be with him. Maybe there was a way to make our own rules. But this could definitely blow up in my face, no doubt about it.

But at minimum, I felt like I'd found out what I needed to know: Minnie was never going to sell those photos. At most, she'd send them to Chance. But probably not even that if I told her I had camera footage of her and me together. Sure, the lights had gone off and ruined most of the shot, but I'd probably got enough video to buy back my freedom.

So in that respect, I was going to call this evening a win.

"Maybe this is fucked up," I told her. "But I liked what we just did. I think I know who you are." She tensed. Fine. Let her have a fig leaf, right? "But what if I'm wrong? If I take off the blindfold, I'll know." I nudged her again with my thigh. "What if I'm disappointed?"

"That *is* fucked up." She laughed. "Daphne, the whole thing is, you've got to stop fucking around. You know you do."

Oh great. A lecture from the good girl I'd just licked to

climax a hot minute ago. The one who tasted like salted caramel. The one who'd blackmailed me at 2 a.m. and didn't care about money.

"Do I?" I made a show of getting comfortable.

I must've dozed. The next thing, a soft kiss on my cheek. The cheek on my face, unfortunately.

"I'm going," she whispered.

I pulled the blindfold off as the door's deadbolt un-socketed. Then I leisurely got up and collected my things, curled back up on the couch, and watched the video of me and Minnie, each glimpse of her face as she came, thinking no one in the world could see her.

TWENTY-FOUR

Here's a fact about me that never made my cutesy bios created for the media press packets: If I hadn't been able to get that surgery, if my dreams of becoming a big star had been dashed? I would've studied science.

It's probably a laughable claim from a girl who worked her ass off for a G.E.D. But I loved the microscopes. I loved the careful observation. I loved making guesses about what creatures would do, and then seeing whether they did it.

The year my jaw was wired shut I couldn't work, so my mom sent me back to school. We had this biology class project where we sexed fruit flies and collected data about how they passed on genetics.

This tiny kingdom of insect, crawling all over each other, sexing each other, their partners revealed by the next generation's recessive crinkled wings, or dominant red eyes — and my only job was to observe and take notes, make guesses about who had slept with whom.

It wasn't all that different than most TV shows. Perhaps disturbingly parallel if you considered my current habitat on a reality show about newlyweds.

In the same way I came to class every morning, fascinated about what might have happened overnight with the fruit flies? Now I opened my bedroom door and watched Minnie go out into the world. I couldn't stop observing her smallest changes in behavior, making guesses as to what might be going on.

She had tried to blackmail me and instead gotten tangled up herself. She must feel like I sometimes felt about myself— as if I had all these plans and good intentions, and somehow my basic instincts were to derail everything.

I wanted to see how Minnie would deal with it. For science.

Also, maybe figure out how I could stop doing that thing where I fucked myself into a corner that threatened to ruin everything I'd worked so hard to achieve. Minnie definitely had this aura of kindness and normalcy surrounding her, like perhaps she'd only stuck her big toe into the waters of blackmail and naughtiness. I could tell by the smudges under her eyes that what had happened was giving her sleepless nights. One morning, I had to wake her to get out to the set, which was totally unlike her.

Also, and this was the part I was least comfortable about, I wanted her again. Maybe the self-destructive part in me had to corrupt her. But I was a little stumped at how to do it. How do you proposition your blackmailer into more sex? I didn't want to just tell her I knew it was her; that felt like she might feel forced, and as much as I wanted her, I didn't want her to get trapped with no way to say no. Lloyd had taught me all about that, and I never wanted to be like him.

These were the things I considered. Weirdly, deciding what to do about Minnie made me feel more tender towards Chance. He would probably never understand, but I felt like I could appreciate what he saw in her. She was nothing like me, and that used to make me jealous.

To be perfectly honest, there was still jealousy in my heart, but now it was more complex. She wasn't just an idea, a competitor. The things Chance adored about Minnie, the way she tasted, maybe even Chance's real or imagined ideas of the little sounds she made in bed? Those were all real to me now.

But I understood how Chance must've felt, like if I played my hand wrong, she might slip through my fingers.

TWENTY-FIVE

On Rand's last day of filming, we had a wrap party planned for him.

As I finished my last scene with him, Minnie frowned severely at us from behind the camera crew. It caught me funny in the chest. Of course, Minnie knew I'd had sex with Rand. Little snoop had photographed us. But it was the first time since the cabana that she looked anything other than jumpy or turned so inward she hardly even noticed me.

Jealous, I thought. And then, *for herself, or for Chance?*

"You are positively scowling." I sauntered up to her.

Of all my lovers on this trip, she was by far the least game at keeping suspicion to a minimum. It made her seem more real, her lack of playing this celebrity secrets kind of game, but I also wanted her to stop.

"I don't like him," she muttered, turning away like a child. Like a jealous lover. Hoped no one around us noticed.

"Me neither," I lied.

Or not exactly lied. I liked Rand fine. But I wanted to soothe her. It all played out on her face; the guilt, the question of whether or not I knew she was my blackmailer, the raw sexuality in the way she met my eye. She was exactly the kind of trouble that could really ruin me.

I leaned in to add, "Not interesting enough for me."

Goosebumps rose along the side of her neck.

At that moment, Rand was taking multiple bows for finishing his last scene. A few scattered applause got him shouting out appreciation to the crew.

"OK," the camera guy for GITZ took over. "From here on out, we'll be stepping in more frequently to get promo for GITZ with Daphne and some others here. Make sure you've signed your waivers if you want to on film for GITZ, Season 2."

People were mostly looking bored, drinking water, murmuring conversations amongst themselves. Rand looked like he didn't know what to do with himself.

It had always been the plan to shoot this kind of show-within-a-show of me backstage or in the makeup room filming my feature debut. But with the chemistry between Audrey and Minnie, the crew was definitely looking to get enough footage for some kind of B-line one or two episode story for the show. In the meantime, they had us doing all the standard operation procedure for fluff reality.

"OK," the camera guy concluded, "We'll be shooting a shopping spree, a few beach shots. Check the schedule if you want to be part. And today we'll be around, just filming so you get used to not looking at us. Thanks, all."

The shopping spree was in part because GITZ was catching enough heat designers had started sending me 'gifts'— expensive handbags, beautiful shoes. An old song I'd recorded when Lloyd had been pushing me into bubblegum pop had even been picked up for a commercial.

The extra attention meant sponsors were lining up to have their products featured in Season 2. Which meant lots of scenes of me trying on beautiful things, or opening a fridge with all the name brand labels carefully facing the camera.

After the structured, memorized requirements of the film for DeltaStar, this part of the job felt easy. But that made it dangerous, too.

You could forget the cameras were there, endlessly watching. The way some people had anxiety dreams about showing up to class naked, I got nightmares I forgot the cameras and picked my nose or fell out of character.

In a way, my fears were worse — there was realistically no way you could get all the way to school without clothes, but I could definitely get caught being too flirty with Audrey or Minnie. And even more terrifying, a comically loud fart would probably make the final cut.

Life was generally full of contradictions, and reality shows definitely mimicked life. As such, just as we were bored and lulled into forgetting the cameras, there was also this unspoken pressure to come up with something really good to catch on film.

The big 'finale' for this section of the GITZ storyline in which I was filming away from Chance, was of course that after all my lonely hearted girlfriend shopping spree fun and becoming a movie star in my own right, I was supposed to be missing Chance. The reveal would be him 'surprising' me by showing up in Mexico.

We were filming that tomorrow. He'd make his grand entrance at a club we would be hanging out in, with all the implications of darkness and drunkenness and sexiness. And of course, an opportunity for me to wear an obscenely sexy clubbing dress.

Despite the sticky situation I was in, I couldn't wait for him to arrive. Theoretically, nobody else on the cast knew he was coming, which I hoped meant Minnie also didn't know.

But before he got here, I had to settle up with Minnie. After all, she did own pictures that could ruin GITZ, and I needed to make sure she would never dare show them to anyone. Especially not Chance.

I put the black socks back on, put a photo up on social media, recreating Minnie's blackmail instructions. She'd left the money at my side after that first night, so I figured she had little actual interest in the cash.

I wrote an obscure comment with the photo about the money I owed her, but hesitated, not publishing.

It was this, or confront her directly. I could prove what she'd done with the video on my phone. That scenario seemed like a lot of tears on her end and me feeling like an asshole. I didn't want that. She'd made this a game, and I wanted to keep playing.

I needed her to reach out to me again. I needed her to get comfortable with the naughty streak hiding under all that good girl.

I wondered what Chance would do if he knew.

I thought about him arriving in a week.

I made sure nobody told Minnie.

Maybe it was revenge. Sometimes I didn't understand my own motives too well, other than it feels right at the time.

On the IG post, I deleted the money reference and posted the image, feeling frustrated. *If* she saw the socks. *If* she knew they were an invitation. *If* she understood I wanted her to meet again, in the cabana, in the middle of the night? It was a lot to get out of a photo of socks.

All day, I studied her.

During a break, I saw her, dug into her phone like a tick.

Eyes wide, thumbs going still, hovering over the screen. Suddenly, this idea hit me.

I signaled to the camera crew to give them the heads up I was gonna pop off the drama. Then I casually walked by Minnie. She was so entranced, she didn't even flick a glance my way. Probably her panties were entirely soaked by my over-obvious socks message. Or she was panicking. Probably both.

I panned to the cameras, giving them my best innocent prank girl grin. Then I snatched Minnie's phone, just like Audrey had a few days ago. This repeat prank would never make the final cut of course, unless I added a pretty good twist to it.

"Daphne!" Minnie jumped. I danced away, playful.

Audrey, bless her camera hogging heart, piled in on the action. "Who you always texting Minnie?"

She got between me and Daphne, which also happened to be front and center of the camera.

"Give me that back, it's not funny!" Minnie whined, going full good girl stereotype. I sweated a little. I had to turn the tables on her quick before she ran away crying like some freaking martyr.

Imagining her, I made Minnie's martyr face: Eyes wide, mouth falling open like she'd slapped me, body going rigid with shock.

"Who are you hiding?" Audrey taunted for the cameras.

Time to get this show cracking.

"Omigod," I said, absolutely devoid of playfulness. The camera moved to get a reaction shot. "You're creeping on Chance."

I let it hang in the air for a moment. Then, with my own wounded good-girl voice said, "Minnie, do you have a crush on my husband?"

One camera swung to catch Minnie's reaction. The other stayed locked on me. A pity, because I had to squelch my triumphant HA! face. 'Good girl' was a weapon, and I'd used her own weapons against her.

"I can't..." She looked about, helpless, groping for any way to save herself. Nothing but cameras, and smug Audrey gasping at the drama, and me, now sitting in the good girl role Minnie formerly occupied. Shit, I couldn't break character, so I had to keep that fragile warble in my voice. But underneath, I was so freaking smug I could barely contain it.

"We can't help who we fall for." Tears stood in her eyes. For a moment, I almost felt bad for doing this to her. Was she talking about me or Chance?

"Oh...My...Dog." Audrey was really doing her best to throw out all possible catchphrases.

"I thought you were my friend," I said because that's how a scene like this had to resolve, the best possible cut-to-commercial kind of cliffhanger. Also, wounded bafflement was the ultimate good girl dagger to the heart.

Minnie sniffled. I thought for sure she'd run away then. That's what girls like her did.

Instead, she stood stubbornly, tears in her eyes, refusing to back down. I wondered if she'd just admitted to everyone she was in love with me. It made my breath hitch.

But of course, she must've been talking about Chance. I hadn't actually looked at her phone. She could've been checking her stock report for all I knew. Except her reaction had been a hundred percent guilty.

"Annnnnd cut!" The camera lenses tilted, the tension dispersing. The light went out of Audrey's face.

"You should get another take," she suggested as the camera guy doled out instructions: they'd want Minnie for some confessional box time, she should meet with the showrunner for some notes on where the storyline needed to go next.

It brought up all these conflicting, confused feelings in me. I'd hurt her, but what I'd done also meant she'd be on the show for sure— spending time in Los Angeles. Around Chance. Around me. Was I delivering her like some gift, painting myself as the supporting actress in their love story, where they'd finally be together every day? Had I hurt her or me?

"I can't," Minnie said, pale and shaking. "I can't talk about Chance on camera."

I handed Minnie back her phone. She gave me this big, shiny-eyed sob like I had broken her heart. On impulse, I hugged her.

"That went perfect," I said.

"You know, people will hate you *so* much," Audrey practically sang at Minnie, probably meaning it as a compliment. I wished I could kick her without anyone seeing. It made me angry, to feel so complicated, to also not know how I felt.

"Don't be silly Aud. Everyone loves a villain. It's what makes the show work," I soothed. "Chance told me there was a bad girl lurking under your good girl shell."

This was a lie. Minnie's eyes got big at the idea Chance and I talked about her behind her back. I hoped that would work towards keeping her mouth shut about those photos.

She did look like she might throw up. With the cameras off, I couldn't hide my smirk. "Come on, Aud. Let's get some lunch and work on our cues for tonight."

When we were alone, I told Audrey Chance was flying in. Predictably, Audrey was more excited to talk about whether Minnie knew Chance was coming (nope) and whether we could ambush Minnie again when he got there (yeah, maybe) rather than what it really meant, which was I wouldn't see her again for a while.

"Oh sure." She waved a hand like shooing a fly when I told her, before diving right back into talk about GITZ and whether it would make her, "famous or, you know, like *famous* famous."

Audrey was easy that way.

TWENTY-SIX

Me: *We're on our way to the club.*

Chance: *I'll be there in an hour. Gotta hit the shower and change.*

Me: *Are you checking into our condo or do they have you somewhere else?*

Chance: *I am this minute sitting on your unmade bed, looking out at the ocean.*

Chance: *Wish you were here.*

Me: *Soon.*

The shuttle bus rocked over speed bumps, engine humming through the seat, distracting. Audrey sat next to me, still, amazingly, talking about all the possibilities for GITZ.

I'd checked the money in my bank account again this morning. After taxes and paying off my credit card bills, I had $350,000 from the first season of GITZ.

When I'd signed with DeltaStar, they'd offered a million dollars, and I'd agreed, breathless. After taxes, that had come out to be a little shy of six hundred thousand.

They'd paid a third for signing, and any day now, the second installment would drop in my account. The final two hundred thousand wouldn't come until the movie premiered.

Nine hundred fifty thousand dollars. In less than a year, I was almost able to pay Chance back.

Those zeros in my account left me giddy. That I could lose them all in a couple of keystrokes— a direct deposit that cash to Chance's account— and be free and clear, the master of my own fate... and also dead ass broke? I wasn't sure how to feel.

I shifted in the seat, agitated. Bad enough I didn't know how to feel about Minnie and Chance. But money and freedom were places I thought I completely understood, could make no errors in judgment.

I did the numbers again in my head: Even if I made exactly the same salary for the second season of GITZ, I'd be able to pay Chance back his million.

Which left me with big decisions to make. What was more important— my freedom, or fame and fortune?

If I paid Chance back, I'd have a couple hundred thousand left to start my new life. But no manager, no leads on anything besides a possible third season of GITZ. If I gave him the money, he'd have no financial interest in me. That would make it easier for him to quit GITZ, the one job I had.

I didn't like thinking how the other side of freedom was maybe being alone. I didn't even have a manager lined up yet.

As Audrey chatted happily away next to me, I got scared. I'd thought I was so close to being free, to being famous and rich. But now I could see I was trapped, my dreams much further away than they'd seemed, and the path to them so much more complicated. Like Lloyd had been before, now it was Chance I'd leaned on for connections. I'd signed contracts, but never actually networked any job but GITZ.

My stomach twisted, but I considered my options of going back to Lloyd. Slimy or not, he'd gotten me the feature deal. He knew people. He was solely devoted to hustling in my name.

I scrolled through my texts. Lloyd hadn't reached out since the night I'd fired him. I'd told myself it was relief that flooded through me, every time my messages buzzed and it wasn't him.

There were so many other people in my life that had messaged me since the last time Lloyd had. I couldn't understand why it bummed me out so bad to scroll back and back in time, until his last message. This was what I'd wanted.

I reminded myself how bad my stomach had hurt every day, knowing he held power over me. How he'd dragged me out at night in skimpy clothes and bright lipstick.

He was probably busy drinking and drugging away his million dollars, buying a whole bunch of shiny suits to wear downtown, telling everyone he'd made me famous, and then I'd dumped him. Probably crying into some new starlet's cleavage like the low rent sleaze ball he was? Good riddance.

Because Mom hasn't texted you either.

A hiccup of shock. I turned to the window, focusing on Audrey talking about fame and fortune and love triangles and the real possibility that she'd find a way to throw a glass of wine in someone's face by the end of next season.

I didn't want to think about how nobody'd even paid

her, and she'd dropped me without a look over her shoulder. Over *Lloyd.*

I didn't want to think about my mom at all.

* * *

REALITY SHOWS WERE nothing like reality. Reality was chaotic, wild, unpredictable, and beautiful. Reality shows were partially scripted, corseted into a story arc, and this strange dance of trust in which the actors depended on the showrunner not to overlay dopey music or a laugh track in when they cried real tears.

Our club shoot was a pretty good example. We shot it in the afternoon so we could rent out the whole building. Then the showrunner and casting director filled it with paid extras who were all varying shades of beautiful and could take directions so that on cue, the whole room would look towards the doors as Chance came through them. Or gravitate off the dance floor when Chance and I went out to slow dance.

That old saying *going to bed with a ten and waking up with a two* was in reverse in reality shows. We all lumbered off the shuttle into the hot afternoon sun and filtered into the black matte painted club. Empty, it smelled of stale, flat booze, the floor sticky underfoot. Like you could catch an STI just sitting on a barstool.

Everyone was sober, nervous, and waiting for the cameras to roll. The lights stayed up, revealing cobwebbed old acoustic ceiling tiles and all the dings in the walls from drunken revelry.

The crew had already been in and adjusted the disco ball and overhead lighting, so there was basically one place I could stand while waiting for Chance to arrive, one place he had to stand when he came in, and one place where we would slow dance, the floor marked with painter's tape.

None of this did anything to soothe the very real nervousness I had about seeing Chance again. If anything, it made the whole thing feel like he and I were pandas in the zoo, with a thousand observers making sure we mated properly once we were reintroduced into our shared habitat.

With a crackle, music started. The lights went out. Then the crowd cheered as things got going, the showrunner hyping on the microphone. This switch flicked on in me.

Now I was Daphne Zak, doing the thing she'd wanted to do since she was a kindergartener going out for cereal commercials. I danced, Audrey at my side, but firmly in the *girls having a good time*, PG way. She just wanted camera time from me now.

Although it was light where I stood and dark where she waited, I watched Minnie. I wanted to hate her, to enjoy her obvious discomfort. I'd exposed her for wanting Chance on what would eventually be a nationally syndicated program. More than that, Chance would see those clips. She had to have a lot riding right now.

For a moment, the lights slid over her face. Her eyes flashed. She watched me, like a tiger in the shadows. The raw, aching desire on her face, the misery, caught me by surprise. Minnie might be in love with Chance, but there was something powerful between us.

Anyone who saw her expression would catch the heat in it. I certainly did, my body remembering everything we'd done. How demanding she'd been, needing as much from me as I could give.

She was like Chance in bed, I realized. Not like Audrey or Rand, who acted as if I was some ride at an amusement park, the Daphne Zak fuckercoaster. Like maybe they'd wanted to take a selfie with me after.

With Chance, it had felt real, but the specialness of that had flown under my radar. He was a bigger star than me, so it seemed reasonable if anyone was gonna fangirl between the sheets, it would've been me.

It was all mixed up in me, missing him, knowing he loved her, missing her, watching her watch me across the dance floor.

I swayed to the music, Audrey brushing against me as we moved with the crowd. I could feel Minnie's eyes in a way I bet the camera would pick up as her hating me. Where she stood, when Chance came through the doors, she'd be in the spotlight with him.

The lighting around Minnie changed. I could tell she didn't notice— it was something you'd know from being in movies, trained to stand in the best lighting. My heart squeezed. She and Chance would sleep under the same roof tonight.

I turned away, surprised how the thought gutted me.

When I looked again, they were hugging, her back to me. Every muscle in his arms defined and gorgeous and terribly masculine, his body mass intimidating. I swallowed, caught off guard. I had missed him so much, even more than I'd realized, and feelings came crashing down all around me, the urge to push through the crowd and...

And what? He was holding Minnie.

Get in between them. I wanted them both, but I wanted them to want me, not each other. I had no idea how to make that happen. Probably, even trying it would go down in flaming wreckage. But that was all secondary to seeing them together and needing desperately to shuck this tiny dress straight to the floor and get between them.

But I stood there. Because before I ever wanted anyone, I'd been taught to stay in the spotlight.

And then she kissed him.

It was a knife in my heart. But also like electricity in my body, a current zapping everything— down my neck and to the ends of my nipples, along my thighs. most strongly between my legs.

Chance pulled back, and I caught the surprise on his face, the change in the way he held her. Everything he felt for her was what I needed him to feel for me. Except I wasn't his safe place. I'd fucked three people since I'd seen him last and we'd been separated less than two months. I was the exact opposite of what he wanted.

And like all storybook villains, I didn't care. I only wanted what I wanted.

He laughed, smiling at her. Although he didn't let go of her, their embrace loosened. He said something to her.

My fault, I thought he said by the way his gorgeous mouth moved.

He brushed the side of her face and Minnie pressed against him, up on tiptoes. I wanted to kill her then. He was mine. I might have fantasies about sharing, but that was strictly about *them* sharing *me.*

He looked up and saw me. I mean, it was scripted. He couldn't miss me. I was all lit up by professional lighting, with staged actors dancing carefully in a circle near me but not too close, and I was wearing a dress roughly the size of a dinner napkin.

But when our eyes met, what he must've seen was all those emotions on my face, all that desire and jealousy and pain. My cheeks went hot.

If he saw it, the cameras did too.

Part of me died with embarrassment. But the look in

Chance's face made my core clench, everything that had been half-triggered by Minnie went swollen and needy for him, remembering what it had been like the last time.

No smile for me. The intensity of his gaze, the tension in his body made me know parts of him must be responding to me the way my body was responding to him. It left me a little breathless that he was still holding her, that what Minnie felt in his arms was actually feelings he felt for me. And honestly, it only seemed fair that if I had to watch them together, she should know that however he felt, pressed against her? That was because of me.

He left her so quickly she seemed to spin, still holding on to him as Chance crossed the dance floor, eyes never leaving mine. It was choreographed this way. I didn't believe in happily ever afters— not with the lighting and the extras instructed to separate out when he arrived. You couldn't believe your own hype, especially not in some Season 2 of a reality show you helped script.

And yet. He left Minnie near tears without a look back. Undistracted by the writhing hopefuls on the dancefloor trying to catch his eye, or the fanboys reaching out to touch him as he passed, Chance came for me. When I threw my arms around him, he didn't merely hug me back. He swept me off my feet, up in his arms, and kissed me. He smelled like sex and wanting.

"Hi," I said.

That was how I knew this part was real life. I didn't have a scripted brilliant catchphrase, or witty remark to close out the scene. I only had this airless, starry-eyed word that meant everything.

"Yeah." He kissed me again, touching me everywhere, holding me close. When we broke, he inhaled against my neck like I was some long lost stuffed animal. "Let's get out of here."

We were supposed to film a whole scene where we danced and kissed and flirted and got to know each other, where he plugged his franchise. Instead, the last part of the club scene and all its painstakingly set lighting was Minnie standing in her little spotlight, looking as though her heart was about to break. The spotlight moved to the center of the floor. But there was no one in it.

Meanwhile, Chance and I barely made it to the employee lounge before he pushed my tiny dress up my thighs and yanked my panties off.

TWENTY-SEVEN

THE REST OF THE AFTERNOON WAS A BLUR; CHANCE's arm constantly slung over my shoulders as we finished some basic clips in the club, touching me, stroking my arm absent-mindedly, kissing me the moment we were free from friendly hellos by everyone in the GITZ crew who hadn't seen Chance since LA. He doled out star struck handshakes to extras who'd waited after filming to say hello or get an autograph. The whole time, the smell of him on my skin, these delicious flashes of what we'd just done—

Pressed against a wall, his hands in my hair.

The heat of his mouth against my throat, club music pulsating through the locked door.

His fingers digging into my ass, my legs around his waist, wedged between him and the wall, as he found his way into me, bumping and nudging against the inside of my thigh as he slid home.

That moment he was perfectly still, both of us barely breathing as my body adjusted to him. This little break in time where we were finally alone together. He'd started moving, slow. Torture.

"...some champagne in the room for you lovebirds," the showrunner was saying to Chance. "I think someone offered Minnie a couch for the night—"

"She can stay," I interrupted.

The showrunner paused, giving me an uncomfortable glance.

Why had I said that? Only minutes ago, I'd been burning with jealousy. She had kissed him. But I wanted her there as much as I wanted Chance there.

I told myself how reckless it was, how there were a hundred different ways this could break my heart. How stupid I'd feel if I woke up at 2 a.m. tonight and they were both gone. And I'd know where. The cabana.

"Well, that's between you," the showrunner said in what might've been a properly scolding tone.

Next to me, Chance gave me a warning squeeze. Or maybe a supportive squeeze. It was impossible to tell. And then all the hellos and autographs had finally slowed to a trickle, and Chance and I got on the shuttle together, snuggled up so that everything smelled like him, so close I could watch the flicker of his pulse, feel the bristle of stubble under his skin. I couldn't stop sighing. Every moment was either me holding my breath, or exhaling in this deep, satisfied way.

Minnie was on the shuttle too, of course, and quickly off when we arrived at the resort. Was she even now packing to move out?

Chance and I made our way to the condo, slow, with him taking in the new digs. He stopped for a moment, admiring the ocean view.

"We're going swimming, right?" He squeezed my hand.

"Every day," I assured him.

"Because I have to go back to Canada to wrap up, and I need to remember warm while I'm here."

I pulled him toward the condo. Maybe I needed to flaunt my win to Minnie. Maybe I needed to prove when we were all together he'd chose me. Whatever I needed, my heart was skipping beats all over the place, and the adrenaline made me want to get him into bed again.

I made sexy eyes at him. "Come on."

He hesitated. "What about..?" He couldn't even say her name.

I leaned into him. "Do you trust me?"

"Maybe." Honesty only made him more alluring. "OK, yeah. I think I do. But I don't want to hurt her."

"You're my husband. She's about as hurt as she's ever going to be."

Those gorgeous eyes narrowed.

"Look," I said. "I've missed you, and I want to find a way to make this work between us. That means making it work with Minnie in our lives."

I pressed my chest against his, tilting up on my tiptoes to kiss him, letting my body brush along his as I did so. He made this primal noise in the back of his throat that sounded like maybe he couldn't control it.

"What do you mean?" he muttered.

"Bet if you put your mind to it, you could figure it out," I breathed.

"What's it like to have everyone you know want to get in your pants?" It wasn't really a question. If anything, he probably knew better than I did.

"Come inside." When I pulled him toward the condo this time, he came willingly enough.

* * *

"CHANCE IS HERE for the rest of the week!" I called as we came in.

"Yay," Minnie deadpanned from the kitchen. I was too happy she was still around to care about her lack of enthusiasm.

I was learning with Minnie I had to pay attention to what she did over what she said. Those hips, bucking against me even while she was feigning some crisis of conscience about blackmail banging me.

I had to remind myself that most people didn't see things as I did— if I wanted something, I went after it, and god help anyone who got in my way.

Minnie wasn't like that. She played it safe. And although it was tempting to think of her as soft, or wishy-washy, or maybe even too prissy to handle me, the part of her that played it safe was also the part of her that made her *feel* safe. If I wanted one I had to accept the other.

Minnie hauled glasses from the cupboard, a bottle of champagne in her other hand. She looked like she was serving drinks at a funeral. The door opened behind us and the camera crew ambled in. Guess we were still on the clock.

"Great idea!" Chance grabbed the bottle from Minnie and popped it. Bubbles foamed and she handed me the glasses. "Let's celebrate! To being back together again!"

To pulling off this magic trick without it blowing up in my face. I raised my glass and drank.

Minnie tilted her champagne glass to her mouth like a shot glass. The scene was perfect for the storyline of me catching Minnie crushing on Chance. She and I stood awkward as hell while Chance filled the nervous silence between us with stories about how his film in Canada was going.

I wondered if Minnie understood I'd invited Chance here because I'd missed him, not to humiliate her. Would she pay me back by handing those photos to Chance?

It might be a smart play: She loved him, she had been exposed for loving him. It would be easy for her to... well, not clear her own name exactly, but she could make us even. But I didn't think she'd do that, because it would hurt Chance.

I thought about the video I had of her, still on my phone, though I wouldn't send it out in revenge. Don't get me wrong, I was plenty bad girl enough to do that kind of thing. But the truth was, I'd watched that video over and over.

It was my new kink, seeing Minnie how maybe she was afraid to see herself. I played it on my phone with my hand pressed between my legs. When push came to shove, I was simply too selfish to ever share it with anyone else. Even if Minnie ruined me with Chance, even if she managed to get those blackmail photos published. The Minnie on the video from that night was someone I thought maybe no one else got to see.

I grabbed the bottle of champagne and topped off her glass. She smiled weakly at me and drank.

"Well, time to turn in!" Chance gave me Hollywood style wolf eyes for the benefit of the crew filming.

I knew my cue: blushing good girl.

"Chance!" I gasped, half-mortified, half-adoring. Minnie's eyes watered as if we'd sucker-punched her. Chance grabbed my hand.

"Goodnight, Minnie!" I wasn't sure if I was trying to make her feel better or alert the camera guys that her reaction was reality show gold.

Chance dragged me to the bedroom and slammed the door behind us. I laughed, understanding the bookended nature of the shot. This was how our wedding night and first episode had ended.

"Nice work you two!" one of the crew called through the door.

Chance and I stood in the semi-darkness. He must've also been remembering our wedding night. Our time in the club had been passionate and risky, private but still swallowed by the storyline of the show. Beyond our bedroom door, the camera crew moved around, packing up. It would just be us, and Minnie soon.

"Hey, come here." He pulled me close and kissed me. More tender than the earlier desperate horniness.

"Missed you," I murmured into his chest.

"Yeah," he exhaled. "Daphne, keeping Minnie here? I said I didn't want to hurt her. Do you?"

"What?" I froze.

"You saw how she looked tonight, right?" He kissed the top of my head. Small jealousy boiled in the pit of my stomach. I thought I could work this out so everyone could be happy, but my theory was based on Chance not fucking it up by taking sides. "Your idea of everyone getting along... it isn't rubbing our relationship in her face. Or is it?"

"I got caught."

Shit. I hadn't planned on telling him like this. But I'd had a drink, and I hadn't expected him to turn the conversation this way. Not after he'd been so easy going when we'd come into the condo.

He tensed. "What do you mean, caught?""Minnie tried to blackmail me, but I've got it hand—"

"What do you mean, *caught*?" Shit, he was angry. This

wasn't going how I'd planned. "What do you mean, *blackmail?*"

"Hold on, just listen."

He moved away, muscles flexing. It was hard to concentrate with things spinning out of control, I wished I hadn't had the champagne. "I'm listening. Start talking."

I tried to find my way back to my plan for telling him. I'd wanted to...

What did *you want, genius? Some sexy intro to bringing Minnie into your shared bed? Because pissing him off seemed like the wrong foot to start on.*

I had to talk fast or he'd shut me out.

"She saw me with Audrey. No one else did. Just her."

That was true. It wasn't the whole truth I'd planned to tell him, but it did seem like the truth he could handle this moment. Rand or photos seemed way too much for our relationship to withstand right now.

He did a double-take as if to check my story. "Who? *Minnie?*" I nodded. "Minnie *blackmailed* you?"

First thought: He couldn't even process her being that bad. Second thought; she hadn't told him she'd caught me. Of course she hadn't. He would've told me right away if I'd been caught. It would've been a fight.

I sat down next to him. Not lovers close now, but the distance a friend sits when they are breaking hard news. Far enough away that they can hug you if you break. Or you can get away fast if they get too angry.

"Tell me," he said too sharply, fist clenched.

"She tried to blackmail me into being faithful to you. She tried to use what she'd seen to ... make me be the kind of wife she thought you wanted."

He slumped. "Why she didn't tell me?"

"Look, I don't know how it works between you and her. What I do know is when I left LA, you and me?" I swung a finger between our chests. "We had an understanding, and you still had Minnie spy on me."

"So, what— you're gonna punish her now? Is that what making her stay in the condo is all about, so she sees you and me sleeping in the same room even though—?"

"You should be worrying about whether you fucked up with me, not if you fucked up with her," I snapped.

"You got caught— the one thing I asked you not to do in an otherwise extremely liberal agreement— and *you're* pissed at *me*?" He stood, pacing again. "You think it's Minnie that's got to learn a lesson here? You risked the show."

"Newsflash! I didn't get caught. You knew from the start about Audrey." I hissed that half-truth, aware of the quiet house around us, that Minnie might overhear. "If Minnie hadn't been paid to spy on me, no one else would've ever known."

He was taking his anger out on me when the person who'd lied to him was her. He'd built her up in his mind to be some paragon of goodness, and he was angry at me even though I'd been the one who'd told been honest the whole time.

Here's the thing about love: If my heart hadn't been involved, I could've let it go. That would've been the smart business decision. I could've let him be mad at me, knowing we'd work it out when he'd had a moment to think things through. If I didn't mind being cast as the bad girl in his heart.

But I did have feelings for him, and the pain of him thinking badly of me because he wanted to think good about her cut me deep. It set this rage off inside me that blotted out the alarm bells in my head warning my relationship with Chance assured my future fame and fortune. Keeping the relationship between us cordial assured my freedom. Burning down my own house this way risked everything.

"She blackmailed me into sex."

The shock on his face felt worth it all, at that moment. Knowing that he would finally see she wasn't so good and I wasn't so bad. "She didn't tell you because I fucked her to keep her quiet."

"What?" He sat on the bed with a thud, face pale.

Triumph drained out of me as quick as it had come. I'd intended to hurt him, get him off his high horse about Minnie. I'd wanted him to love me more than her, and instead, I'd broken his heart.

A loud, disorderly thump on the bedroom door made me jump.

"Crew's gone!" Minnie hollered, sounding a bit drunk, then shuffled away again.

"I need some time," Chance said.

"No, please." The whole argument spun in my head. How had I fucked this up so badly? "I didn't... I care about Minnie. I care about you."

"Save the break-up speech—" He got up, headed for the door.

"I don't want to break up! Don't break up with me." I dodged in between him and the exit and slid my arms up to his neck. "I'm trying to tell you what happened. Stay. I think it's OK. It can be OK if you trust me."

Gently, but also not playing at all, he took hold of my arms and physically removed them.

"Don't leave." I hated myself then. The absolute whining recreation of my mother, who always fucked up every business opportunity by being emotionally desperate for attention, for someone else to make her whole. But I couldn't stop myself. I was losing him, and GITZ, and everything.

Maybe it was better to let him go. Whatever was pent up inside him needed to get free, and that might be real ugly. But I couldn't say the words, even if he was on a crash course to saying things he couldn't take back.

His pointed finger jabbed the air. "I asked one thing of you, don't fuck around. And you fucked the one person you knew would hurt me most. Why, Daphne?"

Maybe if he'd yelled or thrown a tantrum, I would've hated him, screamed terrible things back just to hurt him. But he asked like he was really looking for an answer. "Why do you push me away every chance you get?"

I don't! My throat closed on the words.

He was trying to change me, make me into something I wasn't. I had just moments ago begged him to stay. I had asked him to fly out and be with me because I missed him. I had gotten involved with Minnie because he needed her and I wanted to be part of what he needed. I hadn't wanted to steal her, I'd wanted to share her. I'd wanted to prove I was better.

He panted, angry and flexed, waiting like a junkyard dog on the weakest of leashes. I took a couple of deep breaths. It needed to be the truth for Chance to believe it. Things were fucked up enough without lies or shade or pretend.

"I want to. But I can't let you in. If I do that, it'll make me weak."

I wiped my face, not even knowing what I meant. The silence spun out. I'd said something either so awful that we were broken, or strong enough to keep him around. At least for the night.

"Come to bed," I said, barely louder than a whisper.

"Tell me you want me."

Of all the demands he could've made, all the ways he could've made me pay, this one I understood the best.

He was gorgeous, wealthy, powerful. Everyone wanted him. Maybe someone who only saw that part of him would've figured it for a power play, to bring me to my knees and admit the thing I'd just told him I couldn't give.

But I knew what he was asking because I was the same; a lifetime of rejections, no safe places, being surrounded by people who would use you until they got what they wanted and drop you without a qualm. He was like me; he had everything and nothing at the same time.

My chin trembled, and I broke into the ugly cry as I shook my head. But when he stood there, neither leaving or yelling or saying anything more, my head shakes turned to nods.

"I *need* you. Come to bed." I took his hand, pressing my body against his, pushing him toward the bed and then onto it, bedsprings squeaking.

He grabbed me and pulled me down on top of him.

The electricity burned away everything but tears and need. I kissed his neck, wanting the taste of him in my mouth, the memory of when he'd made me come. Chance might not like me, but he wanted me. I was under his skin and I needed him inside me immediately.

Admitting I needed him ripped me open in some way that felt like I might not survive. I ran a hand over his six-pack. His muscles twitched under my touch. Whatever emotional pain I'd caused him, Chance was ready to go in a way that made me desperate.

He rolled and lay on top of me, not propping himself up

at all, letting his entire weight crush the air out of me, his hard-on a weight between us.

"I'm fucked up about you," he whispered in my ear.

I was hardly in control, my thighs parting, pelvis tilting. We could talk later. That he was here was all that mattered. That he was powerless to resist fucking me even though I'd stolen Minnie from him, even though he could've crept a few feet down the hall into her bed made me slippery with need. I arched my back.

"Say you're mine," he growled in my ear.

"Don't make me into her."

"You want her to know."

I nodded. All my secrets were on sale today.

"You want her to hear me with you."

Face red hot, I nodded again.

He groped at the bedside for his bag, keeping me pinned with the weight of his body. Condoms. It left me breathless having to wait. Underneath everything else, control was what made Chance tick.

An instant later, barely lifting off me enough to put the condom on, he pushed the head of his penis inside me.

That feeling again, of being stretched, of how there was no distance between us, inside or out. I tilted my hips, wanting him fully in me.

He resisted. I thought maybe he was afraid of hurting me, the fit was so snug. I kissed the edge of his jawline, wanting him to know if it was tight, it was only because I was swollen from wanting him, my insides clenched from being so close to coming.

He lay perfectly still, thumb brushing my cheek until I opened my eyes. He stared down at me, moved in a way that made me gasp: *pay attention*, and then pulled back.

I wrapped my legs around his hips, trying to get him

moving, or at least pull him snugly inside me. He would start, that slow fucking rhythm as he watched me, intent. And then he would slow to a pause.

I squirmed. Our bellies pressed together too securely for me to touch myself and force him to either come with me or watch me come all over him, so I pinched my nipple, whimpering a little at the excruciating tease. A faint breeze could've tipped me over.

He grabbed my wrist and pinned it to the bed. I groaned in frustration. He barely moved, but when he did, the stray squeak of bedsprings.

"Say it," he demanded softly in my ear, rolling his hips, pushing deeply into me for a moment before retreating again. "Maybe I don't need a picket fence, but you gotta give me something."

I shook my head. "You like me this way."

I hadn't missed how he'd accused me of wanting Minnie to hear us, but despite his apparent disgust, the idea she'd hear hadn't stopped him. He might be trying to keep quiet, but he was still balls deep inside me. The bed still groaned under our movements, no matter how slow or stilted.

"Minnie made me wear a blindfold," I said. "She told me she loved you, and she came all over me."

Maybe the first thrust was punishment, to shut me up or distract me, but once he started he couldn't stop. And I couldn't stop. I gasped, digging nails into his back, tilting my pelvis to draw him deeper inside. "She didn't know what the fuck she was doing and she still made me come."

Then it wasn't even punishment so much as desperation to get as far inside me as he could. I didn't know if he loved me being bad, or hearing about her being so good, but Chance Zak lost control. Those desperate, furious humps that come from somewhere deep in the most primitive part of your brain, the kind that made you a helpless passenger.

With each thrust, I had to bite his shoulder to keep from making noises that not only would've alerted Minnie, but probably the entire northern wing of the resort.

TWENTY-EIGHT

The next morning, our vibe was strangely bashful. Chance slipped into boxers before prowling to the bathroom to brush his teeth. When he came back, he pulled me close, not saying a word about the night before, but sighing contentedly when I pressed against him.

Outside the bedroom door, we could hear Minnie prepping breakfast, and we both seemed to agree that being late for breakfast or getting caught fucking in broad daylight was just kind of rude.

Still, we got far enough to leave my cheeks pink and give me something to think about for the rest of the morning, on the shuttle ride to a cenote.

While we dipped our toes in the cool water, watching the fish swim lazily by. I thought of how his middle finger had slipped between my legs, a quick caress before he got out of bed again. Morning stubble pebbled his jaw, and I'd thought about what his tongue would feel like in place of his fingers. And what Minnie's tongue had felt like. And that he knew, and we were still OK.

She could barely look at either of us the whole morning,

and it was hard to keep track of her anyway— the GITZ crew wanted shots of me and Chance, jumping into the water, kissing on the rocks along the shore, laughing and caressing each other like newlyweds reunited.

After lunch, the crew took us to a lagoon to get some snorkeling closed set 'date getaway' footage of me and Chance pushing TV-14 limits of pornographic groping for some future GITZ episode. We got caught by a lagoon life-guard who threw a couple of pre-programmed catchphrases at us about no sex in front of the fishes. Because of the closed set, no other GITZ actors were invited. Minnie must've gone back with the rest of the crew to have the afternoon off.

I still had this nub of anxiety inside me about the black-mail photos. Rand had already left for LA, so I didn't have to stress about him telling Chance. But I hadn't been able to talk to Minnie yet, and I was worried about what she might do now.

I hoped she understood that as mean girls as it had been to steal her phone and accuse her of crushing on Chance, it was also the best way to assure that she'd be on Season 2 of GITZ. Also, nobody believed subplots on reality shows anyway. And third, she *was* in love with Chance, and anyone who knew her probably knew, including Chance. But I was worried she might go DEFCON 4 and send him the photos.

Now that I had Chance back, I felt reluctant to rehash the details of the blackmail with him. I didn't exactly feel as though I was hiding Rand; more like it was established fact I fucked around, and Chance had never once asked for an itemized list of all my sex partners. It seemed rude to punch Chance's soft spot with the same painful information, only slightly changing the details.

But as much as I believed this, I also understood the power of those photos if Chance was blindsided by them.

So I had to get a hold of Minnie and make sure that didn't happen.

* * *

CHANCE and I returned to the condo famished after a long, amazing day of getting paid to be in love and on vacation, selling dreams to viewers stuck at home in the cold.

Minnie was prepping dinner when we arrived, chopping in the kitchen, the perfect housewife.

"Welcome home!" she called. "How'd it go?"

"Amazing!" Chance answered, and immediately disappeared into our bedroom. He was nervous! The door closed behind him, so I took my cue and stayed out in the living room with Minnie, wondering if Chance was embarrassed over what he knew about her now.

"Bet he's stripping right there on the balcony to get out of those sandy trunks," I excused him for Minnie.

"That'll be a pretty payday for anyone with a camera," Minnie remarked offhandedly. Then froze like a deer caught in my headlights. Wow, she was no liar at all.

"What do you mean?" I asked, pulse going a little flickery. Was it a threat? Just thinking out loud? Some kind of confession she was my blackmailer?

She busied herself with dinner prep. "There have been a couple paparazzi accumulating around the resort. Security keeps them off the property. I'm sure it's fine. Chance is fine."

I studied her, wondering if there was some deeper meaning. "I guess I didn't think about it too much."

She finally glanced up from her work, eyes blazing with

shocking ferocity, as though she couldn't believe I didn't know my own hype. "Hey, I got a piece of fish for dinner and a bottle of wine."

Holy shit. Like... I was suddenly a little flustered.

She seemed like whatever this game was between us had woken up something in her. I wanted to drop the strange and complicated dance we were doing and drag her back into the bedroom, do things to her in front of Chance, see who Minnie liked better. For that matter, see who Chance liked better. It fucked me up a little to think that way, mixing up all my competitive feelings with my romantic ones.

"I'm starving," I said.

"Me too!" Chance called as he came in.

Minnie ducked her head. This was it. All of us together.

Technically, I wasn't supposed to know she was my blackmailer, much less whether she'd trust me to take her into Chance's bed. It felt like a high-wire act, like I kept inching forward, waiting to see if something would throw me off balance so bad we all fell.

"That lagoon was amazing! They had us going through these caves and cenotes, Min." Chance smelled like fresh soap and his hair was damp. He sounded like a kid coming home from a school field trip. "And the fish! You should definitely go while we're out here."

"We went there for the movie," I laughed, nervous. "Minnie got in and this fish started chasing her around the steps!"

Chance said, "Maybe we could all extend our trip, stay a few days after filming wraps, do some real vacation stuff together."

Everything between my legs melted a little, thinking about real vacation stuff with them. The idea that Chance was offering, even though he knew what had gone on between me and Minnie. Maybe it was an invitation.

Maybe I was seeing something that wasn't there.

From behind Minnie's counter, the chop-chop-chop of dinner prep. She was anxious to see him or guilty about what we'd done together. Fucked up somehow.

"Minnnnnn." Chance sat down next to me at the breakfast bar and leaned in. "Tell me you've got something great for dinner. I'm starved."

An electric current in the air, even worse because Minnie was trying to hide it. From me, from Chance, probably from herself.

All these fantasies, I reminded myself. *And at best, it'll probably end with one of you making an awkward pass that falls flat, followed by everyone sleeping in their proper bedrooms, and a lot of embarrassment tomorrow morning.*

He got up, went to the fridge, moving easily around her in the kitchen, her telling him to get out the wine. It loosened them up, but it made me feel like the odd person out. Watching their delicate glances as they awkwardly danced around each other, Chance working to set her at ease, this agitation started up in me again. I hated that I was so jealous... but it still sucked to watch them flirt. My whole life basically depended on making everyone look at me the most. I chewed my lip, trying to let it happen and not fuck it up.

Minnie laughed—huge, wide-mouthed, totally unscripted. Not from some beautiful angle, but obviously artless and unpracticed. In a movie, she'd never be the lead love interest. Not with her eyes pinched shut and uncontrollable laughter giving her a moment of double chin.

And kind of like I'd known it would be with a girl like her, I found myself thinking how beautiful she was. I ached with it. I wanted her in my life, laughing like that all the time.

Chance must've felt it too.

"I LOVE YOU," he laughed, grabbing her face with his hands, and kissed her on the lips. Right in front of me. "This is perfect."

I couldn't breathe.

I could feel Minnie, not breathing either, across the breakfast bar. I thought about how I'd told Chance I'd tasted her. He'd wanted to taste her too.

She flickered a horrified glance at me. Chance saw. Whatever game we were playing, our cover stories were the thinnest they'd ever been.

"Ummm, here, give me that." Minnie pointed at the wine bottle. "You two should enjoy a glass together. I'll just finish up prep here."

Part of me hated her. Some primitive instinct to kill off all competition for Chance's attention. Or maybe it was because I was my mother's daughter— so fucking needy all the time that my whole world crumbled if I wasn't being admired.

I wanted to climb over the counter and grab her and either fuck her right there on the floor or tear her hair out and make her promise Chance was mine. Maybe both.

I was fucked up, that was for sure. Whatever I'd hoped for tonight, now I was shaking. I had to get out of here.

So I did the one thing actors knew how to do. I faked it. Big smile. Sparkly eyes.

TWENTY-NINE

"I'm going to shower up. But I'll take this," I
tipped my wine glass at them, clinging to the hope this
would all turn out OK. "Don't start grilling until I get back, I
don't eat cold fish."

And because all actors knew how to leave on a line, I
added, "And don't kiss my husband while I'm gone."

"He kissed me!" Minnie flustered, caught between
horror and happiness. I got it; I was right there as well.

"Fine." I turned to Chance. "Don't kiss my girl until I
come back."

And then, because I couldn't stop that desperate part of
me he'd seen in bed, I added, "Promise?"

"Your girl?" He raised an eyebrow, obviously enjoying
my nervousness.

That bastard! But whether he intended it or not, being a
bit of a smug asshole actually stiffened my spine. I mean, he
was right. If I wanted to be free, he got to be free as well.

"I saw her first," he reminded me.

Well I fucked her first, I bit my tongue, but I saw him
catch my vibe anyway. That dare-devil smirk that landed

him the big movie contracts crept over his face. I didn't know whether I wanted to kill him or fuck him, either. Maybe both, with that fucking attitude.

"Scout's honor," he called after me as I went to our room, head high, glass of wine in one hand.

The moment the door closed, I leaned against the while, listening to the hard thud of my heart, trying to get a hold of myself, to not burst into tears like some kid who'd been picked last for dodgeball teams.

What they would do out there, without me? I didn't know if I had the guts to go back and face them. He'd kissed her! My hand slipped down the front of my pants, pressing hard between my legs, trying to calm down all the sparking, frazzled nerves there.

If I walked back out there and they were making out...

The idea that they'd be kissing, holding each other, was worse than finding them all-out screwing. Neither was great, but sex I understood.

My chest hitched in a sob.

I could see it in my head as though I was actually watching: Chance would confront Minnie about the blackmail. She'd waterworks immediately and admit everything. She'd fall into his arms and beg forgiveness. She would say those magic words that would melt Chance Zak: *I've always loved you. I only wanted you.*

Chance would get everything he ever wanted. Even the part he didn't admit to.

I was brutally jealous. I didn't want Chance to fall in love with someone else. I didn't want Minnie to make those little gasping whimpers if I wasn't there.

But I had no leg to stand on. I was the unrepentant cheater here. Chance had tried to get me into monogamy, and I'd resisted like a cat taking a bath. I'd taunted him about Minnie. Tonight, I'd practically thrown them at each other. And left. Omigod, like an idiot, I'd left them alone together.

I inhaled long and slow, feeling like I couldn't breathe, like I was trapped.

You said you were going to take a shower. Take a shower.

No! Go out and get in between them! Stop this!

I pulled myself away from the door, and stripped off my clothes, and trudged to the bathroom.

* * *

WHEN I GOT out of the shower, nothing but silence from the main living area of the condo.

The silence wasn't as damning as squeaky springs or muffled moans, but in some ways, it was worse. Silence might mean kissing. Murmurs of adoration and love so low only they knew what the other said. Silence might mean they'd left to go be alone somewhere else.

Minnie would never torture me by sleeping with Chance in the next room— she'd blush and whine, but she'd pull him out the door, to some secret place, most likely the cabana. Chance would make a note about which of us was kind and thoughtful and *safe* when it came to other people's feelings. And which of us was the bitch who flaunted it.

I swallowed hard. Whatever was out there, I'd have to deal with it eventually.

When I opened the door, Chance was fully dressed, coming through the slider on the patio, freshly grilled fish on a platter. I

sighed so heavily it was almost a sob, tears coming to my eyes. I blinked, feeling out of control and pathetic. The silence had been because he'd been on the patio, and she in the condo.

"You two should have dinner together," Minnie called to him from the kitchen. "Spend some time alone. I think I'll go to bed early."

Whatever had happened between Chance and Minnie while I was gone, it hadn't been the passionate *Daphne Is A Big Loser & We Are In Love Without Her* make-out session I'd played in my head. Minnie sounded defeated.

Can't lie. First reaction was this surge of triumph. He'd chosen me somehow. It rose in me like a firework. But it exploded all these sad feelings for Minnie. She loved him.

"Nah, don't do that," Chance said to her, grabbing her hand and pulling her into my line of sight, to the table, to dinner. I don't think either of them realized I'd come out of the bedroom.

Our eyes met and she gasped, tugging her hand free. Chance didn't let her go, and he smiled at me. Thank god for that guy. Somewhere in all this tailspin of messed up feelings inside me, Chance was right there acting normal, acting like this was OK. He knew how to do that— smooth things over. I thought maybe that's what made him so good in this business. He wanted everyone to be happy, to get along.

Kind of in the same way I always had, I decided to trust Chance, that he was basically a good guy who wasn't trying to hurt anyone. The two of them touching... She was sad and he was fixing it.

It was like a family, I kind of understood then. Or it could be. Maybe that was fucked up, considering our histories. But what did a girl like me know about a functioning family anyway?

"Let's eat," I said.

Minnie hiccupped into a huge, tearful grin. It definitely did not feel like they were gonna run away together. But whatever Chance had done by holding her hand had helped her too somehow.

So we sat down, and we ate. We killed the bottle of wine, and we ordered another. Chance and Minnie told me stories from their childhoods, and soon we were laughing and just...easy. I'd talked to Chance so much about business. I'd rarely seen this side. The whole thing felt effortless and I didn't want it to end.

But exactly like I'd told myself earlier in the night: real-life doesn't turn into porn. Or maybe sometimes it did, but not with all the unresolved drama between the three of us.

Minnie stood up and tottered a little drunkenly. "Wow, I should probably pack it in."

Chance and I glanced at each other, knowing the night was over. Maybe it was for the best— I'd been so fucked up earlier about them getting together. But then I thought about how little time we had left before Chance went back to filming, and I returned to LA.

Maybe after what had happened, I'd never see Minnie again. I could understand that happening. After all, she'd technically blackmailed me, and I was pretty sure both of us knew I knew it was her. We'd had one amazing night, and she was in love with my husband. Tonight, he'd told her he was in love with me. Or something like it, judging by the sadness that still simmered under her tipsy smile.

Because with all those things, a girl like Minnie would probably avoid me for the rest of her natural life after this. However I had broken through her good girl shell, which would heal over like a scar, and she would never want to admit it had happened after this. I didn't want to be her dirty secret

I had to see her again before we left. So when she excused herself to go to the bathroom, and while Chance stacked dishes in the dishwasher, I snuck to Minnie's room, made her bed, and left a pair of black socks in the middle of it. No mistake, with only the three of us here: *meet me.*

* * *

LATER, I was checking my phone in bed when Chance came out of the bathroom in his boxers. One knee landed on the bed, then he crawled across it, nudged my shoulder. "Hey."

I put the phone down.

"Looked like tonight was rough for you," he said.

"What did you tell Minnie?" I curled up on my side to face him. He collapsed on the bed next to me, making the mattress bounce.

"That I was in love with you. Isn't that what you wanted, why you wanted her to stay?"

I had wanted that. But now...

He shrugged. "I thought she had my back."

"I think she was trying to protect you."

"By sleeping with you?"

I punched him lightly in the arm. "You know that's my superpower. And to be fair, she could either tell you what I'd done, which would hurt you, or she could turn a blind eye. She had no authority, and we both knew it. I mean, that was half of me turning the tables on her, proving she couldn't do a thing to stop me."

"Is that the only reason you did it?" he asked.

I shook my head, the covers soft against my cheek. "You wanted me to be her. I was curious. And jealous."

"You really think loving someone makes you weak?" He

did that thing to me again, where he asked it like an honest question, like he wanted a real answer. "You said that last night."

"People take advantage of my mom. For a long time, I couldn't figure why she didn't have everything she ever wanted, why she was always so... sad. But you see it enough times, you know? Like, she'd get burned in a situation, and I'd think, 'OK, that was a bad business decision. Don't do that again'. But it was like she couldn't see the pattern. She'd do the same things over and over. Always let some guy make decisions that were better for him than for her career. Even before Lloyd, there was always a Lloyd, you know? She'd live in a dump with a black eye for a guy who told her she was wonderful. She's..." I shrugged, stirred up to talk about it. "I guess what they call a hopeless romantic."

For most people, that phrase was linked to my mother's name, on account of all the romantic comedies she'd been in as an ingénue. In flick after flick, Heather Conover risked everything for the love of a great guy, or a star-crossed lover, or the billionaire in disguise. She'd been... maybe not the queen of them, but typecast for her bright-eyed optimism and falling head over heels.

But those two words, *hopeless romantic*, always made me think of a fridge with nothing inside but packets of ketchup and soy sauce, of the electricity going out. By ten years old, I'd known if you could scrounge five dollars to send to the utility company, they'd still send your account to a collection agency, but they'd turn the lights back on.

"From what I've seen of your mom, I don't get that impression," Chance said.

Inside, I bristled.

"Oh yeah?" I said, just to see what kind of ditch Chance would dig for himself here. Plenty of people had made the mistake of talking shit about my mom to my face over the years.

"Your mom seems like a mirror."

I frowned. "I don't get what you mean."

But I kind of did. She was my mother, after all. She loved people who loved her. She rose to greatness when someone told her she already was. And when nobody was looking at her, the light in her went out. I'd seen how she'd diminished when Lloyd had been focused on my career.

I would bet cash money that one of these days, when that million ran out, I'd see Lloyd again, hand out. But my mother was different. I thought maybe she didn't want to be near me when other people looked at me first, spoke to me first, called her *Daphne Conover's mother*.

"That's not love." Chance said it like he was trying not to hurt me, winced like he heard how bad it sounded, started again. "Maybe you're afraid to get close to anyone— to me— because you don't want to be like her. I can understand that. But I want you to know, loving someone doesn't feel that way."

I lay there, breathing, sifting through what he meant. "What does it feel like?"

He didn't answer, his eyes on mine. I thought about how fragile my mom was, how *I* loved *her*. I knew in my heart she wanted to love me. That she *did* love me. She just needed some things for herself. I understood that.

I thought about all the times I'd checked my phone, anxious that Lloyd would reach out and try to shake me down for money or some favor. I hadn't heard from him since that night Chance had struck that million dollar deal. Every time, I had to scroll further and further back in time to find his last text. I was supposed to feel relieved. I told myself I was.

Until this moment, I hadn't realized it wasn't his text I'd been waiting for. It was hers.

It had been months since I'd taken my stuff and left her home. I got that she might not want to share the spotlight, but texts were private. She hadn't called to ask what happened, or to see if I was OK.

Maybe Chance was right. Maybe it wasn't that my mother loved too much and too foolishly. It was that she wasn't able to love anyone at all. Not in the way I'd needed. As a kid, anyway.

"I trust you more than anyone else in my life." It humiliated me to say it, but I did it anyway. He was surrounded by people who loved him and looked out for him. But for me, he was the only one.

I said, "I know you want us to be together. But I can't be the way you want."

He pulled back, tense like I'd stung him.

I said, "If you trust me, we can make something that could be good. Like you want. A family."

Now those eyes, in the dim shadows, seemed almost feral. I held my breath, waiting to see if he trusted me. Why would he, after everything I'd done?

Except all I'd done was be myself. If he wanted me, he was going to have to accept me for who I was.

THIRTY

I crept down the steps to the cabana. It was only a little cooler down here, but it got me shivering.

Here was my plan: I'd put the blindfold on, wait, and see if Minnie arrived.

I didn't know what would happen after that, except in a few days, Minnie, Chance, and I would all be going our separate ways. Chance knew it, and Minnie did too. I was on that tightrope again.

I paced a moment, then nervously sat on the couch, the feel of it under me bringing back memories of the last I'm I'd sat here.

My phone buzzed.

Chance: *Where'd you go?*

He must've woken up when I'd snuck out. Or maybe he'd never slept at all as he'd put his arms around me, and I'd snuggled against his chest, listening to his breathing, the beat of his heart.

Me: *In the women's cabana at the pool. Have some business to settle with Minnie.*

Bubbles. Bubbles. I bit my lip, waiting.

Chance: *Come to bed. Settle some business with me.*
Me: *You like me this way.*

I thought I heard something above and froze. Only the gentle sound of waves crashing, a bird call. I checked the time. 1:59.

Chance: *OK.*

Chance: *I'm trusting you.*

Chance: *I trust you.*

Me: *She hasn't shown up anyway.*

Chance: *What are the rules here? Am I talking to you about this?*

Me: *Yeah. I wanna talk to you about her. Is that OK?*

Chance: *It's*

Chance: *weirdly kinky. I'll be telling my therapist all about it next session.*

Chance: *Whatever you do, be smart, don't get caught*

Chance: *or we'll have a messed up story arc for Season 2*

I snickered, curled up on the couch.

Chance: *Hold on. I think she's still here. Lemme check.*

I waited, twisting the edge of the blindfold. Time slunk by. 2:03... 2:07. I began to get really worried. I reread Chance's text, soothing myself. *I'm trusting you. I trust you.*

My phone blew up.

Minnie: *GET BACK TO THE CONDO NOW.*

Minnie: *DON'T COME IN FRONT DOOR.*

Chance: *Holy shit. Minnie just*

Chance: *Lied to my face*

Minnie: *COME TO MY BALCONY, DOOR WILL BE OPEN.*

Minnie: *CHANCE THINKS YOU'RE IN MY ROOM.*

Crap. Crap. Crappitycrapcrap.

Me, to Chance: *You OK?*

Chance: *Yeah. I can't believe she just*

Chance: *Wow. She's a terrible liar.*

Chance: *Honestly, the worst.*

Me, to Chance: *I'm gonna see what's up. Talk to you later.*

I darted up the stairs, across the darkened pool area, along the path to our room.

Through the balcony windows, Chance and my bedroom glowed with soft light, the rest of the condo windows dark, Whatever had happened while I was gone, Chance had gotten hurt.

Like before, I had this overwhelming urge to tell him I loved him, that even if it seemed like I wasn't on his side, I really was, that I thought after this was all done, we could be happy, that we could all get what we needed from each other.

I jogged past the condo's front door. Our place was the endcap suite, every window looking out on the ocean or gardens. When I got to Minnie's room, her balcony doors stood open. Hoping nobody caught me for a burglar, I wedged myself through the bushes surrounding her patio.

"Sh... shhh," she breathed as I scrambled over the balcony railing.

Her eyes wide, movements harried, she helped me over. I reached out to grab her for support as I straddled the rail.

She was so much softer than Chance, both her skin and the muscle underneath. Smaller and more delicate. Her arm wrapped around my waist as I leaned into her. I let myself melt against her, the heavy weight of my breast brushing her arm, knowing she must feel it as well.

"Go slow," she whispered.

Of course. She probably didn't know that I'd spoken with Chance, that Chance knew I'd be here, in her room. I swung my other leg over the balcony and hopped onto her patio, so close our bellies touched.

"He's awake," she warned. "I told him you were in here with period cramps, but he's suspicious. I told him you were asleep."

She leaned in, mouth half-open like she would kiss me despite everything— the fact that theoretically, I didn't know we'd kissed before, or the fact she claimed to love Chance, or that we were out on the balcony in the dark, which would make a crappy paparazzi shot...but still a photo that might be worth something to the tabloids.

She seemed to realize this last one.

"Get inside." She stepped away from me, her eyes clearing as she glanced over my shoulder into the darkness.

"No. Tell me." I tilted my head in the general direction of the master bedroom. Despite her whole paid purpose for being here, she was trying to sneak me back into my own condo. She'd lied to Chance about where I was. "I know he has you watching me. Why?"

"Because it would hurt him. Because I'm in love with him."

And then, in the fresh outdoor air, of her own free will, letting all the lies tumble down around us, Minnie kissed me.

Hesitant and shy and desperate in this completely attractive way that suggested she couldn't help herself. As if she were going against her very nature just to have whatever part of me she dared take.

"Me," I said. "You're in love with me."

She shook her head, still kissing my lips, my cheek, the corner of my mouth. "Shhhhh."

"You were his. But now you're mine. Say it."

"You," she breathed, and I felt it everywhere, this gush of heat between my legs. "I'm falling for you."

She pulled me into her bedroom, into her bed. Every move, familiar from the last time. Except now she was the vulnerable one, the one caught up in secrets.

"It was me." She swallowed, her bottom lip trembling. "In case, you know. You didn't know for sure. I blackmailed you."

It took my breath away. This stupid bravery over something that wasn't a secret to anyone but her. Minnie's dark hair fell across her face, and I brushed it behind her ear, not completely ignorant of what that kind of thing felt like. Her nipples, outlined against her thin shirt.

"He only wanted me to watch out for you, keep you out of trouble. I was so mad at you when I caught you with Audrey, and then with Rand. He's such a massive tool." She scoffed, cheeks flushing with indignation. "Chance didn't deserve that. I wanted you to pay."

"You made me pay. Should I make you pay as well? You inserted yourself into my marriage. You blackmailed me. You made me think I might lose it all."

She squirmed. I kept my mouth closed, letting the silence get so big she had no choice but fill it.

"I'm... I liked it," she whispered, confessional across the mattress. "How messed up is that? I couldn't stop thinking about what you did to me."

I kissed her. I couldn't stop. My hand was under her shirt as she lifted my pajama top, kissing me everywhere, grinding her body against me.

"We can't," she said against me, but we already were.

If I'd had to put odds on a girl like her ever getting into bed with me after what had happened between us? It would've been in the single digits. All my body could remember was the moment she'd totally let go and shuddered against my face. I had to get her there again or die trying. I scratched across her nipple with my nail and she ground against me, this tangle of bed sheets and clothes half off. I slid my thigh between hers, nestled right up against her crotch, and applied a little pressure.

"I heard you. Last night. I heard everything." She tilted her hips against my thigh in that way that drove me crazy, like she didn't want to, but couldn't help herself.

She'd heard me and Chance together. The thought zinged me right between the legs, waves of rolling need as I remembered. Could he hear us now? I thought of all the times I'd heard Minnie moving in her room as I lay in the bed Chance now occupied. What kind of torture was this for him— the heartbreak kind or the massive hard-on kind? Both, maybe. Would he tear through the thinnest veneer of privacy we had between all of us and open the door?

I groaned against her skin. The idea got me so twisted, thinking about him touching himself, listening to us. The fear he might walk in on us. The thrill of what would happen next.

"I'll tell Chance everything," I said.

Minnie went statue still next to me, hands going still. She wasn't ready, I realized.

"You can't. I can't—"

"Be still." There was no more room for dancing around all the things Minnie was lying to herself about what she could or couldn't handle.

"This is my marriage." I bit her earlobe, making sure she knew I was in charge. "I tell him, not you."

"Please..." she whispered.

I loved her then, in this cruel strange way that embarrassed me to admit to myself. I loved bossing her around and

I loved making her do what I wanted. I loved that she looked like she was about to cream her panties even while she was still trying to hold on to all the reasons she thought she didn't want me.

I drifted down her body, feeling her muscles twitch under my palm. I went slow, letting her know way ahead of time where I was going. *Go ahead and stop me,* I thought.

But when I reached her thighs, they parted, inviting me in. Even with Chance in the next room. She was so wet I almost came with two fingers sliding over her.

"Be so very, very quiet."

I watched her, trying so hard not to make a noise. I stroked her over and over, wanting to break her. Wanting her to do what I said and be so out of control she couldn't.

The bedsprings squeaked and she froze. Started up again, needy against my hand, going harder and more frantic until the high-pitched squeals gave her away again. Froze. I clenched my legs together. She had to do this on her own.

Slowly, I stroked around the rim of her opening, sliding up to that pebble of nerve endings, pressing gently down. She jogged her hips against me, her mouth wet on my shoulder, biting to keep quiet. I kept going, listening to her gasps, the squeak of springs, feeling her go over the edge that way she had before, bucking against my hand and groaning into my skin, loud enough that I knew if she had heard us last night, Chance would now.

She kissed me over and over, eyes closing as her breathing slowed. Her face was still a little puffy in a way that made me think she'd spent some time crying.

Everything in me was on fucking fire, but I stayed with her until she drifted off to sleep, my fingers still inside her, moving against her every so often, enjoying her sighs, her body's response.

"Minnie?" I whispered. She didn't move.

I crept out of her bed, through the door, down the short hall. No light shone under the master bedroom door. I opened it.

Chance waited in the dark. Pacing like some wounded animal. The moment the door closed behind me, he pushed me against the wall. He was naked, erect like a baseball bat swinging in front of him.

"Yes?" It was barely a question, a growl against the side of my neck. His cock throbbing heavily against my belly, I nodded. His fist unclenched. Crumpled condom packet inside.

"Yeah. I want that."

I slid my arms around his neck, and he ripped the packet open with his teeth. A moment later, he lifted me by the waist. The heat of him sliding up the delicate skin of my inner thigh, ramming into me made me gasp. He felt like a fever. My back against the wall, he slammed into me, grunting, breathing hard.

"What the fuck did you do?" He demanded in my ear. I couldn't tell if he was more angry or turned on.

He reached for my right hand, drew my fingers into his mouth, and sucked on them. Our eyes met. He knew and I knew.

I came instantly, watching him watch me. His reaction was immediate, jackhammer thrusts that knocked my ass hard into the wall, his lips pulling back to show teeth.

It made me clench around him, coming again, waves on top of waves like I might die from it. His head bent, his forehead on my shoulder, burnt gold hair tickling my cheek, the clean sweat smell of him. My insides clenched against his cock. I loved him like this. Unlike Minnie, Chance definitely wasn't trying to be quiet. He groaned, heaving as he came. Then slumped against me.

We both panted hard, staring each other down, some powerful emotion sizzling between us, making my heart go too fast. That tightrope under my feet wiggling wildly, trying to throw me. He licked his bottom lip, tasted her where my fingers had been, eyes flashing.

Minnie.

I felt him get hard, still inside me.

"Hold on," he muttered, pulling out. He carried me back to the bed, lowering me into it, leaving only to grab another condom from the drawer.

I did.

* * *

THE NEXT MORNING I woke up alone.

Chance was probably running on the beach or doing a morning workout to burn off the booze from last night. I stretched, thinking about last night, bits floating back to me, the mild crash of Caribbean surf coming through the walls of the condo. I put on clothes, my body sore and happy and well-used, then went to the balcony doors and flung them open, sea air billowing in.

"Hey, girl! Last day of filming!" Audrey came up the path, decked out in a million-dollar bikini top and shortie shorts. "You ready to knock this out of the park and get the hell home to LA?"

My stomach fell. Past my feet. Into the ground. Into the center of the earth.

Oblivious, Audrey hollered, "Coming in!"

Sweeping past my balcony, she let herself into the

condo by the front door. I went into the living room to meet her.

Besides me and Audrey, the condo was deserted.

"Minnie?" I called.

No answer. I wandered to the kitchen, opened the fridge. A plate inside with two hard-boiled eggs, cut mango, slices of lemon for my water. Sighing, I pulled it out and took off the little reusable cover. I got it; now that Minnie was officially part of the storyline for GITZ, she might actually be needed somewhere instead of just hanging around feeding me.

Crabby, I nibbled the egg, telling myself she'd made me breakfast. What? Did I want her serving me? To only occupy my bed and the kitchen? I didn't really have a lot of leg to stand on, being pissy.

But I'd wanted to see her this morning, talk to her for the first time without all these secrets and lies between us. I suspected she'd get shy and maybe pull away, try to deny by light of day what we'd done. I didn't want that. I thought about Chance tasting her on my fingers. Heat rose on my face and neck.

"Um, HELL-LO?" Audrey was getting quite an attitude about being ignored.

"Sorry? Egg?" I offered her my other one, even though I was a little possessive over stuff Minnie had made for me.

Audrey wrinkled her nose. "I'm going vegan until the premiere. Speaking of which, am I on the circuit? What's the interview sitch for Season 2?"

I shook my head. "Chance would have a better idea, he's a producer." And then, going for casual, "Where are they? Did I sleep in?"

"Hey, yeah, where *are* they?" She wiggled her eyebrows,

comic seduction. "You lonely? I've been missing you since Chance came to town."

I smiled. I did like Audrey. "Yeah, my schedule's pretty full these days."

She grabbed one of my mango slices and tapped her bottom lip, then put it between her teeth with comically exaggerated sexuality. "Well, if you don't fill this slot, honey, I must inform you there's a waiting list."

My eyes went big, and I laughed. "Who's on your list?" I nudged her.

She ate the mango. "OK, promise not to tell, but Hank."

"The director?!" I squealed.

"He's six months off a divorce and just turned 47. He is so primed for a trophy wife!" She nodded excitedly, then belatedly added, "Don't be mad. I adore you. But this could be my big thing, you know?"

"Holy shit, I get it."

I squeezed her hand, excited for her. Some people might turn their noses up or call her a gold-digger, but Audrey was true to herself, and she knew what she wanted in life. I loved that about her.

"Are you sure we're good?" She made an anxious face, bottom lip caught between her teeth. "Like, don't count me out. I just want to explore this other thing for now."

I stood up and kissed her on the mouth, friendly but to reassure her there were no hard feelings.

"So is everybody filming?" I raised eyebrows around the deserted condo, hoping I came off as casual. It's never good when you're on a job and all your coworkers are missing.

"Well, I was supposed to do a confrontation with Minnie, but it got cut." She shrugged, stealing my last slice of mango. "Instead, I'm doing a scene with Chance this afternoon. I'm supposed to ask him some leading questions about Minnie. He's gonna profess his undying love for you, but also play it like maybe a cliffhanger that he's kind of... curious. I dunno. They're gonna shoot it, see how it plays with a test audience. If it makes Chance look bad, they'll probably cut Minnie's storyline out of the whole show which totally pisses me off."

"What?" I gasped. This was a big change to the storyline plans, and nobody'd told me.

"I KNOW RIGHT?" Audrey rolled her eyes, exasperated. "I'll lose the scene where she slapped the shit out of me, and that was low key gonna make me famous."

"Audrey, I gotta get dressed." I was practically pushing her out the door.

"I can wait if you wanna go over together," she offered. "Maybe you could get them to keep Minnie's storyline, but have Chance reject her and send her home crying or something. That way we could keep the stuff we already shot."

"Yeah, sure OK." I had to think.

"I mean, she was practically crying all rejected anyway. They should've caught it for the camera."

"What?"

"Chance was talking to her this morning. Probably letting her down easy." She lifted a fist to her chest with mock solemnity. "Solidarity, Minnie. Sucks to be cut."

"Just give me a few to put on clothes and let's get over there." I half jogged to the bedroom, stopped, turned back to her. "Where'd you hear the stuff about the script changes?""Chance told me most of it when we were scheduling time to do our new scene. Overheard the rest from the showrunner working it out with the camera crew."

I went into the bedroom, stripping as I moved to the closet for new clothes. Was Chance really going to cut Minnie out of the show? Why was he so pissed?

Why the eff do you think?

I gasped, remembering his tongue swirling around my finger, the way he'd lost control.

I'd pushed him too far. I'd thought he wanted it that way last night, against the wall and again in the bed. Now I could see how jealous he must've been, or angry at himself for liking it. He'd taken it out on Minnie.

THIRTY-ONE

THE LAST DAY OF FILMING WAS TYPICALLY HALF A celebration, half total stress, and frantic last-minute shoots or reshoots. Jubilant calls and people rushing around, camera crew being called from one location to another. This was the big push, the last frenetic climax of all our hard work.

Tomorrow would start a different kind of hectic—everyone packing under a deadline, cleaning up, people departing and disappearing, drunken hookups and tears as quick-made friendships broke up and we headed back to the real world.

I spotted Chance across the location. He was meeting with the director, talking intensely. I got distracted with hair and makeup, and the next time I saw him, he was doing some scenes with Audrey.

I love Daphne, he seemed to say, shaking his head at Audrey's lines. Just like she'd said earlier.

I didn't see Minnie at all. Although in truth, Chance was my top priority. Without him, I'd lose GITZ, and after I paid him back his million, I'd be pretty close to broke, with no representation and no leads on a new gig.

But it was more than that for me now, I reluctantly admitted. Across the set, he flexed, raking his hair casually from his gorgeous face, give Audrey that panty-melting flash of a smile.

If he'd sent Minnie away in tears, if he planned to write her off the script, then he'd chosen me over her.

I didn't understand how he could possibly do that — I wasn't a safe place. I wasn't the good girl, I wasn't the woman he'd written for himself in GITZ, the touchstone to a childhood where everything was good.

It made my heart swell in my chest in a way that felt powerful, but also felt like I might die from so much love for him.

At the same time, I knew he needed her. And I needed her. I had to talk Chance out of sending her away.

I waited anxiously for a free moment to open up between us. When he spotted me, his face broke into a huge grin. In lots of ways, he was so mature and smart and hard-working. It was easy to forget how young he was. He had definitely been working out this morning, and through the tantalizingly thin shirt, his six-pack shifted as he moved across the room. Wardrobe was making their money for sure.

I could sense him being aware of the crowd around us. We were on the clock now: the Chance & Daphne show.

"Hey, babe." He leaned down to kiss me lightly on the mouth.

"I need to talk to you." I fake smiled, but I could tell he knew I was serious. He looked around, pointed at the shuttle bus. "You wanna step inside with me?"

Grabbing his hand, I pulled him to the parking lot and

onto the bus, hearing the sly chuckles and murmured comments about newlyweds.

After five weeks, the bus had seen better days, smelling of exhausted people and old hairspray. But we were alone.

When I turned to him, I wasn't sure what I expected.

Those eyes glimmered, like an animal's. He leaned into me, arm against the wall behind my back, intimidating. I swallowed, nervous. It was so much smarter to keep my mouth shut, a safer play any way I looked at it. Chance was my path to fame and fortune. All I needed was one more season working with him and I'd have enough to pay him free and clear, plus enough to live for a while until I got my next gig.

But even more than that, Chance hadn't been bad to work with. Light years better than Lloyd. He'd treated me fair, hadn't stepped on my lines, or made me look foolish to his benefit. He'd never once mentioned I owed him. And knowing what I did about his need for control, Chance had still never used the loan or his position to make me do as he wanted.

"What?" He was so close, but not touching me anywhere. If I moved at all, we would connect. With the intimidating energy in him, I wasn't sure what would happen. But I'd put money on it involving sex.

"It could just be you and me, and I'd be happy," I said. My voice was shaking. "You don't have to send her away because of me."

"I didn't cut Minnie because of you." His jaw tightened. "I cut her because she lied to me. I don't care that you fuck around."

I opened my mouth to contradict him.

"It gets me here." He made a loose fist, rapped knuckles against his sternum, and underneath that, his heart. His pecs flexed with the movement. His fist dropped to his waist, lower, to the zipper of his jeans. "Here."

He leaned in closer, other arm coming up to press into the wall, caging me. Dark blond hair fell in his eyes.

"She loves you," I said. It was hard to catch my breath.

"I know." He shifted, closer still.

I couldn't believe he was mine. Legally, he was mine. In his heart, he was mine. Standing so close, it was near impossible not to lean into him, close the gap between our bodies, have him in every way possible.

"You love her," I said.

Being near him felt like being drunk— thoughts not making sense in my own head. Part of me was screaming I was making a mistake, this was my happy ending and I was messing it all up. He'd made his choice.

"You love me," he brushed his lips across mine, pulling back, not a real kiss. "Say it."

I nodded, my exhale going shaky. It felt so risky to give him that, to let him see I was weak for him. But if I was gonna be true, we had to both be honest about what was going on between us.

"You love me playing the part you made for her." He'd wanted a good girl he could put on a pedestal. He wanted me in his bed.

I needed him to me and Minnie both for who we really were, for him to dare give up whatever fucked up fantasy he had in his head. Otherwise, how could I trust him not to hurt me, or send me away like he'd sent away Minnie when he'd discovered she was a real person and not the story he'd told himself about her?

He leaned fully into me, muscled pecs against my breasts, hipbone against my belly, making me gasp from the friction. In minutes we'd be some form of naked and the whole crew would make terrible jokes. *When the bus is rockin' don't come knockin'!*

"It should be all of us," I said.

He pulled back. Cold draft of air between us. My stomach sank.

"You love her," he said, half wonder, half hurt.

I grabbed his shirt, twisted it in my fist, so he couldn't get away from me. "So do you."

He shifted, holding himself away from me, and shook his head.

"No. She lied to me. We had this trust, and..." His fist curled at his side. But I'd seen the look in his eyes when he'd put my fingers in his mouth. If he pushed her away, he could keep her perfect. And if he did that, there'd always be someone he loved more than me... even if it was only the idea of a girl he wouldn't speak to.

I couldn't have that.

"So punish her."

"What do you mean?" But the part of him pressed against my belly understood right away, hard and heavy and ready to go. That gorgeously made mouth, so close. I could feel he was nervous and unsure. I got it. This was a big risk.

"Do you trust me?" I asked.

"Yeah," he said.

"Then tell me everything about you and Minnie."

That quick inhale. I waited, that tightrope wobbling beneath us both.

"OK." He nodded, surrendering. "Yeah, OK."

THIRTY-TWO

Two a.m., by myself, in the cabana one more time, thinking about what Chance had told me about him and Minnie, how it'd gone down:

"What's the one thing I sent you here to do, Minnie? Tell me the one thing?"

She'd been tearful, so ashamed she couldn't look him in the eye. "To make sure Daphne didn't screw around."

"How many times did you lie to me?"

She hadn't wanted to say at first. "Lots."

He'd been so angry he'd wanted to punch something. He'd trusted her to have his back. OK, so maybe he'd and I had an agreement, but Minnie didn't know that.

"You know why I asked you to take this job?" He'd asked when he was calm enough to speak without yelling. "Why I paid you a salary and sent you on this dream job where all you had to do was watch Daphne? Because I trusted you. Because I lo—"

Chance had cut his eyes at me then, breathing hard in anger from the memory.

"What happened then?" I'd asked.

She had cried. She had apologized for betraying his trust. She'd apologized for ruining his marriage.

"That's when I realized, she didn't," Chance had told me, almost wonderingly, his breathing slowing, fists unclenching. He'd reached to touch my thigh, like me being there comforted him. "What she did was steal this... I wanted to build this life, to be able to trust each other, to have each other's backs."

"How'd you two leave it?"

He swallowed. "She said she'd do anything to make it up."

"What would she have to do? Are you mad, or are you hurt?"

He'd stood then, agitated, running his hand through his hair. "I don't know. Messed up inside. With you and me, it's different. I need different things from you. But knowing I could show up on her doorstep if I needed it, that's she'd be home for me?"

It felt so strange. Jealousy swirled. I hated not being that place for Chance.

But if I took a deep breath, I could stop myself. I mean, I wasn't even my own safe place. And even when he'd wanted me to be that, I hadn't liked it. I didn't want to spend my life making someone else's breakfast. I didn't want to wait around all day in case he needed me.

I exhaled slowly, but even knowing I didn't want those things, that it was good he wanted Minnie to be that for him, I was... I dunno. I guess I was still self-destructive, or possessive, or needing all the attention.

I tried to breathe through it. I tried to think about Chance. What he'd told me about the casting couch, and the parts of his life he'd never mentioned. His mother. His father. Any aunts or uncles he could turn to. Like me, maybe Chance was alone.

I'd snuck to her room and left those black socks on Minnie's bed as she'd sat all forlorn on her balcony, head-phones on. I thought she'd been coming to the cabana the last time, when Chance had caught her. I thought she'd come again.

I'd brought my phone. I'd brought the blindfold Minnie had left with me on our first meeting here.

Two a.m. came and went, and I sat by myself, in the cool, humid underground air. Above my head, the gentle crash of waves on the beach. The occasional laughter of some partygoer on the beach, or maybe the GITZ crew cutting loose before everything ended here. A shuffle of feet that would get my heart hammering, but then fade into the distance.

"Daphne?" She whispered down the staircase, the word bouncing off the walls, giving it a little echo. Then she was there, in the doorway. "I'm sorry, I couldn't get away—"

"You talked to Chance about us?" I asked.

"What?" She had slept with me, she loved Chance. She would think I was jealous. OK, I was jealous, just not in the way she assumed.

She looked like she might bolt, eyes cutting to the door. I thought about how I'd brought a knife and a video feed down to this room when I'd been the one in trouble. Minnie had only brought herself. "I just had to see you again, before..."

I snatched up the blindfold, afraid she'd leave, that this spell between us would be broken.

"When you caught me, you made me wear this," I said.

Her shoulders came down. The flicker of pulse at her

throat slowed. Scared as she was, this was what she'd come for.

"Now it's your turn. I get to do what I want to you," I said. "So we're even."

"What are you going to do?"

The tremor in her voice was gone. She'd stopped glancing at the door. How she looked only at me, eyes dipping down to catch a glimpse of my breasts, even further down, to my thighs. I thought about Chance up there, alone in bed.

"No," I snapped, handing her the blindfold. "You answer my questions this time."

She put it on.

* * *

I KNEW what it was like to wear the blindfold, to be afraid of losing something important, of not knowing what might happen next.

I flicked off the light, enjoying the sound of her gasp. But I didn't close the door. I wanted Chance to have plenty of time if he came to get a sense of what he'd be getting into. Of deciding if he still loved her, knowing Minnie was more than some story he'd written about her. Whether he'd risk losing that to gain her back.

And I suspected, whether he'd risk letting Minnie see him for who he really was— a real guy, not just some perfect movie star image she could adore from afar.

Maybe he was in the stairwell even now, listening. Maybe what I was planning was wrong. We could be caught by anyone with the door open. But it was a risk I had to take if I wanted Chance to catch us. It was hard to know the ethics of payback on someone who'd blackmail fucked you and was in love with your husband.

I wasn't sure I knew myself, and that frightened me, mostly because my pulsing clit hard-on made it difficult to think about anything other than making Minnie pay and making her come.

As my eyes adjusted to the dim light from the open stairwell, I studied her. From experience, I knew without the lights, the blindfold was a little disorienting— sounds echoed along the walls, touch could come from any direction.

I reached for the hem of her shirt, carefully pulled it over her head. She lifted her arms, revealing her flat stomach, sucked in even more with the shock of losing her clothes, her ribcage outlined for a moment, her perfect boobs. No bra. Delicate pinkish brown nipples.

I drew my fingernails over those ribs that had shown on her inhale, watching her nipples pucker at my touch. "Do you?"

"What?" Already, she panted a little.

"Do you want Chance?"

Let her admit to my face, while we were naked together, she had feelings for him. I wondered if she could do it. The door was open for Chance if he dared come down, but it was also open for her to escape if she couldn't go down this road with me. Now, when I thought of her leaving in a few days, it gave me a bit of relief. If I totally fucked this into awkwardness, at least I wouldn't have to face my mistake too long.

Although I'd be nursing a broken heart for a while if I never saw her again.

Her breathing went more erratic, maybe verging into a

panic attack. I ran my nails across her skin, trying to keep her here, in the moment, her attention only on me.

"I, uh." She took another breath. "I don't."

"Do you. Want to fuck. My husband."

The nerves between my legs lit up with tingles, my core going heavy and swollen with wanting her. My heart raced, watching emotions play across her face. I thought if I slipped a finger into her panties right now, she'd be like warm oil.

Minnie leaned into me, pressing her breast into my hand. She nodded, turning her head away.

"You have to say it. It's dark."

This was a lie. Making her say it was purely because I wanted to break her in every way possible. I wanted Chance to hear if he'd come down.

"Yeah." Barely audible, but loud in the room.

I bent and caught her nipple between my teeth, tasted it just long enough to remember what it had been like before. The feelings were too strong, and all of a sudden I was afraid I would go too fast and maybe scare her or use her, or Chance would come down five minutes too late. He'd walk through that door and it would all be over, with nothing more to see than a tangle of limbs and some smoke wafting off Minnie's crotch.

"I'm the boss," I told her, because fuuuuuuck, I really had to slow down or I was going to come like a prom date, with her not even out of her clothes. "You do what I say."

She reached out, soft touch of her tongue against my mouth. Instantly, I thought of how she had felt on my body. How desperate she'd been when I'd gotten her completely worked up.

"I thought you'd do *anything*," I said, thinking of Chance, how angry he'd been when he'd told me that part.

"I want you to do *anything* for me. It's only fair. And maybe after you do *anything* I want, you won't be so hung up on Chance."

"Are you jealous?"

Without thinking, I twisted her nipple, hard. I had to get out of these clothes. Agitated, I stripped off my shirt, fingers in the elastic of my shorts, sliding them down my hips.

Then, slowly, touching her hips, finding the waistband of her pants, sliding just underneath the ribs of elastic to feel the skin hidden underneath. I tugged the cloth past the widest part of her hips. Her sweatpants slid easily, falling to the ground. Minnie sucked in a quick breath.

I could be on my knees in one move, tongue on her in two. "What do you like about him?"

"I don't want... I don't want to talk about that now."

"What do you want?" I felt like Chance, asking those questions, needing to hear her say it.

"Kiss me."

As soon as our mouths touched, I was against her, nudging her to the couch, pushing her down on her back. I thought of the open door, the stairwell as I slipped my hand up her thigh, between her legs. This might be the last time. This might be...

"Get on top," I told her.

If Chance came— and I wanted him to— I had to give her every opportunity for freedom. I couldn't let her be pinned under me, trapped.

Beyond that, I had no thoughts. I grabbed her ass, diving my tongue in between her slit, starving for her. I needed her, I needed her, I needed...

She did everything I did, and I forced us both to go slow. I couldn't stop, could barely slow down, but the thought

Chance might come kept me edging as long as possible, even when Minnie started making those whimpering noises, nudging against my nose as if she might die from what we were doing.

She tensed against me, going still. At first, I thought I'd pushed her over the edge, that she was coming. My belly clenched in response, clit sparking, needing to go there with her. But instead of tremors down her thighs, that wild clenching of her legs around me, only stillness. Then she slowly began moving against me again.

I dragged my tongue against her, swirling around her completely hard bud of nerve endings, flicking my tongue, tasting her.

She froze again, and so did I, wondering if I'd hurt her, done something too far outside what she liked. All this time I'd thought I was pushing her way past her comfort zone. But this stiffness, this distraction in her, was different.

The darkness had changed. The door was closed.

"Daph," she barely whispered it.

Someone was in here with us.

I hoped it was Chance. Holy shit, if it was the night guard this was going to take a very strange turn.

I could only see part of his silhouette in the darkness, but I knew it instantly. The way he held himself, the way he crossed his arms and pulled off his shirt in one smooth motion. Daphne couldn't see any of it, she was on top and faced away from the door, wearing the blindfold.

I knew what he must see: Daphne, ass up on the couch, head between my thighs. I knew what he'd come here to do, whatever story he'd told himself, whatever plan he imagined — catching her in the act, or catching us both, or breaking her heart and making her pay.

Her legs got the trembles and I knew she must know it

was him, catching us. I licked her long and slow. I could keep her from bolting now, I could compete with all her fears about getting caught.

But I couldn't do anything about how Chance might act.

"Is it still true?" His voice bare and hungry, vulnerable. "That you would do anything?"

And Minnie, who had previously been pressed completely against my mouth, arched her back and presented her most secret parts to Chance. An invitation.

I saw it all, how his breath caught, how he hesitated.

"Say it. Tell me you want me."

Her breath on my thigh. How strange it must be for her, to admit that to him in front of me, in the middle of sex with me, when probably everything she knew about the world would've told her to cover herself, to try and explain.

How vulnerable she was, how deep her feelings must run for him.

He moved, kneeling on the edge of the cushions near my head. He looked at me, his expression unreadable. He reached out to stroke her back until her trembles got less and less. "What about this?"

I didn't know if he was asking her or me. He was looking at me. I wondered if we were ruining everything or not. It was scary as hell, that tightrope. But I wanted it to happen. I wanted to find out what it would be like. Not just in bed, but tomorrow morning. What it would be like if we didn't lose each other after this.

"Yes." She nodded against me, tongue darting between my lips

I put my mouth on her, needing her to touch me, needing to keep the edge of thoughtlessness.

Chance pulled down his pants, cock springing free, so close I could smell the warmth of his skin, the intimate smell of him. I snaked out a hand and ran my fingernails across his thigh, high up, where he was most ticklish.

He looked down at me, unmoving, expression that made me tilt my hips against Minnie almost beyond my control. He was so fucking hot and I knew that look, like no matter what he might do tomorrow, I had him right where I wanted him. But I was afraid about what he might think tomorrow.

My hand on his thigh, I pulled him close. Closer to me, closer to her. He dropped his pants and eased onto the couch behind her.

He put on a condom and I slid my tongue across her one last time, feeling how slick she was. Minnie was breathless and motionless, these hot little pants against my most sensitive parts. I licked her again. Fuck, even if this didn't work out, we were doing this. We were brave as fuck and we were—

Chance slid his cock into Minnie. My fingernails turned to claws in the muscle of his thigh. I couldn't help myself. I wanted this. But I was jealous as hell too. It scared me.

"Don't stop." I didn't know who I meant.

"Is this OK?" Chance said.

"Yeah." She pushed back against him, tits rubbing against my hipbones.

Minnie furiously rolled her tongue along my clit. However much he was turning her on, she was intent on bringing me with her.

"Slow down," I panted, but she only went faster. "Stop. I'm going to come." I tried to squeeze my thighs together. "Stop," I had to beg her.

Chance pulled back, and the next time slid into her, all the muscles in his thighs tensed. She made that noise, that little whimpering noise that before this moment, she'd only made for me.

I knew that feeling. Even the motion of her breath on me threatened to send me over the edge. I didn't want that. I wanted to be with them forever.

I reached up to touch where they connected. Chance groaned. Whatever happened after, this couldn't be undone. It sent this weird shiver through me, tightening my nipples until they hurt, making me totally still.

"Promise you're mine," he said softly. "I can't lose you."

She whimpered. His hand slid around to cup my ass cheek, touching my inner thigh, fingers searching for my opening like he needed to be inside me too.

He thrust hard, throwing a shiver into the whole mattress, making me gasp. "Say it."

"Yes."

For this moment, I was all alone, the two of them totally wrapped up in each other.

And then Minnie's mouth was on me again, desperate and taking me with her, with them. I felt her body clench in those waves, the tilt of her pelvis, her stomach tensing as she pushed me over the edge, her body moving over mine from the impact of Chance's thrusting harder and faster as he came. And I came. And she came.

"I'm yours," Chance groaned.

Minnie collapsed on me, kissing my thigh over and over. I shifted so she could roll over onto the mattress. Her body limp. Maybe she wasn't even fully conscious.

Chance crouched down and kissed me. And kissed me again. And again. Like he couldn't get enough of me. Part of it broke my heart, I was so happy I felt like crying. Part of me was scared to death. We could make our own rules. We had to because the rules for two didn't apply to us.

And honestly, what was more rock star than having a husband and a wife?

Chance brushed my hair away from my face. "I am completely. In love. With You."

"Come on, it's late." I nudged Minnie's comatose ass.

She sighed like one of those fairytale princesses waking up to her happy ending.

"I don't want to." She shook her head.

The tickle of the blindfold against my leg reminded me she still wore it. Some part of her still not fully here with us, accepting what we had done. I got that. Minnie was safe, but she wasn't as brave as me.

"OK then. Sit up." I rolled off the bed, grabbed a pair of panties I hoped were hers and lifted each of her feet to slip them on.

"Stand," I added, dressing her like she was my doll.

She obediently let me put on all her things like she was learning how to be, now that things had changed.

"You OK?" I asked when I was done. Maybe I was reading her all wrong. Maybe what had been perfect for me had broken her somehow. "Are you mad at me?"

She bowed her head a little, and my heart sank. Had we hurt her?

"I'm afraid when I take off the blindfold, it'll be different," she said in this subdued tone. "It'll go back to how it was before. I don't want it to be over."

I leaned in and kissed her.

"OK," Chance said, all practical about everything. "Daph, you go up and see if the coast is clear?"

"Sure." I threw on my clothes and opened the door, sea air warm across my face. I bit my lip, tasting salt and Minnie. From the top of the staircase, I called them up. Chance followed, carrying Minnie in his arms, still blindfolded.

I thought the stakes were extremely low at whatever

o'clock this was, but if someone saw us, there'd be some explaining to do, and maybe some rumors no matter what we said.

I wondered what that meant, that Chance was willing to take that kind of risk tonight, what it meant for us. We hurried through the dark, shivering.

Ahead of them, I opened the condo door and went to our bedroom, leading Chance.

I felt a stab of jealousy again, giving up the privilege of being the only one in his bed, but I wanted him to know this wasn't just a sex thing for me. He hesitated, nodded, followed me inside.

"Get the lights, would you?" he whispered as he put her in the bed, crawled in, and said to her, "Scootch."

I crawled into the bed on Minnie's other side. She reached for me. Chance threw an arm around her, reaching all the way across to hold my hand.

I lay in the darkness, thinking about everything, about what all this would mean tomorrow. I got scared, happy, scared again. But mostly, I just wanted to see what happened.

Chance fell asleep first, the slow rhythm of his breathing, familiar. Bit by bit, Minnie's body relaxed. Her death grip on me, like she was afraid I'd disappear if she let go, loosened. Her mouth fell open the tiniest bit.

I wanted to kiss her. I wanted to snake my hand into the space between her ass and his dick and see what happened when I got them both good and riled up. But I was also exhausted and spent, and content for the moment.

But right before I went to sleep, I took Minnie's blindfold off and threw it off the bed, out of sight.

"No more hiding," I whispered to her sleeping, peaceful face.

* * *

THE NEXT MORNING, I woke up to a kiss. I opened my eyes, Chance's hand on my hip. But it was Minnie who'd kissed me. Chance in the bed behind her.

Minnie smiled. This shy, happy, honest smile.

I kissed her. I couldn't have stopped myself if I'd tried. She kissed me back. In broad daylight. In front of Chance. He snuggled in and kissed her shoulder, grinning at me.

Beautiful boy with a golden curl hanging over one eye. My husband. My partner for Season 2 of GOOD IN THE ZAK. My favorite person in the world.

All of us together, on the same side.

This was going to be amazing.

THE END

If you liked BETTER IN THE ZAK, reviews and ratings are appreciated and welcome.

Read on for a sneak peek of CHANCE IN THE ZAK, available now in Kindle Unlimited.

* * *

CHANCE IN THE ZAK
by Jess Savage

Chance

—Fifteen years ago—

"Hey, Chance." Beau Williams threw his book bag down next to where I sat, against the chain link fence guarding the playground of Sunrise Elementary. "You got a ride?"

Beau was in my second-grade class, but he got pulled

out for accelerated math and language, so I only saw him half the day. Everyone knew he was super smart. I'd missed all of kindergarten and half of first grade going to auditions in LA. Sometimes the other kids thought I wasn't because I didn't know stuff.

I shrugged, squinting my eyes toward the pick-up lane, now empty of cars and busses, the last straggling kids taking off.

"You can call home at the office," Beau said. Hair not combed, collar wrinkled, scuffed up shoes— Beau had all that going for him. He'd get eaten for lunch by the Audition Moms. Didn't seem to bother him, though.

"What are *you* still doing here?" I asked. Most of the cars and all the busses had left.

"I walk home."

I chewed on my lip, stopped. It gave me a red mark on my chin, and casting directors didn't like it. *They can tell you're nervous*, Mom told me once after I hadn't gotten a callback. *They don't like nervous.*

Last time Mom forgot, the playground monitor had taken me to the office and made me call my mom and dad. Nobody picked up either phone. After we'd been waiting a long time in the empty school, the school's office adminis-trator called a police officer.

Turned out my mom just fell asleep, and her phone was in her purse, so it didn't wake her up. She hurried in all frantic and full of apologies. *Understandable!* Everyone said. *Just don't let it happen again.*

The playground monitor was pretty far away, but even from here, I could tell she knew it was happening again.

I thought of all the curse words I'd heard the Audition Moms mutter as their kids flubbed lines in front of the casting director: *Shitshitshit, goddamnit, cheese and rice.* I said them all under my breath.

"What?" Beau leaned in.

"Nothing." The teacher started coming our way, easy to spot because there was hardly anybody left. "Can I go with you?"

Right at the same time, Beau said, "You want to come to my house?"

Beau laughed, eyes widening like I'd farted or something. "Jinx!" And then, "Sure nobody's gonna get mad if you're not here?"

"I'll call." I pulled out my cell phone, pretending I hadn't already called. No answer. "Let's get out of here."

Beau looked amazed at my phone. "Yeah, sure. Come on."

I'd seen these houses out the window of the car, but it was cool to walk past, smell the fresh-cut grass.

"Usually, I walk with my sister, but she's home sick today." Beau held my phone, flicking through all the apps. "You're so lucky."

Big trees lined the sidewalk, cracking the pavement where their roots got too big. You could tell most of the houses were empty in the middle of the day, shades drawn, lights out. Last time Mom had 'overslept' I'd been scared, but now I was mad. When she got to school and found me gone, she'd be sorry.

Beau handed back the phone, talking our teacher's coffee breath and whether I'd heard about the ghost that haunted the bathrooms by the first-grade classrooms (I had) and if I had ever gone in there and counted to fifty (I hadn't).

"Dare you to go in there." He grinned.

"Darers go first."

"We should do it together!" Beau said.

"Yeah!"

"And all the other kids will be like OoooohhoooOooooh!" Beau wiggled until I laughed at how goofy he looked. "And we'll be the coolest!"

Beau stopped in front of a house with a little white fence that went all around, and this yappy dog that sounded like it was going to pass out from excitement when Beau pushed the gate open.

"That's Lincoln. Don't worry about him, he only bites if you're bad," Beau said it like he knew I was good.

"Hi Lincoln," I said.

Beau was already up the path to the front door. "Come on!" And then, "Mommmmm! I'm home!"

The dog followed me in through the front door, barking nonstop. Inside, it smelled like cookies. There was a big green couch in the living room, and on it, a couple blankets piled up. Under them, a girl with eyes so big they seemed like half her head. Her cheeks had two bright pink circles.

"Who are you?" She pulled the covers up.

That was the first time I ever saw Minnie Williams. But the thing wasn't *who* I was but *where*. Because right that moment, it felt like home. Like every apartment my family had lived in since Mason had been a television set, and we'd been acting like a family, and I hadn't known until this moment, when I saw the real thing. It made me feel too much, sad and happy.

My phone buzzed in my pocket. I took it out. "Hold on," I said to the girl. Then, into the phone, "Hi Mom."

"Chance? I'm at the school. The gate's locked. Where are you?"

"I went home with a friend." *See? I don't need you. I can find my own way in the world.*

I did not expect my mother to sob. As soon as she did, I almost cried too. The girl on the couch stared. I turned a little so she couldn't see.

"Don't ever do that to me again!" Mom scolded through the phone. "Where are you?"

Don't YOU ever do that to me again! I didn't say, because even though I was mad, I loved her. "It's OK. I'm at Beau's house."

"Give me the address."

"What's the address here?" I turned back to the girl on the couch.

"Mooooommmmm!" The girl on the couch hollered.

An ordinary woman came out of the kitchen. She was absolutely not like the mothers I'd seen at auditions or the grown-ups who had been cast in commercials with me, who had their hair and makeup done, and she looked nothing like my mother, who sometimes forgot to eat she got so thin you could see all the bones in her chest where her V-neck shirt dipped, and who sometimes forgot to sleep at night, so fell asleep during the day.

I felt like I'd fallen into a whole other world. One where mothers made cookies and let kids sleep on the couch all day when they were sick and didn't get mad if your collar was folded up wrong. Where little barky dogs knew if you were good.

And maybe this was crazy, but all of the sudden, it made sense to me that this was what my house would've been like if Mason had lived.

"Who are you?" Beau's mother asked, a smile on her face.

"I'm Chance." I handed her the phone.

* * *

Continue reading here: CHANCE IN THE ZAK

AUTHOR'S NOTE

Hey, this is a big thanks to you for reading, for showing your support, for making this the best job in the world. If you're into this series, or any of my work, the best way you can help me out is to leave a review with a comment on Amazon, Goodreads, or Bookbub. Thanks again for being here. I appreciate you.

XO,

Jess
jesssavage.com

Jess Savage Bookbub: https://www.bookbub.com/authors/jess-savage

Amazon: https://www.amazon.com/Jess-Savage/e/B08HY63L6X

Goodreads: https://www.goodreads.com/author/show/20692774.Jess_Savage